7-6-98   11

TOOTH AND CLAW

TOOTH AND CLAW

The Second in the new Jim Rook Series

Graham Masterton

This first world edition published in Great Britain 1997 by
SEVERN HOUSE PUBLISHERS LTD of
9–15 High Street, Sutton, Surrey SM1 1DF.
First published in the USA 1997 by
SEVERN HOUSE PUBLISHERS INC. of
595 Madison Avenue, New York, NY 10022.

British Library Cataloguing in Publication Data

Masterton, Graham, 1946–
    Tooth and claw. – (Rook, bk. 2)
    1. English Fiction – 20th century
    I. Title
    823.9'14 [F]

    ISBN 0-7278-5188-8

Typeset by Palimpsest Book Production Limited,
Polmont, Stirlingshire, Scotland.
Printed and bound in Great Britain by
Creative Print and Design Ltd., Ebbw Vale, Wales.

Chapter One

He came out of the kitchen to find his dead grandfather
sitting in the green armchair on the other side of the room.
His grandfather was wearing the same clothes that he had
worn on the last day that Jim had seen him: rolled-up
shirtsleeves and maroon suspenders. The early-afternoon
sunlight turned his glasses into polished pennies. His
tobacco-stained moustache bristled like a yard-broom.

"Hullo, Jim. How're things?"

"Grandpa?" said Jim. He was holding a can of Schlitz
in one hand and a Swiss cheese sandwich in the other.
His tortoiseshell cat tangled herself between his ankles
and almost tripped him up.

"What's the matter, boy?" his grandfather smiled. "You
look like you've seen a ghost."

Jim put down his beer and his sandwich and approached
his grandfather until he was standing close enough to
touch him. But he didn't touch him. He didn't know
much about visitations, but he knew enough to realise
that – if they made any kind of physical contact –
his grandfather would instantly vanish. Visitations were
nothing more than light and memory, mixed.

The sun shone across his grandfather's face, illumin-
ating his grey-green eyes, the wrinkles of his neck, his
white hair cropped as it always used to be cropped, by
the barber on Main Street, in Henry Falls. He had the
same dark mole on his upper lip.

1

"You don't need to be worried, boy. I just came to pay you a friendly visit. Thought we could talk about the old days, and maybe the new days too."

Jim pressed his hand against his chest. His mouth was as dry as a tray of cat-litter and his heart was thumping. "I never thought that I would ever see you again," he said. "Not sitting here in my apartment, anyway. Not to talk to."

"You've got the gift, Jim. You can see anybody, live'n'kicking or dead'n'gone. You know that."

"It just takes some getting used to," Jim told him. Then, "Listen . . . how about a beer?"

His grandfather ruefully shook his head. "Being here is all I can do," he admitted, "and that's not easy. Beer . . . hunh, that's a pleasure of the past."

Jim dragged across the other armchair, a dilapidated brown affair with its yellow foam stuffing trying to burst out of it wherever it was worn. "So tell me," he said. "What's it been like? Do you still see grandma? I mean, is it like heaven, or what?"

His grandfather smiled. "I guess you could say it was heaven, in a way. Every day is different. Sometimes you wake up and you're nine, and it's summertime, and the sun's shining. Other days you wake up and you're old and sick and the rain's running down the windows and you wish that you could die for a second time."

"And grandma?"

The old man shook his head. "I don't see her too much. You see, what you do when you die is pretty much try to settle up your unfinished business, the things you couldn't do when you were alive, or maybe the things you *failed* to do."

"What did you ever fail to do, grandpa?" Jim asked him. "You were the greatest grandpa that anybody could have wanted."

2

"That was your childish eyes, Jim. When I was nine, I failed to collect enough Ralston's boxtops for a Tom Mix six-shooter. When I was nineteen, I lost the girl I should have married to the college football hero. I was passed over for promotion three times when I worked at General Electric."

"You're trying to make yourself sound like some kind of failure. You were never a failure. I always thought you were a winner."

"You did?" asked his grandfather, querulous but obviously pleased.

"I still do. I mean, the fact that you're dead . . . what difference does that make?"

"It makes the difference that I can't touch you any more, boy. I can't hold you, the way that I'd like to. But I can do this. I can give you a warning."

"A warning?"

"It's the least that the dead can do for the living. The dead can see around the curve, so to speak – see what's coming."

"So what *is* coming, grandpa?"

His grandfather licked his lips, the way that old men do. "It's coming out of the east, whatever it is. It's dark, and it's very old, and it kind of *bristles*, if you get my meaning. More like a wild animal than a man; but cunning, like a man is, and cruel, like a man can be."

"So what the hell is it?"

"I can't see it distinctly, or else I'd be able to tell you. But I warn you, boy, it's coming real quick, and when it comes there are people who are going to be wishing that they'd never been born."

His grandfather wouldn't say any more than that – wouldn't, or couldn't. Jim asked "what?" and "when?"

and "where is it going to come from?" but his grandfather lifted his hands because he really didn't know.

They talked for a while more, as the sun gradually moved across his grandfather's shoulders. They talked about the times they used to go swimming in the waterhole close to his grandfather's house. They talked about grandfather's pride and joy, his scarlet-and-cream 1947 Pontiac Streamliner Sedan, which Jim used to polish until it looked as if it had just been driven out of the showroom. They talked about football – and then Jim suddenly checked his watch and said, "My God . . . I'm twenty minutes late. West Grove are playing Chabot this afternoon, and one of my students has made the team."

"Well, then, you'd better get going," said his grandfather. He stood up, and held out his hands as if he wanted to give Jim one last parting embrace. "I hope your boy does well."

"I'll see you again?" Jim asked him.

"I don't know . . . things aren't exactly the same after you're dead. Let's say they're less predictable." He paused, and then he said, "You won't forget my warning, will you? Keep your eyes open. Keep your ears pricked up. You might hear it before you see it."

"Goodbye, grandpa," said Jim, and he didn't make any attempt to hide the tears in his eyes.

His grandfather turned, and as he turned he vanished, as immediately as if he had walked out through the door. Jim stood where he was, staring at the place where his grandfather had been, until the feline formerly known as Tibbles jumped up on the arm of the chair next to him and rubbed his hand with her head.

"Guess you want feeding, you insatiable ball of fur," he told her. "Then I have to run. Russell's never going to forgive me if I miss his first game."

He drew up outside the college football field with an operatic chorus of tires, and his '69 Rebel SST let out an explosive double backfire. He was over twenty minutes late, but he was surprised to find that the game against Chabot hadn't even started yet, and that students and parents were impatiently milling around outside. He climbed out of his car and negotiated his way through the crowd until he found Ben Hunkus, the football coach. Ben was short and bulky, and his close-cropped head looked like one of those pieces of gristle you try to hide under your side salad. He was talking to some of his team, Russell Gloach included. The boys were all looking disappointed and bewildered, and they were still wearing jeans and T-shirts.

"What's up?" asked Jim. "You scratch the game, or what?"

Ben said, "You're not going to believe this, but we've had a vandalism situation. Someone broke into the locker rooms and tore up all of our uniforms. They even broke our goddamned *helmets*."

"You're kidding me. When did this happen?"

"We don't know. Sometime this morning, between eleven and eleven-fifteen. I'm mad. Believe me, I'm mad."

"Do you have any idea who did it?"

"What? Godzilla, by the look of it. You should see the damage."

Martin Amato, the team captain, said, "The second team are lending us their uniforms. The trouble is, most of them are back at home, in the wash, or all crumpled up in the trunks of their cars. I mean, *gross*. And it's going to take us at least another hour to get started."

Martin was tall and square-jawed and handsome. He had curly blond hair and deep brown eyes and a slow, deliberate way of talking. He was supremely dim, but he

5

was one of the best captains that West Grove had ever had, and if the rest of his players had been as athletic as he was, they probably would have won every single game. As it was, the West Grove Community College football team had earned themselves the nickname 'The Fumblers.'

"Did anyone call the police?" asked Jim.

"Unh-hunh," said Ben. "I don't think Dr Ehrlichman is particularly enthused about having a law-enforcement scenario during a college football game."

"In that case maybe I'll go take a look at it myself. Good luck with the game, Martin, if I don't see you before. You, too, Russell."

Russell Gloach gave Jim a friendly salute. Russell was the biggest student in Special Class II, nearly 250 lbs, and he had struggled hard all summer to cut down on cakes and hamburgers to get himself fit enough to be picked for the football team. He was still too slow, but Martin had chosen him because of the sheer effort he had put into his training, and because he had the stopping capacity of a small wall.

As Jim walked up toward the college building, he almost collided with Dr Ehrlichman, the principal, who was hurrying back to his office. Dr Ehrlichman was wearing an off-white seersucker suit and he looked as flustered as the White Rabbit in *Alice*.

"Dr Ehrlichman? I've just heard what happened in the locker room."

"I'm sorry, Jim. No time. I have to take a VIP phone call."

"Ben Hunkus tells me you didn't call the cops?"

"I'd rather we carried out our own investigation first. God *knows* we've had the police around here enough times this semester. You have to think of our reputation."

"Yes, Dr Ehrlichman, I guess I do."

6

Jim pushed his way through the double doors that led to the boys' locker room. A few students were still standing around outside, but the locker room itself was being guarded by the college security officer, Mr Wallechinsky, in his tight brown uniform, blocking the entrance with his beefy sun-reddened arms folded.

"Mr Rook?"

"How's it going, Mr Wallechinsky? I just came to take a look."

"I warn you, Mr Rook. Your heart's going to bleed."

"Don't you have any idea how it happened?"

Mr Wallechinsky shook his head. "Up until eleven o'clock, everything was fine. By half after, somebody had managed to turn the whole damn locker room into a disaster area."

"Nobody heard anything? It must have caused a hell of a racket."

"Nobody *heard* nothing. Nobody *saw* nothing. The last person that anybody saw near the locker room was that Red Indian student of yours."

"Native American, Mr Wallechinsky, if you don't mind."

"Ah, come on, Mr Rook, what's in a name? I'm a Polack, right? You can call me a Polack if you like. There's no name never hurt me."

"All the same, Catherine White Bird is a Native American. Or a Navajo. You can call her either." He paused, and then he said, "So what was she doing here? Did you ask her?"

"Sure. She just came back to fetch Martin Amato's wallet. I guess you know that she and Martin Amato have been dating."

Jim nodded. "Sure." He always did his best to keep up with his students' love lives. It often made it easier to understand why a particular student was depressed, or

7

dreamy, or exceptionally touchy. And he wasn't at all surprised that Catherine White Bird and Martin Amato had fallen for each other – they made a brilliantly attractive young couple. Jim could have fancied Catherine White Bird himself if he'd been fifteen years younger, and he hadn't made it a cast-iron rule never to get involved with any of his female students. Apart from calling Dr Ehrlichman a bureaucratic pinhead, that was the quickest way for any teacher to find himself looking for work.

"Catherine didn't see anything either?"

"Not a thing. And there's no way she could have done anything like this herself."

"You'd better show me," said Jim.

Mr Wallechinsky opened the door of the locker room and let Jim inside. It was gloomy, because the fluorescent strip-lights had been shattered, and there was water hissing all over the floor from three basins which had been completely wrenched away from the wall. There were grey steel lockers lying on their sides, on their backs, and all kinds of angles. But they hadn't just been pushed over: they had been bent and twisted, some of them almost in half. Three or four of them had been gouged and ripped, as if by the teeth of a mechanical excavator.

Heaps of football uniforms were strewn around everywhere, and every one of them had been torn into shreds. West Grove's bright new green-and-orange outfits had been donated by West Grove Screen & Window, at a cost of more than $3,500. Now they were reduced to slews of sodden rags. Even their shoulder armour was torn apart, and their green-and-orange helmets were split open. Jim bent down and picked up one helmet that was crushed like a trodden-on M&M. The mystery was, you couldn't crush a helmet like this with a sledgehammer, or by driving a Jeep over it.

8

The walls of the locker room were scarred, too. All across the far wall, the white porcelain tiles had been scratched right through to the clay. Jim walked across to the wall and ran his fingers down the grooves. There were five of them, in parallel, almost like clawmarks. Yet even a full-sized grizzly bear wasn't capable of making deep scratches on high-glazed porcelain.

Ben Hunkus came in and stood beside him. "Pretty damned tragic, isn't it?" he said.

"No question about it, I think we should call the cops," said Jim. "Whoever did this was totally berserk. Apart from that, he must have had some kind of pick or farm implement that could pierce right through the sides of these lockers. Imagine what could have happened if somebody had disturbed him."

He dropped the smashed helmet onto the floor. "What I can't understand is, why would anybody want to bust up a college locker room? I mean, what the hell *for*?"

"Maybe somebody from Chabot wanted to make sure that West Grove would lose."

"Are you kidding me? Chabot could flatten The Fumblers with shopping bags over their heads. They wouldn't have to do anything like this."

"Listen, Jim, West Grove have a pretty good chance of winning this game. Or at least of not losing by very much."

"Sure, Ben. I'm sorry. But I don't understand this at all."

While Ben tried to heave up some of the fallen lockers, Jim stood in the middle of the room looking around. He was sure that he could sense something, and he wasn't at all sure what it was. It was as strong as that feeling you get when you walk into a room crowded with unwelcoming strangers. It was a deep hostility – almost a *rage*.

"Do you feel something?" he asked Ben.

9

Ben was struggling, red-faced, with an overturned bench. "I feel good and mad, I can tell you that."

"I know. But can you *feel* something, here in this room?"

Ben stopped struggling and looked around. "I don't know what you mean."

"Hm. I'm not sure that I do, either. Do you want a hand with that?"

Ben didn't answer. He was too busy rattling a locker door that had been twisted into the shape of a huge grey bowtie.

He left Ben to his clearing-up and walked back down to the football field. It was a perfect October day – clear and cool, with a light breeze to make the college pennants snap. The West Grove band was playing *99 Red Balloons* for the seventh time, with all the off-key enthusiasm of a Mexican street orchestra. The cheerleaders were strutting up and down in their short pleated skirts and waving their green-and-orange pom-poms. If there was one thing that West Grove could boast, it was the prettiest girls. Prancing in front of them was one of Jim's class, Sue-Robin Caufield, whirling her baton like a helicopter rotor. Jim gave her a smile and a wave and she gave him a winning smile in return. God, he thought, if only that girl could read and write the way she can prance.

He found Martin Amato again, down by the 20-yard line. Catherine White Bird was with him.

"Hi, Mr Rook. What do you think?"

"What do I think? I think I'm going to persuade Dr Ehrlichman to call the police. Meanwhile, tell all of your team to keep on the lookout. We could be looking for nothing more than somebody who gets a kick out of trashing locker rooms. But on the other hand there might be some psycho around who's got some kind of a grudge against you."

"A grudge? Who has a grudge against a college football team?"

"People have had stranger grudges than that," Jim told him. "There was a woman who lived next door to me who used to have a grudge against Lou Costello. She sent him hate mail till the day she died."

Catherine White Bird said, "It couldn't be a student, could it, Mr Rook?"

Catherine had only just joined Special Class II. Up until three months ago, she had lived on the Navajo reservation at Window Rock, close to the border between Arizona and New Mexico, and studied at the Navajo Community College. But her father had won a leading role in a new TV series about the Navajo police, *Blood Brothers*, and she and her two brothers had taken the opportunity to join him in Los Angeles.

Her mother had died when she was fifteen, but one of the first things that she had said when she introduced herself to the class had been, "I look just like my mother. I *am* my mother." In which case, her mother must have been very tall, over 5ft 10ins, with long black hair that fell almost as far as her waist. Catherine had high cheekbones and slanting brown eyes and full, slightly pouting lips. She was big-breasted and long-legged, and today she was wearing a blue checkered shirt and skintight jeans. Around her neck was a silver necklace with an enamel eagle on it.

Jim said, "If it *is* a student, then believe me we'll find out who it is and we'll use his guts for guitar strings."

"My grandmother had a way of finding people who caused trouble," Catherine told him. "She used to have magic bones which pointed them out."

"I don't think we're going to need any magic bones to

find this guy," said Martin. "He's probably bright green, with burst-apart clothes."

"It beats me that nobody saw anything," said Jim. "Whoever did it must have been carrying an axe or something like that. And the noise must have been awesome. All those lockers being knocked over."

"I didn't hear anything," said Catherine. "And I mean, I can practically hear the grass grow."

Russell said, "That thing that Indians do in movies, when they put their ear down to the ground and say 'heap plenty horses coming this way', can you do that?"

"Russell," Jim warned him. "I've told you before about racial stereotypes."

"I don't mind," Catherine smiled. "Just don't let my brothers hear you talking like that, that's all."

"Yes, Russell," said Martin. "You'll end up bristling with arrows."

Bristling, thought Jim. That was the word his grandfather had used. 'It's dark, and it's very old, and it kind of bristles, if you get my meaning.' The truth was, he *hadn't* got his grandfather's meaning, not really, but he hadn't been able to persuade him to elaborate any further. All he had said was 'you'll see.'

Yet there was something about what had happened today, and the strange hostile sensation that he had experienced in the locker room, that made him think again about his grandfather's warning. Maybe this dark, old, bristling menace had come around the curve quicker than he had expected.

The football game started at a quarter after three. Jim sat on the bleachers on the north side of the field with George Babouris, the physics lecturer, and Susan Randall, the head of geography. George was big and bearded and devouring Greek kebabs as if he hadn't eaten for three weeks. Susan was looking as fresh and pretty as a girl in a Norman Rockwell painting: bobbed brunette hair, rosy cheeks, and a red skinny-rib sweater and turned-up jeans. He and Susan had been having an on-off kind of relationship for the past two months. The reality was that they were completely unsuited. Susan was seriously into step aerobics, aromatherapy and ancient maps, while Jim was seriously into Chinese take-out and Bruce Willis movies. But Susan was attracted by Jim's undernourished, dishevelled looks, his scruffy dark hair and his eyes the color of green bottle-glass. She loved the way he pressed two finger-tips to his forehead and squeezed his eyes tight when he was trying to think, and he always made her laugh. She also knew that he was totally dedicated to his students. Once she had sat in back of Special Class II and listened to a tall black youth with dreadlocks reciting *Speaking of Poetry* by John Peale Bishop:

"Traditional, with all its symbols
  ancient as the metaphors in dreams;
  strange, with never before heard music; continuous
  until the torches deaden at the bedroom door."

The youth himself had been awed by what he was saying, and Susan had found it hard to keep back her tears, particularly since he had started in Special Class II as one of the most aggressive and disruptive of students, with a vocabulary that was nothing but a mangled mixture of street-talk and f-words.

"'*Never before heard music,*'" the youth had said, after he had finished, pointing his finger at every member of the class, one by one. "You think what that means, '*never before heard music.*' Shit, you don't know how much I love those words."

Susan turned and laid her hand on Jim's knee. He glanced at her and gave her a tight smile.

"You're looking worried," she said.

Jim shrugged. "West Grove is losing about eight-and-a-half billion to nothing. What do you expect?"

"You're not worried about that, Jim. We usually lose by much more than that."

"I don't know . . . it's this business in the locker room. It gives me a bad feeling, that's all."

"Come on, relax. The police will find out who did it."

"I'm not so sure." He couldn't tell her that his grandfather had appeared to him today, and what his grandfather had said. She just wouldn't believe him. Christ, he could hardly believe it himself – even though he was gradually getting used to the idea that he was able to see visions and visitations that most people couldn't. At the age of ten he had almost died from pneumonia, and his near-death experience had given him the facility to see the spirits that still walk among the living, whether they came to comfort, to protect, or to seek their revenge.

"Do you *know* something about this?" asked Susan. "I get the feeling you *know* something about this."

Jim shook his head. "Just like I said, it gives me a bad feeling, that's all."

Out on the field, Russell had spent most of the game lumbering in unsuccessful pursuit of Chabot's star players. But as the game came to a close, and Chabot's captain Wayne Dooly came sprinting toward the line for a last-minute touchdown, Russell stepped out directly in front of him. Dooly was running too fast to sidestep. He tripped, missed his footing, and collided with Russell with an echoing crash of flesh and body armour. Dooly stood upright for a moment, swaying. Then – as the final whistle blew – he fell flat on his back on the turf. West Grove's supporters cheered and ran out onto the field.

They hoisted Russell up on their shoulders, although it took six of them to do it, and they paraded him around the touchline. Jim stood up and applauded. He had never seen Russell look so happy in the whole time that he had been at West Grove.

Martin came off the field and Jim and Susan went over to commiserate. "It could have been worse," Jim told him. "You did good, considering that you lost all of your uniforms."

"Sure, and considering I've got the slowest, clumsiest team in the entire history of college football. To think – perfectly innocent pigs were killed so that these idiots could kick their skins the wrong way down the field."

Catherine put her arm around him, kissed his cheek and held him close. "You're still my hero," she smiled, and blew him a kiss.

"What are you guys doing now?" Jim asked them. "I gather there's some kind of party in the gym."

"It's a Disaster Party," said Martin. "We're celebrating the longest unbroken run of defeats in community college history."

"No, we're not," said Catherine. "We're going to celebrate the very last game we lose. Next time we're going to win, aren't we? And we're going to go on winning, even if I have to use my grandmother's magic to make it happen!"

"Your grandmother sounds like quite a woman," said Jim.

"Oh, she was," said Catherine. "She could make dead cicadas dance; and she could make it rain. She could walk through a meadow and all the wild flowers would spring up after her."

Jim caught her eye for a moment and she caught his: and in that moment he knew that she wasn't telling him lies – that the stories she had told about her grandmother

15

weren't just pretty stories, they were true. And she knew that he knew. Magic people do.

"Come on," said Martin. "I'm going to have to take a shower. Then we can get down to some serious celebrating."

"We've arranged for you to use the girls' showers," said Ben. "Mr Wallechinsky is going to be on patrol, just to make sure that you behave yourselves. Like, no using the girls' shampoo, or wearing their panties afterward. I don't want a transvestism situation here, to add to everything else."

Russell came up, red-faced and sweating, but infinitely happy. Jim gave him a high five and said, "Well done, Russell. You may have lost the game but you sure made your mark."

Russell said, "'History to the defeated, may say Alas but cannot help or pardon.'"

Jim was taken aback. "That's WH Auden. Who taught you that?"

"You did, sir."

"Did I?"

"It was one of the things that made me train for the team. It was one of the things that made me try to stop eating all the goddamned time."

Jim looked at Russell and saw him for the first time not as a fat, clowning, overweight student, but as a man. He laid his hand on Russell's armoured shoulder and nodded, and that was all he had to do. He didn't smile for very long. A black Firebird had drawn up in the visitors' parking lot, its engine burbling, and two tall young men climbed out. They came walking across the grass with all the purpose of people who have a serious score to settle.

Jim recognized them at once. They were Catherine's older brothers, Paul and Grey Cloud. They came to

16

collect Catherine every day after college, and the only time that Jim had seen Catherine out of college, on the boardwalk at Venice Beach, her brothers had flanked her like bodyguards, conspicuously grim-faced among the smiling roller-bladers and bikini-clad cyclists. This afternoon Paul was wearing a charcoal-grey suit and a black turtle-neck, while Grey Cloud wore a black double breasted coat and jeans. Grey Cloud's hair was tied back in a long ponytail and he wore Navajo jewelry around his neck. Both of them wore impenetrable black sunglasses.

"You're late," Grey Cloud told Catherine. "Do you know what time it is?"

"The game started late," Martin put in. "Somebody vandalized our locker room."

"Excuse me, was I talking to you?" Grey Cloud retorted. Then he turned back to Catherine and said, "I specifically asked you to call if you were going to be late."

"Hey, come on, lighten up," said Martin. "She's not a twelve-year-old."

"Listen, man, stay out of this," said Paul. "This is family and it's none of your business."

"Catherine happens to be my girlfriend. I think that kind of makes it my business, don't you?"

"Catherine isn't anybody's girlfriend and especially not yours. When she does find herself a man, he's going to be Navajo."

Grey Cloud tried to take hold of Catherine's arm but Martin gripped his wrist and forced his arm behind his back. "Get off me, you bastard!" Grey Cloud shouted at him. "You get off me, or I'll kill you!"

But Martin kept hold of him and said, "You listen to me. Catherine's old enough and intelligent enough to be able to make her own decisions about where she wants to be and who she wants to see. You got that?"

Jim stepped up and separated them. "Break it up, OK?

17

If you want to have the second battle of the Little Big Horn, have it someplace else."

"Little Big Horn was fought by the Sioux," said Grey Cloud, in disgust.

"Yes – and the whites were massacred," added Paul.

Martin said, "You listen to me, you guys. Right now, we're having a party. Catherine's coming and if you like, you can come along too. After the party, Catherine and me are going to LA Buzz for some kick-ass chilli. After *that*, I'll bring Catherine home, safe and sound. Now, do you have any problem with that?"

"Catherine – you come home now," Grey Cloud demanded.

Catherine hesitated for a while, and then shook her head. "I want to go to the party. Come on, Grey Cloud, it's only a party."

"Father wants us all together tonight."

"Father wants us all together *every* night. I have to have some life of my own."

"With *these*?" said Grey Cloud, contemptuously, looking around at Martin and Russell and Mark Foley and Rita Munoz.

"These are my friends."

"These will *never* be your friends."

Grey Cloud made another attempt to snatch her arm, but this time both Martin and Russell pushed him away. "Hear this, pal," said Russell. "You try to touch her one more time and I'll sit on your head."

"Yeah," warned Mark. "You ever hear of a tribe called the Flatheads? Well, that's what happened to them!"

"Don't you insult my culture!" Grey Cloud snapped at him, jabbing him in the chest with his finger. "My culture barely survived because of people like you!"

Jim said, "That's enough, guys. If Catherine doesn't want to go home with you, there's nothing you can do about it. So just leave the campus quietly, OK, before I have to do something I don't want to do, like call security."

Grey Cloud gave an aggressive shrug of his shoulders. He looked Martin straight in the eye and said, "I can make you one promise, my friend. If you try to take Catherine out tonight, you won't see tomorrow's sun come up."

"Are you threatening me?" grinned Martin. "Because if you are, you're crazy. I've got all these witnesses."

"I'm not threatening you," Grey Cloud replied. "I'm telling you what will happen to you, just as surely as one moon follows the next."

With that, he and Paul turned around and walked back to their car. They climbed in and drove slowly away, although they paused for a moment so that Grey Cloud could take off his sunglasses and give Martin and Catherine one last steely look.

"Pretty protective, those brothers of yours," Jim remarked.

Catherine was flushed and upset. "They're so angry all the time! They hate white culture, both of them. Especially Grey Cloud."

"Yes, I can see that by his Armani jacket and his Ray-Bans."

"Oh, it's not the accessories, Mr Rook. Navajo have always been good at adapting, at changing their ways. A long time ago they were farmers. Then they became hunters and travellers and raiders. Once they walked. Then they rode horses and carried guns. But what Paul and Grey Cloud don't like is the way that the Navajo are trying to ape white society.

"They think that too many Navajos are forgetting the old ways – forgetting what we are, forgetting what we mean. They think that we're forgetting the legends, and the stories, and the magic. They think that in ten years' time, we won't be anything more than second-class whites."

"And that's why they don't want you to go out with Martin?"

Catherine took hold of Martin's hand, and squeezed it. "They don't want me to go out with any white man. But they won't stop me, no matter what they say."

Martin said, "Listen, I don't want to cause you any trouble."

"I know that," said Catherine. "But you promised to take me to the Disaster Party, didn't you? And you promised to take me to LA Buzz? Don't tell me that you're going to be one of those white men who speaks with forked tongue."

"All right," said Jim, "I'll let you get on with your evening. Martin – too bad about the game. Maybe one day."

"Sure thing, Mr Rook," Martin told him. "And maybe, one day, Gloach will fly."

Jim and Susan went to the Disaster Party for about a half-hour, just to show willing, but Jim wasn't really in the mood for techno rock, flashing lights and noisy students, and he felt like something harder to drink than strawberry punch. "I think I'm a little too old for this," he shouted into Susan's ear. Susan nodded, although she was jiggling enthusiastically to the sound mixes of TYOUSSi and DJ Ham and he could see that she was itching to dance.

Amanda Zaparelli came up and wrapped her arms around him. "Come on, Mr Rook, let's show them what we can do!" But he managed to steer her over to Ray Vito, who had carried a torch for her ever since junior high, and he swept her away in a techno merengue that had everybody clapping and whistling.

Outside, Jim took hold of Susan's hand. The yuccas were silhouetted black and jagged against a sunset as garish as a Hawaiian shirt. "How about coming back to my place?" Jim asked her. "We could pick up some Chinese and a bottle of wine on the way. I've found this great Szechuan place where they do a stir-fried quail you could kill your mother for."

Susan shook her head. "I'm sorry, Jim. I have a whole heap of assessments to do. And we're going on a field trip Monday, to Mount Wilson. I have to get everything ready for that."

"Hey – we're not drifting apart, are we?" Jim asked her.

"I don't think so. We're just like two boats, bobbing on a pond. Sometimes we bump together and sometimes we don't."

"I know. But we haven't had a good bump in ages."

She kissed him. "I like you, Jim. In fact I think I almost love you. But I don't want to commit myself too much, not just yet."

Jim walked her over to her pink Volkswagen Beetle convertible and opened the door for her. He almost felt like proposing marriage on the spot, but he knew what her answer would be, and he preferred to keep on hoping that 'almost love' would eventually flourish into something more. He kissed her and said, "I'll call you later. Maybe you'll have changed your mind."

"I'll be up to my ears in assessments."

"Didn't you know? That's what first attracted me to you – your assessments."

"Good*night*, Jim," she said, emphatically.

Jim watched her drive away, waving to him as she went. He stood and watched her until she had rounded the curve in front of the college, and then he walked thoughtfully back to his car. Maybe he should ask his grandfather about her. Maybe the dead knew more about love than the living. It was always worth a try.

He made himself a tuna sandwich and watched sports for the rest of the evening, while the feline formerly known as Tibbles sat on the arm of the chair opposite, her eyes locked onto every tiny movement his sandwich made. When he had finished it all she gave him such a death-stare that he put her outside the front door of his apartment and told her not to come back until she stopped feeling so resentful.

He went to bed early and had a sleepless, sprawly night. He dreamed that his grandfather was walking away from him along Electric Avenue, moving in a strange, eerie glide. He kept calling his grandfather to stop.

"What do you mean it bristles?" he kept shouting. "You said that it bristles. What did you mean?"

But his grandfather wouldn't stop, and wouldn't turn around. He kept on gliding away down the street, and all the sky was luminous purple, with a bone-white sun.

He heard an alarm-bell ringing, and he thought he ought to warn Susan that something terrible was going to happen. The trouble was, he didn't know how to find out where she lived. He started to run, and then he realised that his telephone was ringing, and that he wasn't running at all, but kicking against his sheet like a small boy in a tantrum.

He sat up and dislodged the receiver. "Yes? Who is it?"

"Mr Rook? Mr Jim Rook? Sorry to disturb you, sir. This is Lieutenant Harris."

"Lieutenant Harris?" He groped for his bedside lamp. "What the hell time is it?"

"It's a little after seven-thirty, sir. I hope I didn't wake you."

"No, no. I'm always awake in the middle of the night."

"Well, it's pretty much morning now, sir. And I'm afraid I've got some real bad news for you."

Jim rubbed his eyes and pinched the bridge of his nose. "Bad? How bad?"

"Just about as bad as it can get, sir. Martin Amato was found dead on Venice Beach this morning."

Jim felt a terrible tingling surge of dread. "Dead? Martin? I can't believe it. Are you sure it's Martin?"

"His father's just identified him, I'm afraid."

"Well, what happened to him? Was it some kind of accident?"

"I don't think so, sir. It looks like he was attacked by some kind of animal. And when I say animal, I mean something very wild, and very mean, and very, very strong."

"What do you want me to do?" asked Jim.

"It'd be a help if you came down to the morgue, sir. Martin's girlfriend is here . . . Ms Catherine White Bird? She's in a real bad state and she keeps asking for you. I also think it's going to be worth your while talking to one of our counsellors – you know, so that you know how to break the news to Martin's fellow students."

"Yes," said Jim. "Yes, I'll come down right now."

He replaced the receiver and sat on the edge of the bed and he was literally shaking. Animal, Lieutenant Harris had said. Very wild, and very mean, and very, very strong. All Jim could think about were those deep scratches on the walls of the locker room, and the way that the lockers themselves had been twisted and ripped open as if by huge and powerful claws.

23

Chapter Two

Lieutenant Harris said, "This way," and opened the door to a small waiting-room with two beige couches, a collection of *National Geographic* magazines and a faded framed poster of an orange grove. Catherine White Bird was sitting in the far corner, her arms crossed tightly across her chest and her face rigid. She looked as if she were just about to make her first parachute jump.

Standing by the window was Henry Black Eagle, Catherine's father. He was as tall as his sons, with silvery-black hair that hung long over his shoulders. He had the same high cheekbones as Catherine, although his nose was much more hawklike and his cheeks were deeply lined. He wore a fringed black buckskin jacket and black jeans.

"Mr Black Eagle, this is Mr Rook, Catherine's tutor from West Grove," said Lieutenant Harris.

Jim held out his hand. "Of course, we've met. How are you doing, Mr Black Eagle? I watch your TV show whenever I have the chance."

He turned to Catherine and said, "How are you feeling, Catherine? Is there anything you need?"

She looked up at him with desperate eyes. "I just want Martin back, that's all. I just want you to tell me that this is all a dream."

Jim sat beside her and put a comforting arm around her. "I'm so sorry. I don't know what to say to you.

Martin is such a great guy." He didn't correct himself and say "*was.*"

Lieutenant Harris was cleaning the edge of his thumbnail with his teeth. "She says she and Martin took in a chilli at LA Buzz and then they went for a long walk on the beach. The last time she saw him was when he dropped her off home."

"So why did he go back to the beach? He lives in the opposite direction."

"Who knows? His car was parked about a half-mile away."

Jim said to Catherine, "Did Martin tell you he was going back to the beach?"

Catherine tearfully shook her head. "He kissed me goodnight and then he drove off. I can still see his face, the way he was laughing."

Her father said, "Why don't you come home now, Catherine? There's nothing more that you can do here."

"I don't want to leave Martin. I can't."

Henry Black Eagle said, "Catherine, this was a terrible thing to happen. But Martin's gone now, and nothing can ever bring him back. Besides, he could never have been yours, you know that."

Jim frowned at him. "What makes you say that?"

"Because, Mr Rook, Catherine is already spoken for. She has been pledged in marriage since she was twelve, and when the time comes she will have to honour that pledge."

"I thought that only Indians from India believed in arranged marriages."

Henry Black Eagle didn't answer. Instead, he reached out his hand and took hold of Catherine's shoulder. "Come on now, Catherine. Your brothers are waiting for you."

"Please, dad. I don't want to go. I want to stay here a little while longer."

Jim said, "Why not let her stay, Henry? Let me have a talk to her, and then I'll bring her home. I think she could use a little unburdening, if you know what I mean. Come on, now. Be a guy."

Henry Black Eagle puckered his lips so that they looked as if they been sewn together by headhunters. But then he said, "All right. So long as you bring her back no later than noon," he said, checking his gold Rolex Oyster.

"I'll be on time, honest Injun," Jim promised, and then flushed bright red when he realised what he'd said. Whatever he thought about it, Henry Black Eagle didn't reply, but nodded curtly to Lieutenant Harris and walked out of the waiting-room.

Lieutenant Harris turned back to Catherine. "Pretty serious individual, your dad. It's strange that, isn't it? On TV he always seems like such a fun guy."

"On TV he speaks from a script," said Catherine, and there was a flatness in the way she said it that made Jim think that she had often clashed with her father before, and often said those same words before.

A uniformed patrolman came in to tell Lieutenant Harris that the medical examiner wanted to talk to him, so that Jim and Catherine were left alone. Jim said, "You want to talk about what happened last night?"

"I've told you everything. We left the Disaster Party and then we drove to Venice for a chilli. Afterward we walked on the beach for a while. I've never dared to go there at night because of all the local lowlife. But with Martin I felt safe. With Martin I *always* felt safe."

"Your family didn't care for him too much."

"It wasn't Martin in particular. They've never liked *any* boy I've dated, *ever*. If they had their way, I'd go back to Arizona and do nothing but sit outside a *hogan* all day, weaving blankets."

26

"This guy you're supposed to be marrying . . . what's he like?"

She shook her head. "I only ever saw him once. He lives out by Fort Defiance. Dad took me to meet him on my twelfth birthday, and said 'This is the man you're going to marry.' Can you believe that? It was very dark in the trailer where we met, and all I could see was a very thin young man, naked to the waist. That's all I remember. Except that my father cut our wrists and pressed them together and said that our blood was now joined forever, no matter what happened. I think I cried. In any case my father never took me to see this man again and I kind of forgot all about it. I never thought that I really *would* have to marry him. But when we came here, and I started to date Ray, and then Martin . . . well, it's all come up to the surface again."

"You don't even know the guy's name?"

"No. And I've never wanted to know. I want to marry somebody I fall in love with. I want to marry somebody here in LA. I want some fun, you know? I don't want to spend the rest of my life sitting in some trailer park in Arizona."

Jim said, "You realise you're old enough now to do whatever you damn well like?"

"Try telling that to my dad. Try telling that to Paul, and Grey Cloud."

"You'll work it out, I'm sure of it. And if you can't work it out, come back and talk to me again. Right now you shouldn't be worrying about your family problems, anyway. You should be trying to come to terms with what's happened to Martin. It's been a hell of a shock, hasn't it, and it's going to be days before you're ready to start accepting that it's really happened. Weeks before you stop crying all the time. And *months*, believe me,

27

before you can go through a whole day without thinking of him, even once."

Catherine's eyes welled with tears and her shoulders started to shake. "He's dead," she wept. "He's dead, and he's dead, and he's dead."

Jim held her close, and smelled the light musky perfume that she wore. He didn't particularly like it, but it was just what young girls wore, and whenever he smelled it again he would think of that bare waiting-room with its beige couches and its faded framed poster.

"You remember me talking a couple of weeks ago about Edna St Vincent Millay?" he said, in his softest voice. "She wrote a sonnet that I sent to my sister once, after her husband had died of a heart attack. It ends up:

Thus in the winter stands the lonely tree,
Nor knows what birds have vanished one by one
Yet knows its boughs more silent than before:
It cannot say what loves have come and gone;
I only know that summer sang in me
A little while, that sings in me no more."

Catherine lifted her head and looked at him, her eyelashes clotted with tears. "That's so sad," she said.

"Yes, but it tells you that you're not alone, that other people grieve too. It tells you that other people understand the pain you're suffering."

Catherine took out a balled-up tissue and wiped her eyes. "They won't let me see him. Could you ask them if I could see him, just one last time?"

"Well, I'll ask Lieutenant Harris, see what he says. I can't promise you, though."

He got up, and he was about to leave the room when the door opened and Catherine's brothers came in. They were both dressed in black T-shirts and black jeans. Grey

28

Cloud's was emblazoned with the initials DNA – not for dioxyribonucleic acid, but for *Dinebeiina Nahiilna Be Agaditahe*, the Navajo legal aid corps.

"What do you two want?" Jim demanded. "Don't you think you've caused enough trouble already?"

"We've come to take our sister home," said Grey Cloud, taking off his sunglasses.

"Well, you're going to have to wait," Jim told him. "We're not through here yet, and your father's given Catherine permission to stay till twelve."

"Do you have some kind of hearing impediment? I said we've come to take our sister home."

Jim stepped up to him so that their faces were only six inches apart. "You listen to me, you punk. Your sister has experienced a traumatic shock and she needs all the understanding she can get. What she doesn't need is you two swaggering in here like two medium-grilled John Travoltas and putting her through even more stress. So back off. You can wait, if you want to, and give her a ride when she's ready. Otherwise put an egg in your boot and beat it."

"You don't talk to us like that," put in Paul, jabbing his finger at Jim's chest. "This is our country, man. Not yours. You don't have the right."

"Aren't you forgetting what you said to Martin in front of half-a-dozen witnesses at yesterday's football game? I'm sure my friend Lieutenant Harris is going to be very interested in that."

"Threaten him? I didn't threaten him," Grey Cloud retorted. "I simply told him what was going to happen to him if he kept on dating Catherine. It was a prediction, *capiche*? You can't arrest anybody for making a prediction."

"Oh, no? Well, here's another prediction: if you don't back off and give Catherine the time she needs to get over this shock, your nose will be mysteriously broken before the count of ten. Besides, what the hell kind of Navajo word is '*capiche*'?"

Grey Cloud angrily clenched his fist but his brother Paul held him back. "Come on, man, this isn't worth it. We can wait for five minutes."

"Thank you," said Jim, trying not to sound sarcastic. "I'm going to talk to Lieutenant Harris and while I'm gone maybe you can find it in your hearts to be good to your sister."

"Mister, you don't know *how* good," Paul told him.

Lieutenant Harris was standing outside the morgue door, talking to Dr Whaley, the medical examiner, a balding, stoop-shouldered man with lopsided spectacles and a huge mournful nose.

"You and the rest of your faculty must be feeling pretty shaken," said Dr Whaley. "I never saw anything like this, not in thirty-two years with the coroner's office."

"Catherine wants to know if she can see him."

"I don't think that's very advisable. But you can, if you like."

Jim glanced at Lieutenant Harris, but all Lieutenant Harris did was to shrug and say, "It's up to you. You haven't had breakfast yet, have you?"

"It's just that I'd appreciate another opinion," said Dr Whaley. "And I mean *any* opinion, whether it's medical or not. I've already called Jack Skipper from the LA Zoo. He's going to come and take a look and see if he can't identify what kind of animal might have inflicted these kind of injuries. I'll tell you, it wasn't a dog, and that's for sure."

He led Jim busily into the chilly, green-tiled autopsy room, his rubbers making echoey squeaks on the floor, and Lieutenant Harris followed. There were two stainless-steel tables set side by side. One was empty. On the other lay a body, under a green hospital sheet. Dr Whaley walked around it and switched on his bright pivoting lamp.

Lieutenant Harris said, "Martin Amato was found at approximately 5 a.m. by two joggers exercising their dog on the beach. When you see his injuries you'll understand that whoever or *what*ever attacked him killed him almost instantly."

"Judging by his body temperature, he hadn't been dead for more than two hours," said Dr Whaley. He took hold of the edge of the sheet, and then he said to Jim, "Are you ready for this?"

Jim nodded, and Dr Whaley slowly drew the sheet down the whole length of Martin Amato's naked body. Or what was left of Martin Amato's naked body.

His head was unrecognizable. One side of his face had been torn completely away, exposing his teeth and part of his jawbone. Most of his scalp had been wrenched off, too, leaving a clotted red tangle of skin and hair. But it was his chest and stomach that horrified Jim the most. There were four terrible rips – three or four inches deep in places – which crossed the front of his body diagonally from his left shoulder to his right thigh. They were parallel, like a clawmark, but what kind of animal had claws that could cut through the muscle and bones of a young man's ribcage, snagging his heart and puncturing his lungs, before slicing his insides into hideously decorative ribbons? Reds, blacks, yellows and sticky beiges.

Jim stared at Martin's body for almost a minute without saying anything. Then he turned away, and he heard Dr Whaley replacing the sheet.

"Well?" asked Lieutenant Harris. "Any ideas? You ever see anything like that before?"

"I thought mountain lion at first," said Dr Whaley. "But mountain lions don't only claw their quarry, they

31

bite them, too – and there are no teethmarks anyplace at all. What was done to that poor boy was done with no more than three extremely powerful blows – either with an animal claw or an implement that resembles an animal claw."

Lieutenant Harris said, "Besides that, how the hell could a mountain lion get to Venice Beach? We've had no reports of lions missing from zoos or private menageries or movie animal companies. And the interesting thing is that – apart from the pawprints left by the joggers' dog when it first approached the body – there were no tracks in the sand that resembled anything like the spoor of a very large lion-like animal. Only human footprints, that's all, and some bicycle tires."

"And there were no eye-witnesses that you know of?" asked Jim.

"We've already started knocking on doors, and we'll be putting out an appeal on the news – but no, not so far. The kind of people who frequent Venice Beach in the middle of the night are not normally the kind of people you might describe as concerned citizens."

Jim glanced back at Martin's body. "I think I'd like to get out of here," he said.

Lieutenant Harris took him outside, and they stood on the steps in the sunshine so that Jim could take three or four very deep breaths. "God," he said, "I hope it was quick. I hope he didn't suffer."

"Almost instantaneous," said Lieutenant Harris. "Just imagine the shock to the system. Wham. He didn't stand a chance."

"There's something I have to tell you," said Jim. "I'm not supposed to report this without going through Dr Ehrlichman, but I think the sooner you know, the better. Just before yesterday's football game against Chabot college, somebody broke into the boys' locker room at

West Grove and smashed everything to pieces. They tore washbasins away from the walls, they ripped steel lockers to pieces. What was more, they left deep scratches in the tiles – scratches that went right through the glaze into the clay. Scratches that looked like clawmarks."

"And this wasn't reported to the police?"

"Dr Ehrlichman wanted an internal inquiry first. We've had quite a bit of police trouble lately up at West Grove. Mainly minor stuff – speed, crack, petty theft. But he wasn't keen to have a black-and-white rolling up in the middle of a major football event."

"What you're trying to tell me is that the lacerations you saw on Martin Amato's body reminded you of the scratches you saw on the locker room walls?"

Jim nodded. "There's something else, too, although I don't know whether it's related. Martin's girlfriend is a full-blooded Navajo. Her two brothers came to the college yesterday and there was an argument between them. One of her brothers made a threat that if Martin didn't leave Catherine alone, he wouldn't live to see the next sunrise."

Lieutenant Harris whistled. "Who heard him say that?"

"Me . . . and maybe seven or eight other students."

"In that case, I think I'd better have a talk to these brothers of hers. Where can I find them – any idea?"

Jim heard footsteps and looked around. "Speak of the devils," he said. Walking toward them were Paul, Catherine and Grey Cloud. They came up close and then stopped.

"Sorry, but we're tired of waiting for you, Mr Shoulder-To-Cry-On," said Grey Cloud. "We're taking our sister home now."

"I told you before. Your father said she could stay."

"Sometimes our father says things that he doesn't really mean. We're going."

"Well . . . I don't think so," put in Lieutenant Harris. "I'd like to ask you two gentlemen a few questions first."

Grey Cloud gave Jim the coldest of stares. "Has somebody been talking to you, lieutenant?"

"Somebody did mention something that you said to Martin Amato at yesterday's college football game."

"I told him to stay away from our sister, yes," said Grey Cloud, without hesitation.

"And you said that if he didn't, he wouldn't see another sunrise?"

"That's correct. But it wasn't intended as a threat."

"I wouldn't call it a term of endearment."

"It wasn't. I didn't like Martin Amato at all, and I'm not going to pretend that I did. But if you warn a man not to walk across the San Diego Freeway and he insists on doing it, what do you say to him? You say the same thing: 'you won't live to see another sunrise.' That isn't a threat. It's simply a prediction."

"But why should dating your sister be such a risky enterprise? Who else was going to take objection to it, if not you?"

"Some things just can't be explained," said Grey Cloud.

"I'm sorry . . . you're going to *have* to explain them. Whatever you want to call it, you made a threat against Martin Amato's life in front of witnesses and the next morning he was found dead."

Grey Cloud said, "My brother and I were both at home last night. All night."

"Can anybody vouch for that?"

"My father and my sister."

"No other independent witnesses?"

"A friend called me from New Mexico just after 2 a.m. He forgot how late it was. His wife had just had a baby boy."

"You'll be able to give me his name, won't you?"

"For sure. And his telephone number, too. Henry Red Jacket. He called from the Wide Ruins reservation."

Lieutenant Harris jotted it down. Then he thoughtfully scratched the back of his neck. "There's still one point you haven't made clear. If you didn't have anything to do with Martin Amato's death, then who do you think did? And what made you so sure that he was going to die?"

Paul said, "Don't forget that we're Navajo, lieutenant. We can feel the rain coming days before the clouds appear. We can hear people approaching hours before they arrive."

"So? What difference does that make?"

"Martin Amato had the look of death on him yesterday, that's all. It was almost a certainty."

Lieutenant Harris pointed his pen at him, warningly. "Let me advise you, my friend. You may be able to predict all of next week's winners at Santa Rosita, but that's not going to help you in a court of law."

"You're arresting us?" asked Grey Cloud.

"No, I'm not. But I'm going to want to talk to you again. Do us both a big favor and stay at the same address until I advise you otherwise."

Catherine looked as if she were about to say something, but then Paul and Grey Cloud took her arms and hustled her down the steps to their waiting car.

"What do you make of those two?" asked Lieutenant Harris.

"I'm not sure. I guess if you want to understand them, you have to look at life from a Navajo point of view. They're trying to protect their culture. They're trying to keep their bloodline pure. That's why they don't approve of Catherine dating whites. Apparently she's already betrothed to some guy out on the Navajo reservation – has been for over five years."

"Damned pretty girl," Lieutenant Harris remarked, as he watched her being driven away. "Seems like a waste to me."

"Do you think her brothers might have killed Martin?" asked Jim.

"I'd like to think so. It would make my job a whole lot easier. They had motive, for sure. They might well have had the opportunity, too. If Grey Cloud's friend called from New Mexico at 2 a.m. and spoke for twenty minutes, he still would have had plenty of time to drive down to the beach and meet up with Martin Amato."

"Why didn't you pull them in?"

"Think about it. The real question is – *how*? Those guys are fit, and they're tough, but even they wouldn't have had the strength to rip a man's body open with one blow. Not like that. As you say, they might have had some kind of special implement – but even so . . ."

"So what are you going to do?"

"Urgent priority number one is a cup of strong black coffee. Then I'm going to do what I always do. I'm going to go plodding around looking for witnesses and circumstantial evidence and in the meantime I'm going to be keeping a close eye on those two jokers."

He laid his hand on Jim's shoulder and said, "A word to the wise . . . if I were you, I'd keep your eyes open. If they *were* the perpetrators, they're not going to be thinking it's a million laughs that you told me what they said to young Martin at the football game."

He checked his watch. "After the coffee, I'm going to take a photographer and a forensic officer and I'm going to go over to West Grove and check out that locker room. Maybe you're right. Maybe those clawmarks match."

"What if they do?"

"Then I really don't know *what* the hell we're looking for."

Jim had almost forgotten that it was Sunday. He drove back to his second-story apartment in a pink-painted block just off Electric Avenue, parked his car, and wearily climbed out. The morning was hazy and not particularly warm, but three or four residents were already sitting on the dilapidated sun-loungers by the pool, reading newspapers or knitting or listening to Sony Walkmen. Jim said hi to Miss Neagle, the middle-aged woman who had taken over old Mrs Vaizey's apartment. Miss Neagle was wearing huge dark glasses and a scarf on her head, and her big dimpled thighs bulged out beneath a 1960s-style swimsuit with brown-and-white flower patterns on it.

"Hi, Miss Neagle."

Miss Neagle lifted her sunglasses and smiled up at him. Her lipstick was so bright she looked as if she had been eating strawberry jelly. "Good morning, Mr Rook. You seem a little under the weather."

"I didn't sleep too good, that's all. Tossing and turning most of the night."

"Ha! You don't have to tell *me* about tossing and turning. I'm a martyr when it comes to tossing and turning. Sometimes I just dread the sun going down."

"How about sleeping pills?"

"No, Mr Rook. There's only one sure cure for tossing and turning."

"Oh, yes? Then why don't you try it?"

She lowered her black-blotched eyelashes coquettishly. "I would if I could, Mr Rook, believe me."

Jim suddenly realized what she was talking about, and gave her a quick, humorless smile. "Can't always have what we want, Miss Neagle."

As he walked toward the steps that led up to his apartment, he was narrowly eyed by Myrlin Buffield, from Apartment 201. Myrlin used to have a belly that hung over

37

his shorts like a tide of slowly-melting marshmallow, but he had been working out at Gold's Gym lately and now the tide had crept back upward, giving him an extraordinary puffed-up look, as if he were constantly sucking in his breath. He still had the same slicked-back hair, though, and the same dagger earring. He was pretending to read *Men Are From Mars, Women Are From Venus.*

"Hi, Myrlin," said Jim.

"You ain't been creeping out of your apartment nights and spying on me again, have you?" Myrlin wanted to know. "I was sure I heard somebody creeping outside of my apartment last night and I was pretty damned sure that it was you."

"Sorry, Myrlin. My creeping days are over."

Myrlin was deeply suspicious of Jim, almost to the point of paranoia. Ever since old Mrs Vaizey had held a séance in Jim's apartment, and had left it thick with incense smoke, Myrlin had suspected him of being a drug addict or a dabbler in the black arts, or worse – especially since, soon after, old Mrs Vaizey had disappeared, and had never been seen again. Only Jim knew what had happened to her, and Jim was never going to tell anybody, ever.

Jim went up the steps and along the balcony until he reached his apartment. The feline formerly known as Tibbles was waiting for him outside the door with an expectant look on her face. He hadn't had time to feed her before he went out. He unlocked the door and she dashed straight into the kitchen and waited by her bowl with her tail sticking up in the air like a witch's broom.

Jim opened the icebox and was just popping open a cold can of beer when he heard a rapping at the door. It was Miss Neagle, wrapped up in a pink toweling robe. That wasn't so extraordinary: she often came up in a variety of highly informal attire to borrow coffee or sugar or orange juice. But what was extraordinary was that she was wearing a pink lobster SpaceFace hat, complete with eyes and claws. It had been a favourite of old Mrs Vaizey's.

"Hi, Miss Neagle."

"Hi yourself."

"That hat sure brings back some memories."

"I like it. I found it in my apartment when I moved in."

"Suits you. Well, it would suit anybody who wanted to walk around with a lobster on their head."

"Of course . . . that wasn't all I found."

Jim said, "Oh, no?" Then, "How about a beer?"

"A beer? I hope you know me better than that."

Jim blinked at her in surprise. Apart from exchanging a few words around the pool every day, he hardly knew her at all. "Okay, then," he said. "Whatever."

"Bourbon, straight up. No rocks."

Jim unscrewed the Wild Turkey and poured a generous measure into a highball glass with Miami Parrot Jungle printed on the side. Miss Neagle came over and took it and said, "Why don't we drink to *very* long life. With the emphasis on *very*."

"All right. *Very* long life."

Miss Neagle leaned forward and stared into Jim's eyes. "You don't recognise me, do you?"

"Sure I recognise you. You're Miss Neagle from Apartment 105."

"Yes, I am. But I'll tell you what else I found in my apartment when I first moved in, apart from this hat. I found Mrs Vaizey."

"Excuse me?"

"She was still there, Mr Rook, at least in spirit. Very faint, almost faded away. But when I was lying in bed that very first night, almost asleep, she *spoke* to me."

"She *spoke* to you? What did she say?"

39

"She was kind and she was sympathetic, and she gave me all kinds of encouragement. You see, I was very depressed when I first moved here. I was almost flat broke, and a man who I loved very, very dearly had just died of cancer. Sometimes I thought about ending it all. But Mrs Vaizey gave me comfort and friendship like I've never know before. She made me feel that I wasn't alone any more."

The feline formerly known as Tibbles was rubbing herself frantically against Jim's leg, desperate for food, but all Jim could do was stare at Miss Neagle with his beer half-raised to his mouth.

Miss Neagle sipped her whiskey and smiled at him. "Mrs Vaizey was about to fade away completely, the way that all spirits do, after a while. But I didn't want her to go. I loved her. I needed her. So I let her in. I don't quite know how it happened. I just sort of . . . let her in. Miss Vaizey is here inside of *me*, Jim." She tapped her forehead. "She's still here . . . she's still with us."

"I don't believe this," said Jim. "You're trying to tell me that you're Miss Neagle *and* Mrs Vaizey, both?"

"Got it in one. And it happens more often than you'd think. A spirit who isn't yet ready to fade away finds somebody who's still alive who desperately needs her. Somebody who's sick, maybe – or suicidal, like I was. Both of them benefit. The spirit gets to stay here for a whole lot longer, and her host gains all of her memories and all of her lifetime's experience."

Jim walked back into the living-room and circled Miss Neagle in deep suspicion. This was beginning to sound like some kind of very eccentric shakedown. "If this is true, that you're yourself and Mrs Vaizey both, then of course you'll know what special talent Mrs Vaizey had."

"That's right. Of course I do. She could tell people's fortunes . . . with tea-leaves, or the Tarot, or by reading palms. She was also a damned good knitter."

Jim thought: she was right, but that wasn't really much of a test. If Mrs Vaizey's son had left her lobster hat behind, he had probably left her Tarot cards and her knitting patterns, too.

"You know what her maiden name was?"

"For sure. Duncan, Alice Duncan – born January 17, 1919, in Pasadena, the second of seven children."

"And you know how she died?"

Miss Neagle nodded. "She suffered. She never told you how much she suffered, because she knew that she'd upset you. But she suffered, believe me."

"You know how, and why?"

"One night, her spirit left her body, looking for a voodoo *houngan* who was trying to take possession of one of your students. Unfortunately, the *houngan* was waiting for her."

Jim stopped pacing, and looked Miss Neagle right in the eyes. "You're in there, aren't you?" he said. "You're really in there."

"Yes," said Miss Neagle. "I'm really in here." And she lifted her hand to his cheek and touched it, very gently, not in the way that a woman like Miss Neagle normally would, but in the way that a grandmother would, or an elderly friend. Jim took hold of her hand and squeezed it. "Welcome back," he told her.

"I'm not sure you're going to say you're so happy to see me when I tell you why I'm here."

"What's the matter? Don't tell me *you've* seen something frightening coming to get me, too."

"Who else has told you?" asked Miss Neagle, in the querulous tones that Mrs Vaizey would have adopted.

Jim said, "My grandfather was here yesterday morning.

41

My *dead* grandfather. He told me to watch for something dark and old and *bristling*."

"Then that's much more serious than I thought."

"What? What's more serious?"

"People's relatives hardly ever make visitations from the other side unless those people are in desperate danger. I mean, why should they come back? They've had a whole lifetime of struggle and conflict, they don't want any more. But for me – no, it was your aura that worried me."

"My aura? What's wrong with my aura?"

"When you came walking around the pool just now, you had the most threatening aura I've ever seen, alive or dead. You were completely surrounded by a swirl of dark, dull colors – like – like *tentacles*, thrashing around in a muddy river – and there was a dreadful feeling of *cold*, too. That's why I came up to see you."

"So what does that mean?"

"It's very serious, Mr Rook. It means that something awful is going to happen to you – and whatever it is, it's already begun. That's why your aura has started to grow darker, the same way the sky grows darker just before a storm. It can feel the threat that's coming toward you. It can *sense* that you're soon going to die."

"I'm going to *die*? And *soon*?"

"Unless you can find a way of saving yourself, yes."

"Come on, now, what the hell is all this about? What does 'soon' mean? Sometime in the next half hour? Tomorrow? Next year? And *how* am I going to die?"

Miss Neagle shook her head. "I can't tell, not exactly, unless I read the cards."

"Listen," Jim protested, "I don't have any intention of dying. Not sooner. Not even later."

"Nobody does, Jim. *I* didn't, any more than you do now. We're all frightened of pain. We're all frightened of darkness. Why do you think I'm clinging onto this life, by staying with Valerie?"

"Valerie? Who's Valerie? Oh – I see who you mean. Miss Neagle. Yes, for sure."

Miss Neagle said, "You don't have to find out how you're going to die unless you really want to. Most people don't."

"But how can I save myself if I don't know what it is?"

"You want me to read the cards?"

"Of course I want you to read the cards. You think I want to go out, turn the corner and find myself torn to pieces by something old and cold and bristling?"

"Just because your grandfather said it was bristling, that didn't necessarily mean it was something that could tear you to pieces. It may be nothing more than a detail . . . just part of the omen, not all of it. It may be nothing more than a hairbrush, lying next to your bed when you're dying."

"Somehow I don't think so. He said '*bristling*' like he really meant it."

"All right, then," said Miss Neagle. She took a pack of cards out of her bathrobe pocket. She had obviously come prepared. "How about here, on the table?" she said, and Jim pulled out two dining-room chairs so that she could spread the cards out in front of her. Jim had never seen anything like them before. They were colored picture-cards, like the Tarot, except that the drawings they bore were even stranger, and more obscure. There were demons on stilts and dwarves with copper pans on their heads and pale, naked women with their eyes blindfolded, surrounded by huge black-beetles. There were minstrels in extraordinary heaped-up hats and sad-eyed knights carrying hideous witches on their backs. Some of the cards showed nothing but deserted landscapes, with only a shadow falling across them to indicate that somebody was just about to enter the picture.

"Pretty weird deck," Jim remarked, as he sat down beside her.

"Weird, yes, but very sensitive. You don't see many like this. They were secretly devised in the fourteenth century on the orders of Pope Urban VI – supposedly to help his cardinals to flush out an infestation of demons in hundreds of Italy's churches. Because of that it's called the Demon Tarot. The demons hid themselves in the cellars and the belfries, and only the cards could tell you where they were. Whether that's true or not, I don't know. But I've known these cards to sense that a wife was going to attack her husband with a breadknife, six hours before she actually did it. And once they warned that a little girl of six was going to die in a house-fire."

"And did she?"

Miss Neagle nodded, sadly. "Her mother wouldn't believe me. I tried to find out where she lived and take the little girl away, but by then it was too late." She paused, and then she said, "That was the last time I used this pack, until today."

"You're scaring me," said Jim, trying unsuccessfully to smile.

"I'm scaring myself," Miss Neagle told him. She shuffled the cards, tapped them three times, and then started to lay them out in an H-shaped pattern, 21 cards in all. The feline formerly known as Tibbles had been watching her closely, but now her fur rose up on end, and she let out a soft hiss of disapproval.

"One of these cards has to represent you, the significator. This one looks good – the teacher. It's the card I used to choose for young, well-educated men – especially *single*, young, well-educated men."

The card showed a man with a strange, serene look on

his face. He was wearing a long cloak that was decorated with all kinds of objects, like kettles and hourglasses and loaves of bread. A young woman was sitting in front of him, cross-legged, with a golden ear-trumpet in one ear, into which the man was pouring green oil from a green-glass bottle.

Miss Neagle placed the card face-upward in the centre of the H-pattern. Then, slowly, she turned the rest of the cards face-up, too.

"This is tomorrow," she explained, lifting up a card showing a man in a complicated black-velvet bonnet, looking out over a stormy estuary. On the man's back a shadow had fallen – a shadow like a large hand. "And this next card is the number four." Three noblemen in masks were standing in a cemetery; but almost invisible amongst the gravestones and the monuments was a grotesque grey figure with horns and a strange trumpet-like protrusion instead of a nose.

"So far this means that the next significant event in your life will not take place until four tomorrows have passed."

"So I won't be killed until Thursday? Is that it?"

"I don't know, Jim. Let's carry on."

She picked up the next card and showed it to him. A pale man was walking across a desert with the rising sun behind him. On closer inspection, Jim saw that the desert floor was composed entirely of intertwined human bones. Miss Neagle said, "Whatever is going to harm you, it's coming from the east."

"Is that good or bad?"

"It may be not significant. But all evil spirits come from the east. You should never build a house with its front door facing east."

"What's that? *Feng-shui*?"

"Not at all. It's simple survival. You don't want demons flying into your house every time you open the front

45

door, now do you?" She leaned forward over the cards, frowning. "Now here's an odd one."

She showed Jim a very dark card, almost black. Jim held it up and his cat abruptly jumped off her chair and ran into the bedroom. Jim got the feeling she would have closed the door behind her if she could have done. He peered at the card intently, and he could just distinguish a rough, shaggy shape with two reddened eyes. More significantly, though, he could see a claw lifted into the air – a claw like a bear's claw, only bigger, with viciously hooked nails.

"Well?" he asked Miss Neagle.

"Well . . . this is what is coming after you, I presume. A beast of some kind. I don't know why it's coming after *you* in particular, but it is. Feel the card again – no, feel it. It's warm, isn't it? It's actually warm. It's charged with psychic energy. It *knows* you.".

She was right. The card *was* warm. In fact it was so warm now that he could hardly hold it. He was about to hand it back to her when it suddenly curled up and burst into flame. He dropped it into the ashtray and both of them watched as it was reduced to a curled-up wafer of black ash.

"How the hell did *that* happen?" asked Jim, flapping away the smoke.

"I told you. Psychic energy. The card acted as a cable between whatever this thing is that's coming to get you, and you yourself. And like all cables when they get overloaded with energy, it burned out."

"Well, I'm real sorry about your deck." He reached into his back jeans pocket for his wallet. "Is it worth very much?"

"They're irreplaceable. If my son had known how rare they were, he wouldn't have left them behind. But he never did like me telling fortunes."

"Oh, shit," said Jim. "I'm sorry."

Miss Neagle was gathering up the rest of the cards. "You don't have to be. I haven't lost any. That card didn't belong to this pack at all."

"I don't understand."

She laid her hand on top of his. "I've never seen it before now. It just appeared by itself. Now, is that a warning, or is that a warning?"

Jim gave her a long, grave look. Then he stared at the ashes in the ashtray. "You mean . . . ? You'd better tell me more."

Chapter Three

The cards could tell him only three ways of avoiding the 'old, cold bristling' thing that was following him. The first was to seek the advice of two friends. The second was to travel on a long journey, although they didn't say where. The third was completely cryptic. If he were going to survive, a game would have to be played, and both sides would have to admit defeat.

"A game? Do the cards say what kind of game?"

Miss Neagle shook her head. "I'm as mystified as you are. But I get the feeling that these three instructions are *progressive*, if you get my meaning. Once you've sought the advice of your friends, you'll know where you have to travel, and once you've travelled there, you'll know what kind of game has to be played, and why both sides have to lose."

Jim sat back. "You say these cards are supposed to be the best?"

"You want to try a second opinion from the regular Tarot? Or the tea-leaves, maybe? Or Sydney Omarr?" She was being sarcastic. Sydney Omarr was a professional astrologer with a 1–900 phone line.

"Unh-hunh. I think I'll stick with the Demon Tarot. At least it's offering me *some* way out. I just wish I knew which two friends it's talking about. That would be a start, at least."

"Maybe it's talking about two lecturers from college."

"Sure. And maybe it's talking about Bill and Gordon from Joe's Bar & Grill. It could be talking about anybody."

Miss Neagle put her cards away. She closed her eyes for a moment, and then she suddenly leaned forward, propping her head in her hands. "Miss Neagle – Valerie – are you okay?"

For a moment, she didn't say anything. "You want a glass of water?" he asked her. "Another shot of whiskey? How about some iced tea?"

"I'm all right," she said, at last. "It was a hell of a strain, that's all, trying to do what Alice used to be able to do."

"How's Mrs Vaizey?"

"She's okay . . . but she's exhausted, too. She found it tiring enough reading the cards when she was alive. Now she has to guide my hands and make my brain work, and I'm not a psychic sensitive, the way she was."

Jim laid a hand on her shoulder and smiled at her. "You did very well, Valerie, thank you. You don't mind if I call you Valerie?"

"Sweetheart, you can call me anything you like." She knocked back her whiskey in one gulp and prepared to go. As she went to the door, however, she said, "This thing that's supposed to be after you – this *beast*," she said. "Do you believe in that?"

"I wouldn't have done, not until this morning."

"You really think it's real?"

"Yes, I do. I don't have any idea what it is, or why it's after me – but, yes, I think that it's really real."

She kissed him, and this was definitely Miss Neagle kissing him, not Mrs Vaizey. This was the kind of half-serious kiss you got from a boozy, fortyish woman in a bar. "You're an interesting man, Jim. You don't mind if I call you Jim? One of these days you and I ought to sit down together with a bottle of wine and a plateful of spaghetti and ask each other the meaning of life."

Jim said, "Tell me one thing, before you go."

"What's that, Jim?"

"Do you argue at all? You and Mrs Vaizey, inside of your head?"

Valerie knew back her head and gave three short, barking laughs. "You *are* an interesting man, aren't you? Yes, we argue all the time. But it's a whole lot more entertaining than arguing with yourself."

Jim gave her a wave as she tottered back along the balcony in her little pink high-heeled slingbacks. Then he went back into the kitchen and opened up another beer. *Two friends?* he thought. *Which two friends? And where do I have to travel?*

There was one thing he knew for certain. He had to act fast, because he was now totally convinced that there was a beast looking for his blood; and that it was the same beast that had slaughtered Martin Amato on Venice Beach.

He picked up the frail fragments of ash from the ashtray, the remains of the playing-card, and sifted them through his fingers. They silkily fell back again, and formed the shape of a black, horned creature, with tiny, demonic eyes.

* * *

He arrived early for his first English tutorial on Monday morning and when his class came in he was standing at the window with his back to them, staring out at nothing at all. He hadn't slept well. He was wearing a crumpled pair of tan-coloured chinos and a green checkered shirt which looked as if he had salvaged it from the bottom of the laundry basket. His hair stuck up at the back and no amount of smoothing it down would keep it down, even with spit.

Special Class II were unusually quiet as they took their places, although he could hear the murmur of the names 'Martin' and 'Catherine' and he knew what they were all talking about. Before he turned around he waited until all the murmuring and whispering had stopped, and there was nothing but an occasional cough or the squeak of a sneaker on the composition floor.

At last he stepped up to the front of the class and looked at all of them, one after the other. Greg Lake, pulling his usual faces over in the corner. Greg suffered from a lack of co-ordination, and it was a constant effort for him to show his feelings with his facial expressions. At the moment he looked as if he were sucking on a particularly sour lemon candy.

Amanda Zaparelli, olive-skinned and sultry, with a husky smoker's voice, a liking for very strong perfume and lots of it, and a chronic inability to tell the difference between an adjective and an adverb. "You should of seen me walk into the room. I was so strutly." "Give me that quickly cigarette, will you?"

Jane Firman, pale and dyslexic and given to sudden bursts of frustrated tears. Titus Greenspan III, serious and bulgy-eyed. Titus tried harder than almost anybody else, but he always took everything too literally. If he read that 'the noon sun drilled a hole in my head' he would put up his hand and ask why the narrator hadn't dropped dead on the spot, spilling his brains all over the desert.

Sharon X, in a voluminous black djellaba-like dress which he could only presume was a Black Muslim mourning outfit. John Ng, moon-faced and serious, with a white carnation in a jelly-jar in front of him. White was the Vietnamese colour for death.

Jim looked at them all, one by one, and studied them all. They didn't have any idea how much their predicament could hurt him. Sometimes he wished for their sake that they didn't have to grow up and leave college – and, in particular, that they didn't have to leave his class. They were so characterful, so individual, so full of inflated hopes and wild ambitions. They wanted to be celebrities. They wanted to appear on TV and live in big, pink-washed houses. But he had so little time to teach them – so little time to help them overcome their turtle-slow reading speeds and their painfully limited vocabularies, not to mention their stuttering and their word-blindness and their horrifying ignorance of history or geography or world affairs.

"What's the capital of Chile?" he had asked Ricky Herman.

Mark Foley had shot up his hand and said, "I know! Con Carne!"

Jim loved them, all of them. But he hated the culture which had led them to believe that reading was unimportant, that correct spelling didn't matter, that any dumb poem which *they* wrote was just as good as any dumb poem that Marianne Moore or Robert Lowell had written. He hated it most of all because it didn't allow them the gift of expressing themselves, especially at times like these.

Very quietly, he said, "Yesterday, we all suffered a terrible shock and a loss so painful that it's difficult to put it into words. Martin Amato was found murdered on Venice Beach in the early hours of Sunday morning. He was a son, a brother and a friend. He was a civil engineering student and captain of the football team. He was twenty-one years and two months old."

Jim paced to the back of the class, where Sue-Robin Caufield was sitting. She wore a black scarf around her arm and she was biting back the tears. She and Martin had dated for a while, before Catherine came along.

"What do you say about somebody like Martin? He was reliable. He was considerate. He took himself too

52

seriously. He wasn't a genius, but that never affected his unquestioning loyalty to his college, to his team, and to all of his friends. He was the kind of regular guy who had the potential for happiness, and self-fulfilment, and to make a lasting contribution to society.

"Now all of that has been taken away from him – and from us, too. And because of that our lives are going to be poorer, and more doubtful, and less trusting of the world we live in."

He walked up to Catherine's desk. Today she was wearing her hair tightly braided with a black ribbon, and a black dress. Her eyes looked puffy from crying.

"Are you all right?" he asked her. "You can be excused this class if you want to."

"I'm okay," she whispered, without looking up. "Please . . . I'd rather stay here."

Jim stayed beside her for a moment, watching her, and then he turned to the class at large. "Today I want you all to write me a short poem about Martin. I want you to use that poem to express in words everything you feel about him, or any other friend that you've lost."

Muffy Brown put up her hand and said, "Excuse me, Mr Rook, sir, but isn't that kind of like *cynical*? I mean Martin's been dead for no more than a day and you're turning his death into *classwork*?"

Muffy was small and pretty with a personality like a roomful of bouncing balls. Earlier this semester she had worn the most elaborate braids that Jim had ever seen, but now she had shaved her head almost bald except for a flat crewcut on top, and acquired a silver ring through her eyebrow.

Jim said, "Listen to me. If you can express your feelings about Martin's death in writing, you'll be paying him the greatest compliment you ever could. If you can put down the shock, and the anger, and the sense of unfairness . . . if

53

you can learn to convey your grief to other people . . . not only will you be improving your communicating skills, you'll be helping yourself to come to terms with what's happened. You'll be making it clear that Martin's death touched you and affected you . . . and you'll have found a way of telling the world just how much."

He picked up one of his books and said, "After Allen Ginsberg's mother died, he wrote a long poem called *Kaddish*, which was filled with anger and bewilderment and relief, too, because his mother had been mentally sick. He used it as a way of honouring her, of remembering her – and of coming to terms with the way in which she had changed from being a pretty young girl 'sitting crossleg on the grass – her long hair wound with flowers –' to an elderly woman 'too thin, shrunk on her bones – new broken into white hair – loose dress on her skeleton – face sunk, old! withered – cheek of crone –'

"But finally, he says to her, 'There, rest. No more suffering for you. I know where you've gone, it's good.'"

He lowered the book, lowered his head. "For Martin's sake, and for your sake, too, write something that comes right out of your heart."

There was silence in the classroom. Then, almost as one, everybody brought out their pads, uncapped their pens, and began to write. Jim had never seen them so subdued. He went back to his desk, sat down, and started to write something himself. But he wasn't writing a poem about Martin's death. He was writing "2 Friends? Who? Journey? Where? Game in which both sides surrender? What?"

He sat with his head in his hands for a long time, trying to make sense of what he had written. After a while, however, he looked up. Most of the class were bent diligently over their work, although he could see that most of them had written no more than two or three lines. Still, for Special Class II, two or three lines was something of an achievement. Russell seemed to be the most inspired – or the most deeply affected – because he had already filled one sheet of paper and was on to his next, his tongue clenched between his teeth like a small boy trying to hook a maggot onto a fishing-hook.

When he looked toward Catherine, however, he saw that she wasn't writing at all. She was sitting up quite straight, her head tilted back, looking toward the ceiling. There was an extraordinary smile on her face, almost a radiance, as if she were supremely happy.

Jim watched her with gradually-increasing curiosity. She kept on looking at the ceiling, and she started to sway her head from side to side in a strange, repetitive movement that reminded him of something but he couldn't think what. *Shock*, he thought. *She's going into shock.*

Immediately, he stood up, tilting back his chair so that it fell onto the floor with a sharp, echoing clatter. The class all looked up at him, but he raised his hand and said, "Don't worry. It's okay. Just get back to your work."

He went back to Catherine's desk and stood over her. "Catherine? How are you feeling? How about going outside for a couple of minutes? Maybe you could use some air."

She didn't answer, so he cautiously reached out and touched her shoulder. "Catherine – come on, how about seeing the nurse?"

Slowly Catherine turned her head. As she did so, she closed her eyes. But when she had turned completely toward him, she abruptly opened them again. He felt a shrill sense of fright and he couldn't stop himself from taking one step away from her. Her eyes were totally expressionless, as if she didn't know who he was – or even *what* he was. He had never known anybody look at him like that before, and he couldn't even think what to say to her. What do you say to a painted portrait, when it stares at you; or a snake that stares back at you, in the reptile-house?

"It's all right, Mr Rook," she told him, in the softest of voices. "I don't need to see a nurse. I'm fine."

"All the same, maybe you'd better go home. This only happened yesterday morning. Shock can last for days or weeks or even years."

"I want to stay here," she insisted. "Please, Mr Rook, I'd prefer to stay here."

"OK, OK. But if you start to feel dizzy, or anything like that—"

"*I have to stay here*," she hissed at him. "*Don't you get it? I have to stay here!*"

"All right!" he told her, lifting both hands in instant surrender. "If you want to stay here, then stay here. That's fine by me."

Catherine continued to stare at him as he retreated along the aisle. He picked up his chair and sat down at his desk, giving her one last, long look of concern. She was still in shock, no doubt about it, but he didn't want to distress her more than she was distressed already, and he didn't want to disrupt the tutorial. He would have a quiet word with her later, when she was on her own.

He went back to his conundrum. *2 Friends? Who*? What he didn't see was the drop of blood that suddenly appeared between Catherine's tightly-pressed lips and quickly slid down her chin. It dripped onto her notepad and made a red splattery mark.

She wiped her mouth with the back of her hand. Then she lifted her head again and continued to stare at the ceiling, her eyes still expressionless, as if she were listening to a long message that came from a long, long time ago, and far, far away.

He was leaving college at four o'clock that afternoon when he saw Catherine waiting beside the parking-lot, clutching her books close to her chest, her head bowed and her long hair blowing in the warm afternoon wind. He walked up to her and said, "Waiting for your brothers?"

She nodded. This time she wouldn't even look at him.

"Come on, Catherine, you've had a hell of a rough time," he told her. "You don't have to come back to college until you feel like it. Maybe you should talk to your doctor. Or better still, you could have a word with the college counsellor. Did you ever talk to Naomi? I know she looks a little – well, *eccentric*, what with those glasses and that hedge of a hairdo, but she's a terrific listener. She's a real sane person too. Not one of these whackoes who's going to tell you that you're suffering from sublimated guilt or something."

Catherine raised her head. Her eyes were streaming with tears, so that some of the strands of her hair stuck wetly to her cheeks. "What if I *am* guilty?"

"Guilty of what? Guilty of being the last person to see Martin alive?"

"He wanted to stay with me. He wanted to sleep with me. But I said no."

"So what are trying to tell me? If you'd let him sleep with you, he wouldn't have gone back to the beach, and he wouldn't be dead?"

"I didn't know what to do. If I'd let him sleep with me, and Paul and Grey Cloud had found out—"

"Catherine, you're a big girl now. You're way past the age of consent. If you wanted to sleep with Martin, then there's nothing that Paul and Grey Cloud could have done about it."

She shook her head. She really was exceptionally pretty, especially with her hair floating across her face and her eyes glistening.

Jim said, "You can't let your brothers rule your life. All right, I know they're family. I know they think that have your best interests at heart, not to mention the racial purity of the Navajo. But look at me. I'm part German and part Scottish and part Hungarian. You may be Navajo, but first and foremost you're Catherine, your own person. Only *you* can decide what's best for you."

"That's not the point. If Paul and Grey Cloud had found out that Martin and I were sleeping together, they would have beaten up on him, I know it. Every time I've gotten friendly with anyone, they've frightened him or chased him away. Martin was the first boy who wouldn't let them push him around. If it had ever gotten really serious between us – I don't know. It all scares me. It scares me so much. That's why I didn't let Martin into the house."

Jim said, "You weren't to know what was going to happen to him. How could you? You were doing your best to protect him."

She lifted her head, her mouth tightened with grief. Jim said, "Here," and took a travel pack of Kleenex out of his coat pocket. He pulled one out and dabbed her eyes for her. It had been a long time since he had dabbed a woman's eyes.

"I killed him," she said, her voice choked with grief. "I should never have dated him. I should never have fallen in love with him."

"Come on, Catherine. You didn't kill him. It was bad luck, that's all. Everybody knows that the beach can be risky at night."

He dabbed her eyes again, and it was at this moment that he heard the throbbing of a tweaked-up V8 engine, and her brothers' black Firebird rolled into the parking-lot and stopped close beside them. Paul and Grey Cloud climbed out in their black jeans and their sunglasses, came over to Catherine and stood either side of her.

"Well, well, the Cheeryble Brothers," said Jim, referring to the irrepressibly optimistic characters in *Nicholas Nickleby*.

"The what?" asked Grey Cloud, taking off his sunglasses.

"Forget it. I don't expect you to know anything about Dickens."

"Dickens? They sound like hotels for people like you," Grey Cloud retorted.

"Well, well, a sense of humour," said Jim.

Paul came up close to him. "Catherine is coming here for the education, man. She's not coming here to look for a date. She's not here to look for any kind of counselling, either. And most of all she's not here for some kind of indoctrination into the white man's way."

"What she chooses to make of her time here is up to her, wouldn't you say?"

"No, I wouldn't say. And if I were you, I'd stick to teaching English and stay out of the rest of her life, OK?"

"Otherwise what?"

"Otherwise you remember what happened to your college football captain."

"That's a threat," said Jim.

Grey Cloud shook his head. "That isn't a threat any more than what we said to Martin Amato was a threat. That's just another prediction."

Jim took Susan out that evening to St Mark's, on Windward Avenue, for a steak dinner and an evening of live blues. He liked St Mark's because it was a friendly, jostling, casual place and dinner didn't usually cost more than $30 a head, so long as he didn't drink too much Stag's Leap chardonnay. They sat at a cramped corner table and tried to hold a conversation while King Jerry and the

Screamers gave a deafening rendition of *The House of the Rising Sun*.

Afterward, Jim drove Susan home. They sat outside her house in Jim's Rebel SST with the engine quietly burbling.

"Thanks for coming out," he told her. "I needed something like that to get my mind off Martin."

"That's OK. I enjoyed it."

He touched her shoulder. "Listen," he said, "you know what you said earlier, about boats bumping?"

She looked at him with her head slightly tilted to one side and he knew what her answer was going to be. Girls who want to bump will immediately give you a kiss: they won't look sympathetic.

"I'm sorry," she said. "It's just that – I don't know, Jim. Our relationship doesn't seem to be going anyplace."

"Where do you want it to go? Paris? Rome? Van Nuys?"

She smiled and shook her head. "It's not a question of where I want it to go. It should have a dynamic all of its own. But all we seem to be doing together is nothing very much."

Jim propped his arm on the back of his seat, and faced her directly. "So what are you saying to me? That you want to stop doing nothing very much, and do something else instead? I'm only a college teacher, Susan. My only dynamic is to turn semi-literate kids into people who can express themselves."

Susan said, "Yes. I know. And I've always admired you for what you do. But the truth is, Jim—" She paused, and then she said, "The truth is that I've forgotten why I fell in love with you."

He felt a cold snail-like sensation in his stomach. It made him feel like a teenager all over again. "Is it important that you remember *why?*" he asked her. "I mean, so long as you do?"

"That's the thing about it, Jim. I don't. Not any more."

"The other day, you said you almost did."

"Well, I've been thinking about that, and I don't think I'm being fair on you. Almost just isn't enough, is it?"

"Almost is better than nothing."

"Jim . . . I don't want to hurt you, that's all."

"You're right. Better to face up to it. We don't want to live out a lie, do we?"

"No," she said, lowering her eyes.

"Come on, we can still pass in the corridor and say 'hi' to each other. We can still watch college football games together. We can still chit-chat over cups of poisonous coffee at faculty get-togethers."

"Jim—" she said, and took hold of his hand.

He took a deep breath. "Don't worry," he said. "I'll live."

Although it suddenly occurred to him that if he didn't find the *2 Friends* within the next twenty-four hours, he would almost certainly die.

He knew that something was wrong as soon as he reached the top of the steps and started to walk along the balcony that led to his apartment. His front door was ajar, and there were hundreds of soft, crumbly fragments tumbling out of it, like snowflakes, except that they couldn't be snowflakes, with the late-evening temperature still well over 60 degrees.

He approached his front door cautiously, tightly rolling up the copy of *Esquire* that he was carrying so that he could use like a club. He listened, but he couldn't hear anything except for the occasional surge of studio laughter coming from Myrlin's television in the next door

61

apartment, and the swooshing of traffic. Somebody was playing a guitar somewhere, and somebody else was whooping with laughter.

He reached the door and the snowflakes blew around his shoes. It was only then that he realized that they were tiny fragments of multicoloured plastic foam. He bent down and picked one up and squashed it between his fingers. It looked as if a pillow had been ripped open and emptied all over his floor.

"Pusscat?" he called, in a low, hoarse voice. He waited, but there was no response. He tried whistling, but there was still no reply. It was a damned nuisance, having a cat that refused to answer to her own name. She had suddenly stopped, about eighteen months ago, and Jim had even taken her to the vet to find out if she were deaf. The vet said, "Just cussedness, that's all."

Jim stretched out his hand and eased the front door open wide. It must have been kicked open, because the lock housing had been splintered right out the doorframe. Inside, it was almost totally dark, and he stood for a long time wondering if he dared to go in. There had been a spate of drug-connected robberies along this stretch of Electric Avenue in the past few weeks, and two innocent householders had been shot, one of them fatally.

"If you're in there, you'd better come out!" he called. "The cops are coming and I'm armed!"

Still there was no response. Jim reached around the door and felt for the light-switch. He took a deep breath, and switched it on.

At first he couldn't understand what he was looking at. Then – as he took one step into his apartment, and then another – he realised that the whole place had been torn apart, as if by a gang of enraged baboons. The snowflakes had come from his couch, which had been comprehensively gutted, right down to the springs. Polyurethane foam was scattered everywhere, ankle-deep in places. Pictures had been pulled from the walls and smashed. His television lay on one side, the screen cracked and two of the legs wrenched off. His CD collection had been pillaged, his books thrown everywhere, his venetian blinds reduced to collapsed concertinas.

It was the same in the kitchen. The refrigerator door had been pulled right off, and food strewn everywhere. A large jar of tomato-juice had been emptied across the floor like blood.

Most chilling of all, though, were the scratch-marks across the kitchen cabinets. The light oak doors had been viciously gouged by something which must have resembled a huge claw. Even the formica work-surface had been scratched – over an inch deep in places.

Jim picked up a broken picture-frame containing a photograph of his cousin Laura, with whom, when he was younger, he had fallen hopelessly in love. The glass was smashed and a claw had torn away half of Laura's face. He looked at it for a moment, and then let it drop back onto the floor. It was as if his entire life had been ripped to shreds – as if everything he had ever thought or felt or worked for had never counted for anything, and this was fate's way of showing him so.

There was worse to come. He went into the bedroom and his bed-covers had been sliced into shreds, his pillows burst apart. In the bathroom, the mirrors had all been smashed into kaleidoscopes and the washbasin pulled free from the wall – although, thankfully, the pipes hadn't been fractured.

He was just about to close the bathroom door when he noticed a reflection in the shattered mirror of his medicine cabinet. A dark reflection, on the other side of the door. At first he thought that it was just his robe, which he usually hung up there. Then he realised it was something more. His robe seemed to have a thick fur collar.

With a terrible feeling of dread, he looked around at the back of the door. His robe was there, yes. But it didn't have a fur collar. The feline formerly known as Tibbles had been hung on the same hook, right through her wide-open mouth, up through her palate and into her brain. Her eyes were wide open and glassy, and her teeth were bared in an agonized snarl.

Jim bent over the bathtub and up came half-chewed steak and string potatoes and broccoli, as well as an acid gush of bile and chardonnay.

After a few minutes of choking and gasping, he wiped his mouth on a towel and made his way back to the living-room, treading on broken glass and CDs and books. He found the telephone behind the sofa, and by some miracle it was still working. He took Lieutenant Harris's card out of his coat pocket and dialed his personal number.

He was still waiting to be put through when a figure appeared in the doorway. It was Miss Neagle, in a gauzy pink nightdress, with a ruffled collar.

"My God, Jim, what happened here? You look like you've just had your own personal earthquake."

Jim said, "Not far from it, Valerie. You know what you said about this dark thing coming to get me – this old, dark bristling thing? Well, it's almost caught up with me, believe me. If I hadn't have gone out tonight—"

Miss Neagle stepped her way carefully through the wreckage. She stood close to Jim and laid a hand on his shoulder. "I'm so sorry . . . you must be devastated."

"Devastated isn't the word for it. I'm terrified, too. And my cat – whatever it was, the damn thing killed my cat."

Miss Neagle sniffed – a long, inquiring sniff – and it sounded more like Mrs Vaizey sniffing. "I can still smell it," she said, after a while.

Jim sniffed, too, but all he could smell was Folger's coffee, spilled all over the kitchen floor. "It's left a *smell*?" he asked her.

"Not a real smell . . . it's more like a spiritual aroma. Sometimes, when I stand close to somebody who's done something really evil, I can pick up a terrible sour kind of odour, like rotting meat. Other times, I can smell when somebody's happy. It's very warm, and floral."

Jim sniffed again. "So what does this smell like?"

"It's an animal, although it isn't an animal. It has a very strong musky odour, like a bear. I can smell its aura, too. It's very fierce, almost berserk. I don't think anybody could stop it, even if they tried. It has incredible determination. It would go through brick walls to get at you, if it had to."

She paused, and frowned, and then she said, "And yet, you know – and yet –"

"And yet what?"

"I don't know. I can smell something else. A sense of *confusion*, maybe."

"It wasn't confused enough to tear up everything I own. Even my goddamn pajamas."

Miss Neagle looked at him and raised an eyebrow and now she looked just like Miss Neagle, and not at all like Mrs Vaizey. "Oh . . . I didn't know you wore *pajamas*."

Jim said grimly, "I don't, do I? Not now."

Just then, his call was connected. Lieutenant Harris sounded as if he had a headcold coming, and kept clearing his throat every few seconds. "Harris? What's the problem, Mr Rook?"

"Somebody just tore up my apartment, the same way they tore up the locker room at West Grove."

"Jesus, I'm sorry. Is there very much damage?"

"They killed my cat and they ripped up everything I

own. Furniture, books, paintings . . . there isn't anything left intact."

"Did anybody see anything?"

"It's probably just as well that they didn't. Whoever did this could rip your lungs out with one blow."

"What makes you think it was the same person that tore up the locker room?"

"I've got very similar scratches here, and clawmarks. And who the hell has the strength to pull the door off an icebox?"

"Listen," said Lieutenant Harris, "I don't want you to touch anything. I'll send a patrol car around as soon as I can, and I can get down there myself in twenty minutes. OK? But don't touch anything."

He put down the phone. Miss Neagle was prowling around the apartment, sniffing and sniffing, her arms held out almost like a ballerina. "What else can you smell?" Jim asked her.

"I smell *two* animals, not just one. I can't understand it. I can smell dog, as well as bear. Two distinctly different spiritual aromas."

"So what does that mean? That *two* animals came here and trashed my apartment, instead of one? What difference does that make?"

"It makes a whole lot of difference, Jim . . . because one animal is very strong and determined but the other feels as if it's fighting an inner battle with itself. That's all part of the *confusion* I was talking about."

"I don't follow this at all," said Jim. "I'm just going outside to wait for the cops."

But as he tried to pass, Miss Neagle clutched his arm and said, "The dog aroma comes from very far away – hundreds of miles. It must be tremendously powerful to make itself felt at such a distance. The bear is very dangerous, Mr Rook, but it's the dog you have

66

to be wary of. The dog is going to do something really, really bad."

Jim looked around at his apartment, at his disemboweled furniture, at his shattered pictures, at his ripped-apart books. "You're telling me that this isn't really, really bad? Quite apart from the fact that I'm supposed to have less than three-and-a-half days to live."

"Something worse is going to happen, believe me."

Miss Neagle stared into his eyes and they weren't her eyes. They were pale and lucid as Mrs Vaizey's. "You don't even know what this thing can do to you, Jim. These animals can take your spirit, as well as your body. When you die, you expect to be back with your parents, don't you, and the people you always loved? You expect to be back in those old familiar places where you used to play when you were a boy? But if you give your spirit to *these* beasts, Mr Rook, you won't know anything but pain and darkness, for ever and ever. There *is* an afterlife, believe me, but if you let these beasts get hold of you, you'll wish to God that there wasn't."

Chapter Four

Jim spent the night on the couch round at George Babouris'
house in the less desirable part of Westwood. George was
big-bellied and black-bearded and catastrophically untidy.
His living-room was strewn with cast-off sneakers and
discarded sweatshirts and empty pizza boxes, as well as
heaps of books and students' coursework. It looked only
marginally less devastated than Jim's place.

George got up early and came padding through to
the kitchen in a Homer Simpson T-shirt and a pair
of baggy shorts, scratching his behind and puffing on
the first cigarette of the day. Jim looked up frowzily
from the couch and said, "What time is it, George, for
Christ's sake?"

"Five-thirty. I always get up at five-thirty. It gives me
time to have a little bit of life outside of college."

"Five-thirty is so damned early it's practically still
yesterday."

"Yes, but think what you can get done. I'm writing a
book at the moment. I can write two or three pages every
morning before I have to start thinking about banging
Newton's Law into those sloping foreheads in Applied
Physics. Here, look—" he said, and passed Jim a handful
of crumpled, coffee-stained paper.

Jim rubbed his eyes and peered at the title. *The Lute
of Apollo: The Complete History of Bouzouki Music*. He
handed it back without comment.

"You see?" said George. "I went to the library and found that nobody has ever published a definitive book on Greek café music – not even in Greece. So I thought, here's a gap in the market, I'll write one myself! I'll be famous! Maybe they'll make me President of Greece! How about some coffee?"

Jim dressed and went to college almost an hour earlier than usual because George fried himself a huge breakfast of corned beef hash which filled the whole apartment with greasy smoke, and then insisted on playing *bouzouki* music so that Jim could learn to appreciate how much it spoke of the sun, and the wine-dark sea, and a land where men were men and had seriously hairy chests and women did all the work.

Alone in his classroom, he sat in the dust-speckled morning sunshine marking essays. He had given up smoking seven years ago, but he had never felt more like a cigarette. He had asked Special Class II to write him a critical assessment of *Treasure Island*. Mark Foley had written, "Long John Silver was this cool dud with 1 leg, leder of the pirates. He wants to rip off all of the treasure but Jim Hawkins stops him. He should of kill Jim Hawkins but they had a bond, lik a father and son should of been."

Jim always found it extraordinary how his least able students were able to get right to the nub of a story. They ignored the plot and felt the pulse of it. Beattie McCordic, who always interpreted everything she read from a radical-feminist point of view, had written that 'there are no women pirates in *Treasure Island* which is ridiculous because in real life there were plenty of them and some of them were real ballbreakers.' But she went on to say 'that doesn't mean that the story is anti-feminist. The way Jim Hawkins behaves is influenced all the way through the story by his mother, who is quiet but strong

69

and very moral. There are two main characters in this book: Long John Silver and Jim Hawkin's mother, even though she only appears right in the beginning and right at the very end.'

After two or three essays, he stopped marking, and stared out of the window. He thought of the feline formerly known as Tibbles and he felt so angry and sad that he could have cried. But while he was looking out of the window he saw a dark-blue Chevrolet Caprice turn into the parking-lot, and Lieutenant Harris climb out. Lieutenant Harris put on his dark glasses, combed his hair, straightened his coat, and walked toward the college buildings like a man who was very pleased with himself.

Two or three minutes later, there was a knock at the classroom door. "Mr Rook?" said Lieutenant Harris.

"Sure, come on in," Jim told him. "You look like the cat who got the caviar."

"Well, I thought you'd like to know that we've made a breakthrough in the Martin Amato homicide."

"That's good news. That's really good news. Did you make an arrest yet?"

Lieutenant Harris triumphantly lifted one finger. "Let me tell you something, it was classic procedural police-work. We did a house-to-house down at Venice Beach, and then we staked out the boardwalk and stopped every single cyclist and jogger and skater. We interviewed every bodybuilder on Muscle Beach and every rollerblader in the Graffiti Pit."

Jim put down his pen and waited for Lieutenant Harris to finish complimenting himself on the trouble that he had taken.

"In the end, we found two young guys from Idaho, of all places. They had hitch-hiked all the way from Boise in the hope of becoming movie extras. Saturday night they didn't have anyplace to stay so they tried to sleep on the beach. They were lying in their bedrolls when two men ran right into them."

Lieutenant Harris picked up the small plaster bust of Shakespeare on Jim's desk and peered at it closely. "Who's this? Don't tell me. That guy from *Star Trek*."

"Lieutenant," Jim said, impatiently.

"Oh, sure. Well, there was a scuffle between these two young kids from Idaho and these two guys who had run right into them. It wasn't much, and the kids wouldn't have thought anything about it, except that when the two guys had gone running off, one of them found that his hands were covered in blood. The first thing he thought was that one of the guys had stabbed him. So he went to a local bar and washed it all off, and found that he hadn't been stabbed at all. The blood must have come from the other guy."

"Suggesting what?"

"Suggesting that the other guy had either cut himself badly – or else he'd very recently cut somebody else, and gotten himself splattered in their blood."

"And?"

"And he couldn't have cut himself. The blood must have come from somebody else."

"How do you know that?"

Lieutenant Harris gave him a triumphant smile. "Because the two kids on the beach positively identified him as Catherine White Bird's brother Grey Cloud – and it didn't take much to establish that Grey Cloud didn't cut himself that night. His partner they identified as Paul – Catherine's other brother."

"You're kidding me. Those two pretend they're tough, but I don't believe they'd go that far."

"They did it, Mr Rook. That's obvious. They didn't like their sister going out with a white man, so when she

71

refused to give him up – that was it. Tribal honour was at stake, or whatever."

"You've arrested them?"

Lieutenant Harris nodded. "Suspicion of first-degree homicide. I'll admit that I still don't know how they inflicted those wounds on Martin Amato, but they were down on the beach at the time he was killed, and Grey Cloud was covered in blood. We're running a DNA and haemotology test right now, and if that blood turns out to be Martin's . . . well, that's all folks."

"What about the locker room? What about my apartment? What about my cat?"

"In those instances, Mr Rook, I believe that we're looking for somebody else altogether."

"But the scratches match, don't they?"

"There's some superficial similarity, but we haven't finished our forensic tests yet."

"Lieutenant," Jim protested, "these incidents are all connected. That locker room was trashed by the same person who killed my cat and trashed my apartment, and the same person who killed my cat and trashed my apartment is the same person who murdered Martin Amato."

"I have a problem with that," said Lieutenant Harris.

"Problem? What problem?"

"At the time your cat was being killed and your apartment was being remodeled, Paul and Grey Cloud were having dinner at home with their father and five friends from their father's TV show."

Jim stared at him. "So what do you conclude from that?"

"I conclude that the two cases are not connected."

"What if Paul and Grey Cloud *didn't* do it? They could still be connected then."

"*Yes*, Mr Rook,' said Lieutenant Harris, with thinly-disguised impatience. "But they're not, and we're going to prove that they're not, and once we've done that, Paul and Grey Cloud are going to get what's coming to them."

The door opened and David Littwin cautiously put his head around it. "OK to come in, Mr Rook? I thought I'd come in early to finish off my poem."

"Sure, come in, David," said Jim. "Lieutenant Harris was just leaving."

"I may need to talk to you some more," said Lieutenant Harris. He was obviously upset that Jim hadn't clapped him on the back and acknowledged him as the greatest procedural detective since Maigret.

"Sure, any time," Jim told him. Lieutenant Harris hesitated by the door for a moment, and then left. Jim went back to his marking.

Sherma Feldstein had written, 'I think *Treasure Island* should be banned as the only physically-challenged person in the entire novel is presented as a villain. That is, Long John Silver, who only had one leg, not his own fault. This novel will further reinforce prejudice against the physically disadvantaged by presenting them as greedy and immoral and prepared to use their disabilities for nefarious gain.'

Jim gave her an extra point for good spelling and vocabulary, and for correctly using 'nefarious', but he simply didn't know how to mark her for suggesting that *Treasure Island* had been written as a diatribe against the disabled.

He felt the same way about Lieutenant Harris. Maybe Lieutenant Harris was right, and Martin *had* been murdered by Paul and Grey Cloud. There was strong circumstantial evidence against them, after all. But it seemed to Jim that Lieutenant Harris was doing what Sherma Feldstein was doing – closing his eyes to everything except his own prejudice.

There had been no discrimination against Long John

Silver in *Treasure Island*. In fact, he had dominated all the other characters – while Paul and Grey Cloud seemed to Jim to have a mission that white men might not fully understand, but which amounted to very much more than attacking anyone who tried to be too friendly with their sister.

When the class assembled, there were three absentees. Titus Greenspan III had another bad attack of asthma; Seymour Williams had gone to his great-aunt's funeral at Forest Lawn; and Catherine White Bird had simply failed to show. It wasn't hard to understand why.

Jim didn't tell the class that Catherine's brothers had been arrested. They would find out soon enough, and he was more interested in teaching them how to cope with their grief. Revenge could wait until later.

"You want to tell me how you got on with your poems?" he asked them. "Did you find them difficult? Did you find that they helped you to express how you feel?"

"I think it's better to smash something when you're feeling that bad," said Ray. "You know – break a window, kick in a door. It gets rid of your frustration better."

"So you felt frustrated by Martin's death?"

"Frustrated? You're kidding me, aren't you? I felt like *why*, man? The guy was so young. Like he had his whole life in front of him, and he happens to walk into some whacko who kills him. I just wish I could of been there. I just wish I could of saved him. I just wish it was Saturday afternoon again and he was still alive."

"So what did you do? Did you write a poem or did you smash something?"

"I did both. I went home and I wrecked my old Spanish guitar. I smashed it up against the wall until it was nothing more than matchwood and strings."

"And did that make you feel any better?"

Ray shrugged, and said, "Yeah. It made me feel better."

"How about your poem? Do you want to read it to us?"

Ray fastidiously picked the gum out of the side of his mouth and stuck it under his desk. He picked up a well-folded sheet of paper and cleared his throat. Usually, the rest of the class would have barracked him, but today they were silent. They knew he wasn't very articulate but they knew how he felt.

"This is called, like, *Smashed-Up Guitar*:

'I smashed up my guitar today
So that I would never have to play
Any more songs for you

I don't want to play the chords
Or even sing the words
You wouldn't hear me even if I wanted you to

You're just like my guitar
Smashed-up, that's what you are
Your only song is gone and we're all missing you.'"

"That's good, Ray," said Jim. "That's probably the best piece of work you've produced this term. You've made a really vivid analogy about your guitar being broken and silent and Martin being broken and silent, too."

Ray suddenly flushed scarlet – the first time that Jim had ever seen him embarrassed. He retrieved his gum and bent over his desk with his face covered by his hands.

"Anybody else?" asked Jim.

John Ng hesitantly put up his hand. "I've only written something very short," he said. "It's not exactly a *haiku* but I guess it's kind of like it."

75

"Go on, then."

" 'The grass
Misses your tread
The sand
Misses your running shadow
But the wind
Welcomes you.' "

"Do you want to explain that a little?" asked Jim.

"Well . . . I'm just trying to say that when you leave the earth, there's another life waiting for you. Not a life that you can see, just like you can't see the wind, but just as exciting."

"So you believe in a life after death?"

"Of course, Mr Rook. The same as you do."

Russell said, "Mr Rook, sir? Do you want to hear mine? It's pretty long. Sixty-two verses. I call it *The Ballad of Martin Amato.*"

There was a quiet groan from Mark Foley. The last ballad that Russell had written was a blow-by-blow account of the plot of *Waterworld*, and it had gone on almost as long as the movie itself. But Jim said, "OK, Russell, let's hear it." He didn't think it would do the class any harm to have a little light relief.

" 'This ballad is just starting
It's the story of a boy called Martin
Of the crop he was the cream
And he was captain of the football team.
Martin was tall with a ready smile
He was so tall that he stood out a mile
As you know his surname was Amato
Which was why he was often kidded and called
Tomato.' "

76

Russell went on and on, and the monotony of his rhyming wasn't helped by his halting delivery. Jim found himself looking out of the window and thinking about Mrs Vaizey and the warnings that she had given him through Valerie Neagle. God, it was Tuesday morning already and he was supposed to be killed on Thursday – and he still didn't have any idea of who his '2 Friends' might be or where he was supposed to be travelling. It gave him a terrible nagging feeling of frustrated dread. Don't talk to *me* about frustration, Ray. Don't talk to *me* about smashing things up.

Russell was still droning on when there was a knock at the classroom door and Dr Ehrlichman's secretary came in. "Mr Rook? I'm sorry to interrupt your tutorial, but there's a visitor for you."

"Okay, thanks, Sylvia. Listen up, everybody. Let Russell finish reading his ballad and then I want you to read the poem on page 32 of *Gasoline* by Gregory Corso."

He left the class and walked along the corridor in the wake of Sylvia's overpowering perfume. When he reached the principal's office he found to his surprise that Henry Black Eagle was standing there, waiting for him. Henry Black Eagle's face was as serious as an axe-hacked oak.

"I don't like to disturb you, Mr Rook. But I have to ask you a very great favour."

"Well, you can *ask*," said Jim, cautiously.

"Can we talk in private?" asked Henry Black Eagle, looking over Jim's shoulder at Sylvia, who was pretending to check Dr Ehrlichman's diary while keeping one dangly earring cocked to hear what they were saying.

Jim said, "Sure . . . why don't we take a walk?" and led him out through the hallway to the front entrance. They walked out past the tennis-courts, under a hazy sun.

Their conversation was punctuated by the *plick-plack* of students playing mixed doubles.

"Lieutenant Harris told me that your sons had been arrested," said Jim.

Henry Black Eagle nodded. "The police came this morning, just after six o'clock. I've already talked to a lawyer here in Los Angeles, but I sent to the DNA for a Navajo lawyer, too."

"I gather that two hitch-hikers saw Paul and Grey Cloud on the beach just about the same time that Martin Amato was murdered."

"That's true," said Black Eagle.

"You mean they *were* there?"

"Yes, they were. But not to kill the Amato boy, believe me."

"Even though they'd already threatened him? I mean, I was a witness to that. They specifically told Martin that he wouldn't live to see another dawn."

"I know. But you misunderstood. They never had any intention of causing the Amato boy any harm."

"They had blood on them, that's what Lieutenant Harris told me."

"I know. But I can swear to you that they didn't commit any crime."

"So what *were* they doing down on the beach?"

Henry Black Eagle stopped. "They were protecting their sister, as they always do."

"Protecting her from what? From the animal that killed Martin?"

"Yes, in a way."

"So what is it, this animal? And why is it trying to hurt her?"

"This is the reason that I've come to you for help," said Henry Black Eagle. "Apart from the fact that Catherine thinks that you're a very inspirational teacher, she tells me that you have a gift. Her classmates told her that you can see things that other people can't . . . spiritual things."

"Well, that's partly true. I sometimes have – I don't know, *visions* and spiritual intuitions. But what does that have to do with this animal?"

"This animal, Mr Rook, is not a real animal. It comes from the spirit world. It is like a curse, of a kind."

"A curse," said Jim, trying not to look too unimpressed. "Do you want to tell me more?"

"I think you should talk to Paul and Grey Cloud. They are both much more involved in Navajo spiritualism than me. But you can see my problem, can't you? How can I prove that my sons didn't kill this Martin Amato boy when he was killed by something that you can't see, even if you could be persuaded to believe in it?"

"So what do you think *I* can do about it?"

"Talk to Paul and Grey Cloud, please. At least hear what they have to say. Even if you don't do it for their sake, or for my sake, at least do it for Catherine's sake. She knows that her brothers didn't murder Martin, and she doesn't want to see them go to prison for it. She also wants the beast to be sent back to the spirit world, so that it won't hurt anybody else."

"I'm going to have to think about this, Mr Black Eagle. I had a very, very bad horoscope this week, concerning beasts. Apart from that, my dead grandfather came to my apartment two days ago and sat and talked to me, as close as you are now. He warned me to watch for something old and cold and bristling, and that sounds like a beast to me."

"Please, Mr Rook. If there were any other way – if there were any other person who could help us, I wouldn't ask. But you're the only one who can see the beast. Nobody else would stand a chance."

Jim stopped and pressed two fingers to his forehead,

the way he always did when he was thinking something over. Then he said, "OK . . . I'll go talk to Paul and Grey Cloud – see what they have to say. But I can't make you any guarantees. Not until I know what this is all about."

"Let me give you something," said Henry Black Eagle. He reached into the pocket of his fringed buckskin coat and took out a thin silver whistle on a frayed cord made of twisted hair. "Here . . . it belongs to Grey Cloud, but he wouldn't have been allowed to give it to you down at the police station."

Jim took the whistle and turned it from side to side. "What is this? What does it do?"

"It works like a dog-whistle, way beyond the range of human hearing."

Jim blew it; and Henry Black Eagle was right, it was silent. But there was a man walking a Labrador bitch only fifty or sixty feet away, and the bitch took absolutely no notice, even when Jim blew it again. "So what kind of dogs does this call?" he wanted to know.

"Please . . . you'll understand more when you talk to Paul and Grey Cloud."

Jim said, "All right. But I'm not making you any promises. And I'm scared of dogs. So if this whistle calls anything more aggressive than a chihuahua, you can forget it."

"You make jokes in the face of death."

"No, I don't. Death is just about the biggest joke of all. The only trouble is, it never makes me laugh."

He arrived at police headquarters just before noon. His car let off a deafening backfire, and two policemen who were climbing out of their patrol car instinctively ducked. "Sorry," he said, with a wave of his hand.

"You want to get that muffler fixed before somebody shoots back," one of the officers warned him.

80

"Sorry," he repeated, and went up the steps to the front desk.

Lieutenant Harris was on the way out. He looked hot and unhappy. "Mr Rook – I really appreciate all of the assistance you've been trying to give us, but I don't think that you're going to be doing anything at all constructive by talking to those Navajo boys."

"I don't think they did it," said Jim.

"Oh. That's supposed to be constructive, is it? They made a death threat against Martin Amato in front of independent witnesses. They were seen by more independent witnesses at or near the crime scene at the time the crime was committed. They have blood on their clothes which I have learned within the past fifteen minutes is the same group as Martin Amato's, type O. And apart from that, they're uncooperative, aggressive, and their lawyer's just arrived and he looks like Sitting Bull."

"Sitting Bull was a Sioux."

"Whatever."

Jim said, "I still want to talk to them. Come on, lieutenant, the family trust me. I might be able to throw some light on what really happened."

Lieutenant Harris wiped perspiration from his forehead with the back of his hand. "OK . . . but don't take longer than ten minutes – that's if they agree to talk to you. And when you're through, don't say one single word to the Press. You got that? Not even 'no comment'. I'm not having this case prejudiced by the media, no way."

"You can trust me, lieutenant."

Lieutenant Harris was about to push his way out through the revolving doors when he stopped. "By the way, we checked the clawmarks in your apartment and measured them up against the clawmarks in the locker room. They were similar, but they didn't exactly match."

"What do you mean?"

81

"I mean that the damage in the locker-room was inflicted with a similar-type claw or instrument as the damage in your apartment, but there was quite a difference in measurement."

"Measurement? Like what?"

"Whatever trashed your apartment had a claw span of well over eleven inches. The widest claw span we found in the locker room was just over six."

"What about the clawmarks on Martin Amato?"

"They were different again. Eight, maybe nine inches at a stretch."

"So what conclusion do you draw from that?"

"None, so far. I'm just telling you."

"Maybe you should be looking for three different animals. Or one animal that can grow dramatically in the space of a single weekend."

Lieutenant Harris stared at him long and hard, one eye squinched up in an unconscious impersonation of *Columbo*. He didn't attempt to disguise the contempt in his voice. "Mr Rook, if you can find me any living creature whose claws grow five inches in a matter of three days, then please let me know, because I can get in touch with Ripley's Believe It Or Not. Meanwhile, if you really have to talk to those two Native Americans, why don't you see if you can't persuade them to confess that they *did* murder Martin Amato, and tell you how they did it. It would save the taxpayer money. It would save *them* money. We could go fishing instead of sitting in court. Anyhow – I have to go. Sergeant! Take Mr Rook through to see our Native American guests. Ten minutes max."

The big-bellied sergeant came forward with a long loop of keys hanging from his belt. "This way, sir," he said, with deep condescension, his moustache cropped like a brand-new nailbrush. He led Jim through a swing door, past the squadroom, and through to an interview room at

82

the back of the building. There was a plain table scarred with cigarette burns and four plain wooden chairs. The window was covered with wire mesh.

"Just take a seat, sir," said the sergeant. "We'll bring your friends up momentarily."

Jim stood by the window and waited. Outside he could see the rear end of a squad car and the corner of a brick wall, and a narrow rectangle of intensely blue sky. He wondered what it would be like to be locked up for the rest of your life. Better to be dead. But he didn't want to think about being dead, either – not with death breathing so coldly and quickly down his neck.

The door opened and the sergeant and another officer brought in Paul and Grey Cloud, handcuffed and shackled. The sergeant told them to sit down, well away from the table. Then he said to Jim, "Remember what the lieutenant said, sir – ten minutes and no longer. No smoking, no passing of any smoking materials, foodstuffs, books, gifts or documents. No physical contact whatsoever."

"All right if I breathe a little?" asked Jim.

"That's optional," said the sergeant, and left the room, leaving the other officer standing by the door, his hands behind his back, his eyes fixed on nothing at all, slowly and irritatingly masticating a large wad of chewing-gum.

Jim sat down. "I guess you probably know that your father came to see me. He said that you needed my help."

"We wouldn't have called for you at all," said Grey Cloud, proudly lifting his head. "But Catherine insisted – and, so long as we're locked up here – there is no other way open to us. You will have to be our eyes and our ears, our legs and our voices."

"Your father mentioned some kind of animal."

"The spirit-beast, yes. The beast that nobody can see, even when it kills them."

83

"It's going to be hard to explain that to a jury."

"That's why we've come to you. We need you to tell people that the spirit-beast *does* exist. That's our only hope of proving that we're innocent."

"Maybe if you took a polygraph test," Paul suggested.

"Wait a minute," said Jim. "What gives you the idea that I believe you?"

"You're prepared to admit the possibility that we *might* be telling the truth," said Grey Cloud. "Otherwise you wouldn't have come."

"OK – there's an outside chance that some kind of spiritual force may have been responsible for Martin Amato's death, instead of you two. I'm probably the only person on the planet who thinks so. But I believe that the West Grove college locker room and my apartment were both trashed by the whatever it was that killed Martin, and I don't care for the way that the cops are trying to suggest that they weren't. That smells of railroading to me. But I'm going to need a whole lot more proof before I start taking lie-detector tests and standing up and swearing on the Bible that an invisible creature from the spirit world ripped Martin's lungs out, and not you. After all, you were down on the beach at the time when he was killed."

"I promise you we had nothing to do with it," said Paul. "We didn't even *see* it."

"You were covered in blood."

"It was hard not to be."

"You were right there – right after it happened?"

Paul, soberly, said, "Yes. He was still pumping it out like a gusher."

Jim ran his hand through his hair. "You've got trouble here, guys. No question about it."

"All right," put in Grey Cloud. "You saw the body. What do *you* think killed him?"

Jim hesitated. "A bear, maybe, or a mountain lion."

"It certainly wasn't done by humans, was it?"

"Not unless they had some kind of fancy claw."

"Well, sure," said Grey Cloud. "But can you imagine the strength you'd need to do something like that? And what happened to this fancy claw? Did we throw it away? Did we bury it? Is it hidden in our house?"

"OK," said Jim, "supposing you find a way of convincing me that this spirit-beast exists. What do you want me to do about it, apart from making a laughing-stock of myself in front of a court of law?"

"We want you to arrange for the curse to be lifted, so that the beast returns to where it came from."

"Oh, yes? And how can I do that?"

Grey Cloud said, "You will have to make a journey – a journey that will take you many miles in distance, and a long, long way inside your soul. You will have to learn what it is to be a Navajo. You will have to acquire the great understanding."

Seek the advice of two friends, thought Jim. Travel on a long journey. But then he said, "Don't you think one of your own kind would be better at this? A Navajo? Somebody who believes in this stuff already?"

Grey Cloud shook his head. "Too many Navajo have lost their faith. They should be looking for their spirits, but all they want is automobiles and housing developments and factories. When white men first came to our land, they defeated us not only by slaughtering us and giving us white men's diseases, but by shaking our faith in our gods. One by one, all of our deities lost their power to defend us. Even Gitche Manitou the Great Spirit was rendered powerless and silent. How could he speak to people who no longer listened? We used to hear his words in the wind, but after the white men came all we heard was train-whistles and traffic and radio shows. In the same way, where can the spirit of water survive, when the rivers are poisoned by industrial pollution? There is no place for a spirit of fire when men have atomic bombs.

"The spirits are still there, but the people are blind. Only *you* can see them."

"Well, this all sounds very mystical," said Jim, "but I'm not at all sure that I can do it. I'm not at all sure that I *want* to do it."

"I'm sorry," said Grey Cloud, "but you *have* to. You know that you do. Not just for our sake, but for yours, too. If you don't go looking for this beast – this beast is going to come looking for you. It knows that you've been protecting our sister – and, what's more, it knows that you can see it."

Jim wasn't sure that he believed any of Grey Cloud's warnings or not, but they gave him an uncomfortable feeling that he was being *watched* – or, worse than that, that something very dark and malevolent was *sniffing him out*. He glanced up at the window, but the shadow he had seen out of the corner of his eye was only the shadow of a nodding leaf.

"So where am I supposed to journey to?" he asked. "And what am I supposed to do when I arrive?"

"You have to journey to the Navajo capital of Window Rock, in Arizona. Take Catherine with you, and three other friends. My father will pay for the air fares. When you reach Window Rock, you will meet a man called John Three Names. He will take you to Fort Defiance, which we call the Meadow Between Rocks."

"Then what?"

"Then he will take you to the man that Catherine is supposed to marry."

"So Catherine's betrothal has something to do with all this?"

Grey Cloud said, "Yes. The man that Catherine is supposed to marry has gone to a wonder-worker and conjured up the spirit-beast to prevent her from forming any attachments to anyone else."

"I see."

"You don't believe us? It's true! He was so angry and jealous that he would have done anything to stop anybody else from touching her."

"Supposing I *do* believe you?" said Jim. "Why did your father promise this guy that Catherine was going to marry him in the first place? Is he rich, or what? I mean, that's not a Navajo thing, is it? Arranged marriages?"

Paul paused, and then he said, "Our father did it because our mother was dying of ovarian cancer. The man said that he knew a wonder-worker, and that the wonder-worker could intercede with the spirits to save our mother's life. All he wanted in return was to marry Catherine and breed children with her."

"And your father agreed to that? Without asking Catherine what *she* wanted?"

"He was losing his wife, Mr Rook. He was losing our mother. He was desperate."

"But your mother died anyway, didn't she?"

"Yes, she did. The spirits obviously thought that it was time for her to die. Afterward, my father went back to the man she was supposed to marry and asked if Catherine could be released from her betrothal. But the man said that a sacred promise was a sacred promise. Our father begged him, but he refused to change his mind. He said he wanted Catherine and he was going to have her, whatever it took."

Paul said, "We lit out of Window Rock overnight, leaving most of our possessions behind. Catherine didn't know why and we weren't going to tell her. We came here to Los Angeles and my father was lucky enough to get that part in *Blood Brothers*. The studio needed a full-blood Navajo and he was a full-blood Navajo, and he could act."

"But then?"

"Then we had messages that this man was going out of his mind with jealousy, and that he was going to ask the wonder-workers to put a curse on Catherine, so that no other man would ever be able to touch her. If they did – well, you saw what happened to Martin. The spirit-beast destroyed the locker-room, as a warning, and then, when he refused to be intimidated, it killed him."

Jim stood up and walked back to the window. A small puffy cloud had appeared in the rectangle of blue sky, and the squad car had gone. "This is a seriously weird story, I'll tell you that."

"Believe me, Mr Rook, this is the truth. Would we tell you a lie, when our freedom is at stake? We might even go to the gas chamber if they find us guilty."

"Think of Catherine, too," said Grey Cloud. "Think of all the other people who could get hurt."

"Yes," said Jim. "Including me."

"Will you help us?" asked Paul. Behind him, the police officer sniffed and carried on chewing his gum.

Jim said, "I don't know. You haven't told me what I'm supposed to do when I meet this spirit-man. How am I going to persuade him to give Catherine up?"

"John Three Names will explain all of that. But the main thing you have to do is make him an offer. Money, mainly. But some other promises, too."

"I'm sorry, guys. I think I need to know much more before I say yes or no."

"Mr Rook – it's far too complicated to explain right now. But I promise you – it isn't anything difficult."

"All right, maybe it's not difficult. But is it *dangerous*?"

Grey Cloud gave an evasive shrug; but Paul said, "It won't be dangerous if you remember everything that John Three Names tells you."

"I don't know," said Jim. "I'm still not sure about this."

Paul clenched his handcuffed fists and banged them on his knees. "You *must!*" he said. "*You have to*! There isn't any more time and we don't have anybody else."

"Excuse me. You may not have anybody else but I just get the feeling you're not telling me everything you know."

"There's nothing else *to* know. You go to Arizona, you talk to this guy, you make a deal with him, and that's the end of it."

"So why do I have to take three friends?"

"To take care of Catherine, that's all."

"Can't Catherine take care of herself?"

"Mostly . . . but with all this going on, we think it's a good idea for somebody to keep a close eye on her. That's why we always picked her up after college. You know, just in case."

Jim said nothing for at least a minute. The guard sneezed twice. Paul and Grey Cloud watched him with tightly-contained unease. He didn't understand this situation, not at all. But he took his grandfather's warning very seriously, and he took Mrs Vaizey's fortune-telling very seriously, and it seemed as if he were following the destiny that they both had predicted for him.

"All right," he said, at last. "Let me talk to your father again. Then I'll see what I can do."

He found Henry Black Eagle at Universal Studios, on the set of *Blood Brothers*. A small scrubby area of backlot was supposed to be the Navajo reservation in Arizona, although Jim could easily see the *Psycho* house on the horizon, and coachloads of tourists being trundled around the *Jaws* pool and through the parting of the Red Sea.

Henry was sitting in the front seat of a dusty blue-and-white police car drinking coffee from a styrofoam cup and smoking a cigarette. Jim leaned over the roof and said, "I talked to your sons. It looks like I'm going to Arizona."

Henry nodded, without looking up. "Thank you, Mr Rook. One day, you'll get your reward for this." He checked his watch, and said, "There's a flight to Albuquerque at seven tomorrow morning. I can get you a charter from Albuquerque to Gallup. John Three Names will meet you there and drive you the rest of the way."

Jim said, "There's only one thing I'm going to ask you. What kind of a character is this man who's supposed to be marrying your daughter?"

"Clever. Devious. He can twist your mind like a helter-skelter."

"How old is he? Do you know where he comes from?"

"He's as old as he looks. Where he comes from – well . . . where do any of us come from? The trees, the rocks, the dust on the ground."

"Does he have a name?" asked Jim. "It seems a little odd, flying all the way to Arizona to meet a guy and I don't even know his name."

"Well, he has several names, as many Navajo do, but most of the time they call him He Who Speaks To Animals, or Dog Brother."

"And what does he look like? I mean, how old is he? Like, what can I expect?"

"You can only expect the unexpected, Mr Rook. He's a very devious man, very unpredictable. You should take care not to upset him."

At that moment, a podgy assistant director in a sweaty green *Blood Brothers* T-shirt came waddling up and said, "Come on, Henry. We're ready to shoot the explosion scene."

90

"OK," said Henry, and eased himself out of the car. "How about it, Mr Rook? Do you want to watch?"

"Yes, sure. I'd love to," said Jim. He followed Henry and the assistant director to a small corner of the lot where an elderly black Lincoln Continental was already tilted into a ditch. In the driver's seat sat a dummy with a blue flowery dress and a blonde wig, slumped over the steering-wheel. Special effects technicians were still fiddling with wires and detonators, and the camera crew were standing around, switching on dazzling photo-floods and then switching them off again, smoking and drinking bottles of Evian water.

On the other side of the set, on the porch of a 'sheriff's office' that was nothing more than a front wall propped up with joists, Jim caught sight of Catherine, wearing a yellow checkered shirt and jeans, talking to a script assistant. "You brought her to work?" he asked Henry.

"What else could I do? Her brothers are in jail. Somebody has to watch over her."

"She could have come to college. We keep a pretty good eye on our students there."

Henry said, "Yes, I know," but that was all; and then the assistant director came over to put him in position.

Just before the clapper-board snapped, however, Henry turned to Jim, and the expression on his face was unlike anything that Jim had seen before. Haunted, haggard, almost pleading. Jim looked over at Catherine. She was still talking with great animation to the script assistant, flicking back her hair and moving her hands. She was just as beautiful as ever – her hair gleaming, her eyes bright. But Jim was sure that he could see a shadow around her. A dark, dim shadow – much bigger than she was – and *hunched up*, as if it were trying to hide itself within her.

The longer he looked at her, the clearer the shadow became. It followed every movement she made, but it

91

was obviously another being altogether, a being that was imitating her, in order to stay concealed. Jim couldn't take his eyes off it.

He was standing right next to the best boy, who was wearing a *Blood Brothers* baseball cap backwards and trying to sort out a wildly frayed arrangement of multicolored electrical wires with a pair of pliers.

"Let me ask you something," he said. "That girl over there . . . the one in the yellow shirt. Can you see kind of a *shadow* all around her?"

The best boy peered at Catherine, and then looked back at Jim as if he were two fajitas short of a Mexican picnic. "Shadow?" he said, as if he didn't know what the word meant.

"It's nothing," said Jim. "Forget it." But after the best boy had gone back to his electrical spaghettini, he looked at Catherine again, and there was no doubt that there was a dingy shadow flickering over her. Even when she got up from her seat and walked across the set, the shadow followed her, like smoke, like clouds, like a black-and-white movie projected over her face.

She saw him, and waved, and he was still watching her when there was a deafening explosion, and the Lincoln blew up in a scorching ball of orange flame. The windows were shattered, the tires caught fire, and the hood was flung twenty feet up into the air. Jim turned around just in time to see Henry Black Eagle rolling away across the dust with a gun in his hand.

When he looked back, Catherine had disappeared behind the dust and the smoke and the milling crowd of extras. But he glimpsed the shadow, sliding across the front of the 'sheriff's office', and it was crouched, and angular, with a jagged, bristly outline.

Chapter Five

He met Susan in the corridor outside the geography room and asked her if she was interested in a trip to Arizona.

"Arizona? Why on earth should I want to go to Arizona?"

"I don't know. You like cacti, don't you? And the weather's pretty good."

"The weather's pretty good here. Besides, I'm right in the middle of the busiest semester I've ever had. And also, I thought that you and I were taking a raincheck."

"Well, it won't be just us. One of my students is coming along. In fact, two or three of my students may be coming along. We're visiting the Navajo reservation at Window Rock."

Susan shook her head. "I can't believe you sometimes. You are the most – I don't know. You are the most off-the-wall person I ever met. Sometimes I feel like you arrived here from another planet, and you haven't quite learned how Earth people behave."

"All the same, how about coming to Arizona?"

"No, Jim. I can't."

"I need you, Susan. I wouldn't ask you if I didn't need you. And I'm not talking about sexually. I'm talking about *needing* you, okay? Like needing your support."

"Why?" she demanded.

"Well . . . I'm taking a couple of my girl students away

with me, and I think it would be more appropriate if they had a female chaperone."

"I suppose you're taking Catherine White Bird?"

"Of course. I mean, this was what inspired the trip in the first place, her being a full-blooded Navajo and everything."

"And a very alluring full-blooded Navajo, too."

"What am I supposed to say? That she looks like the back side of a totem pole?"

"OK. Who else is going?"

"I don't know. I haven't asked them yet. But I really wanted you."

Susan said, "This won't work, Jim. You and I, we're just not suited. You say tomayto and I say tomato."

"I know that. But that's not the point. I need a clear-thinking, intelligent, responsible adult on this trip. I need a woman who can keep an eye on two or maybe three young girls in a difficult situation. I need somebody with a good grasp of ethnic cultures and the ability not to annoy me. You were the only person I could think of."

"Window Rock, you say?" she asked him.

"Window Rock . . . and maybe Fort Defiance, too. You know what the Navajo call that? 'Meadow Between Rocks.' It's going to be really, really interesting."

She looked up at him and he wished desperately that she were in love with him, but that was fate. "I don't know why I'm saying yes," she told him. "But, yes. When were you planning on going there?"

"Oh . . . there's no rush. I'll pick you up tomorrow at five o'clock."

"Tomorrow? I can't go tomorrow. In any case, my last lecture doesn't finish until twenty after four."

"I meant five o'clock in the morning. We're catching the first flight to Albuquerque."

Susan opened her mouth and then closed it without

saying a word. She watched Jim walking off down the corridor to his classroom and she thought to herself that she might like him more than she had ever admitted.

"I'm taking a short cultural trip to the Navajo reservation in Arizona," he announced to Special Class II. "The reason I'm doing it is to find out more about Catherine's background so that I can help her develop as an English student. Of course I've done the same for several other members of the class . . . Rita, you remember when I spent some time with your family and friends, so that I could get a better handle on Spanish culture. John . . . you kindly invited me to spend a weekend with your Vietnamese friends, and I enjoyed every minute of that, except that I was so clumsy with my chopsticks that I kept dropping *thit bo to* on my shoes.

"I can take two of you with me. One of you should be a girl, so that you can share a room with Catherine. The other – well, it doesn't matter. Girl or boy. Whoever wants to come."

Sharon X put up her hand. "Please, sir, I'd love to. I'm so interested in oppressed cultures."

"OK . . . anybody else?"

Mark Foley cautiously lifted one finger. Mark was cocky and funny, but he was one of the least academic students in the class. He was shorter and slighter than most of his contemporaries, with a pale, bruised-looking face and badly-cropped blond hair. His jeans and T-shirts were always very clean, but most of them were worn out and frayed. The sole of one of his trainers flapped when he walked.

"You, Mark? You want to come along?"

"Well, sure. I never flew before. It won't cost anything, will it?"

"No . . . Catherine's father is generously picking up

95

the tab. All you need is a couple of changes of clothes and a toothbrush."

"Hey – think your dad'll let you go?" asked Ricky Herman.

"I don't care what my dad says," said Mark, defiantly. "I'm going anyway."

Jim said, "If you have any problems with your father, Mark, just have him give me a call." He had dealt with Mark's father before: a real Bluto type who owned a run-down body shop in Santa Monica. He spent all day thumping second-hand Chevies into shape and all evening sluicing down jugs of draft beer at KC's Bar. He had told Jim to his face that as far as he was concerned Mark's English course was a waste of time because Mark spoke English already, didn't he? and poetry was 'all that faggot stuff'.

"Mrs Whitman will be taking over while we're gone . . . but there's a special project that I want the rest of you to do for me. I want you to find out all that you can about the Navajo people and Navajo culture, especially their religious beliefs. See if you can find out the names of their spirits and any colorful stories about them. When we come back, we'll be able to discuss what we've discovered in Arizona with what you've managed to discover here."

Ray Vito said, "Have a good time, Mr Rook. Bring us back some firewater and a couple of squaws."

"You and your racial stereotyping," Sharon protested.

"Yes, Ray – you should be ashamed of yourself," put in Ricky. "You greasy spaghetti-eating opera-loving Eyetie."

Jim stood back in amusement as the entire class started to shout racial insults at each other. Sometimes it did them good to come out with all the words that nobody was allowed to use any more. It made them realise that most racial slurs were only words, and that what really mattered was how well they got along and how much they liked each other. After a few minutes they all collapsed in laughter.

"Right, then," said Jim. "That's enough political incorrectness for one day. I'll see you Friday morning, hopefully."

He take a long last smiling look around the classroom, trying to give himself a clear picture of every face. After all, this might be the last time that he would see them.

*   *   *

Their flight from LAX was delayed for nearly an hour and they arrived at Albuquerque International Airport just before lunch. As they crossed the concrete apron the temperature was over 93 degrees and the wind was as dry as a whip.

All through the flight, Catherine had been unusually quiet and thoughtful. Jim caught up with her as they approached the terminal building and said, "Catherine – hey – are you all right?"

She brushed back her hair with her hand. "I think so. But frightened, I guess."

"Frightened of what? This guy you're supposed to be betrothed to? We'll sort him out."

"I'm more frightened of me."

"You? Why should you be frightened of you?"

She turned to him, and looked at him intently through her windblown hair. "I feel like there's something inside of me . . . something that's making me feel confused. Like I'm angry about something but I don't know what. I felt it the last time I dated Martin, I don't know why. But here I can feel it much more."

Jim thought of the dark, jagged shadow that had followed her at Universal Studios. "Maybe it's just your

97

age. When you're young, you know, you *do* feel confused."

"I don't know, sir. It feels like more than that. It feels so black. It feels so *angry*. It's like a wildness in me, do you know what I mean?"

"A wildness," said Jim. "A wildness that comes out of nowhere at all?"

Catherine said, "Yes. That's it. That's exactly it."

"Let me talk to you later," said Jim. "Meanwhile, let me see if I can fix up our connecting flight."

"Hey, it's hot here," said Mark, wiping his forehead with the back of his arm. He was carrying an old grey canvas sports bag, but his Nike trainers were brand-new and shining white. When his father had heard about his trip to Arizona, he had taken him straight out and bought them for him. "I think it's a total waste of time but you ain't going to show me up by going nowhere with no flappy shoe."

Sharon was wearing a shocking-pink T-shirt and white satin shorts and she looked like an Olympic athlete. "I'm so excited," she enthused. "I mean, isn't it beautiful here? So warm!"

Susan gave her a smile. Susan, as usual, was looking very Doris Day, with a blue headband and a crisp sleeveless white blouse and a pleated skirt in yellow-spotted cotton.

"Jim?" she called. "Don't forget the infantry."

Inside the chilly air-conditioned terminal, with its highly-polished floors, Jim went to the West New Mexico chartered airline desk. An overweight woman with a huge blonde lacquered hairstyle turned around and called, "Randy! Mr Rook and party!"

Out of the back office came a wiry-looking pilot with a deep tan and a snow-white crewcut to match his snow-white shirt. "How're you doing, folks? Anybody want to use the fixings before we go? Don't like to see my passengers fidgety, that's all."

He led them back out onto the heat-baked concrete, where a twin-engined Golden Eagle was waiting to fly them to Gallup. Mark sat up front with the pilot while Jim sat next to Catherine and Sharon and Susan sat in the back. They waited their turn on the runway behind the rippling backwash of a Boeing 737 – then, when it was their turn, Randy took them up 'like a flea hopping off a dog's back'. Immediately they angled west-north-westward, with the sun filling the Golden Eagle's interior with dazzling light.

"Said you're headed up to Window Rock?" asked Randy.

"That's right," said Jim. "We're on kind of a college field-trip. We're doing a project on the Navajo way of life."

"These days, that's not much different from any other way of life," Randy remarked. "Don't be disappointed if you don't see nobody in feather headdresses and bone breastplates. Window Rock's pretty much the same as anyplace else around here. It's got motels and restaurants, and a fairground, and a bank, and a community building and an FHA housing development. They've even got their own medical college these days.

He sniffed, and then he said, "Don't forget to buy yourself a rug, though. You can't visit the Navajo reservation without coming back with a rug. Teec Nos Pos, they're the best."

Jim remembered that Catherine had given a talk in class about Navajo weaving, and told them that rugs from Two Grey Hills were easily the finest, with more than 80 wefts to the inch. But this morning she stared out of the window at the dry, wrinkled ground below them, and said nothing. Once or twice she glanced at Jim and gave him a tight, uncommunicative smile, but that was all. Jim was trying his best to make her feel protected, but he didn't really know what he was supposed to be protecting her from.

He had seen a jagged shadow around her – a shadow that nobody else could see – but he had no idea what that meant. Was she actually possessed by this smoky, bristling spirit? Or was it nothing more than an omen – a spiritual warning that the beast was hunting for her, too? The trouble with signs and messages from the other side, they were never spelled out in plain English. Everything was communicated by hints, and suggestions, and faces seen in distant windows.

"Did you ever fly before?" Randy asked Mark.

"No, sir, never. Today's my first time. I thought I was going to be biting my nails but I wasn't."

"I mean did you ever fly an airplane before? I mean, like, yourself?"

Mark violently shook his head. "No, sir! I don't even own a *car*."

"Well, you have to start sometime," said Randy. "Take hold of the controls, let's see what you can do."

"Me?" said Mark, in a very much higher voice than he'd meant to. "I can't. Supposing I crash?"

"You won't crash. You don't have the experience to crash. Come on, take hold of those controls."

Mark gripped the controls so tightly that there were white spots on his knuckles. The Golden Eagle dipped a little, and tilted to one side, and the engines gave a threatening drone. But the pilot said, "Relax, you're doing fine. Just keep her on an even keel, that's all. Like, resist the temptation to nosedive."

Gradually, Mark gained confidence, and began to fly the Golden Eagle straight and reasonably smooth, with only one or two stomach-disturbing dips and swoops. The pilot showed him how to use the pedals and how to adjust his speed. "You're a natural, boy. You should make yourself a career out of this."

Jim watched and smiled. He had never seen Mark so excited. He thought – God, if only more people took a little time with boys like Mark, and showed them what they were capable of doing, instead of always telling them that they were dumb and useless.

"What do you think, everybody?" Mark called back. "Think I'm a pretty good pilot?"

Sharon said, with a big wide grin, "You know something, Mr Rook? I've never been so scared in my whole life."

They were flying over the last slopes of the Cibola National Forest, only a little more than 10 miles away from Gallup. Jim looked down and he could see their shadow dancing through the trees. "Little more height," Randy told Mark. "That's it. Want to make sure we clear that ridge up ahead."

Mark pulled the controls back, but as he did so, the Golden Eagle's port engine let out a loud burp, and then another, and another. Randy checked his instrument panel and lifted his sunglasses so that he could see the engine nacelle more clearly. "Well," he announced, "we're not on fire, I'm very happy to say, and we've got plenty of gas. Guess we might have a fuel-line blockage."

The engine burped even more loudly, and then sputtered, and abruptly died. Susan reached forward and took hold of Jim's hand, and squeezed it hard. Jim turned around and said, "It's OK, don't worry. You too, Sharon. This kind of thing happens all the time."

Randy said, "Don't panic, folks. All we have to do is feather the prop, and land on the other engine. You can't crash one of these babies even if you wanted to."

Susan said, "I hope that's not famous last words."

Jim tried to smile at her but found that he couldn't. He

could feel his sweaty shirt clinging to his back. He had never liked small airplanes, and he had been clenching his fists and curling his toes ever since they had taken off from Albuquerque. The plane suddenly tilted to port and the starboard engine let out a low-pitched moan of protest.

Sharon moaned, too; and Mark said, "Oh, shit. Oh, shit."

"Let's keep our heads here, folks," said Randy. "We still have plenty of height and we're only five minutes away from Senator Clark's Field at Gallup. This may be a little on the rough side, but there's nothing to get hysterical about."

The plane plunged again, and then soared upward, leaving Jim's stomach about a hundred feet below. Mark sat in the co-pilot's seat grim-faced, with his hands tucked firmly into his armpits. Susan was gripping Jim's hand so tight that her fingernails were digging into his skin, and Sharon had her hands over her face, although she was peeping out from between her fingers. When he looked at Catherine, however, she was sitting calm and still, her chin slightly raised, and her eyes staring straight ahead.

"Catherine?" Jim asked her. "Catherine, are you okay?"

Catherine didn't answer, but Jim was sure that he could see that shadow around her, even though the airplane cabin was filled with sunlight. She looked almost as if she were wearing a ghostly funeral veil. She was staring straight ahead, straight at the instrument panel, and her lips were moving, as if she were whispering something.

"*Coyote . . . Coyote . . . Coyote . . .*" that was all he could catch, over and over again.

"Catherine?" he repeated.

He reached out to touch her, but as he did so, all the indicator lights on the Golden Eagle's instrument panel winked out, and all the dial-pointers dropped back to zero. The starboard engine rumbled and shuddered and abruptly

102

cut out. They were swallowed by an eerie quietness. All they could hear was the whistling and the buffeting of the wind.

Randy jiggled the switch to restart the starboard engine, but nothing happened. "Nothing," he said. "All the damned electrics are dead. Never known this happen, never."

"Can you glide in?" Jim asked him.

"I don't know. The way we're dropping, we won't make Senator Clark's Field."

Mark said, "Oh, shit! We're not going to die, are we?"

"Die? Hell, no!" the pilot told him. "We're going to belly-flop in somebody's alfalfa, that's all." But Jim could tell from the way he spoke that Randy's mouth was dry, and that he was just as frightened as the rest of them. They had one last ridge to clear, which meant that they would have to maintain enough height to fly over a line of tall, jagged trees. But the Golden Eagle weighed over 3½ tonnes and it felt to Jim as if it were dropping out of the sky as promptly as a grand piano. The trees rose higher and higher in front of them, and soon they were almost brushing the upper branches.

They were never going to make the ridge. They could all see it now. They were already below the level of the taller trees, and there wasn't even a gap between them which Randy might have tried to fly through.

Susan whispered, "Oh my God, Jim. Oh my God." Sharon was holding her head in her hands, and her eyes were wide with panic. Jim felt sick with fear and helplessness, and a wrenching grief, too. He had come out here to save himself, and Catherine – but now they were both going to die, and they were going to kill Susan and Mark and Sharon, too.

"You got to brace yourselves," said Randy. "With any luck, the trees'll act like a cushion."

You know they won't, thought Jim. They'll smash us to pieces, and there won't be anything left for the rescue services to pick up but arms and legs.

Jim turned to Sharon and Susan. "Take your shoes off, then heads down, hands over your neck." The Golden Eagle lurched and dropped as Randy tried one last desperate effort to gain a little more height.

Jim looked at Catherine. She was still sitting up straight, her eyes fixed on the airplane's instrument panel. The shadow around her was even more distinct now, blurry and patchy, as if he were viewing her through a black-and-white photographic negative. What was more, her eyes were totally black, with no whites showing whatsoever.

"Catherine!" he shouted at her, and gripped her wrist – but then he instantly recoiled. He hadn't felt the smooth slim wrist that he had expected. He had felt something thick and cold – something that was bristling with coarse, matted hair.

"Catherine, listen to me! It's Jim Rook! Listen!"

"Tell her to brace herself!" Randy shouted. "For Christ's sake, we're going in!"

"Catherine!" Jim yelled. "Catherine! You have to listen to me! Catherine!"

He reached across and tried to turn her face around, but as soon as he touched her cheek he shouted, "*Ah!*" and whipped his hand away. Catherine's cheek had been rough and whiskery, and he had distinctly felt *teeth*.

"Catherine, if you're in there, Catherine, try to fight it!" Jim screamed at her.

"Jim? What on earth are you doing?" said Susan. "Jim! Get your head down, you'll break your back!"

Every cockpit window seemed to be filled with nothing

but rising trees. Mark was still gibbering "shit, shit, shit," under his breath, and Sharon was praying to Allah.

Catherine can't hear me, thought Jim, desperately. She may be there but she simply can't hear me. She's an animal now, not a human being. And how can you make an animal hear you?

He suddenly patted the front of his shirt and felt the whistle that Henry Black Eagle had given him, dangling around his neck. He lifted it up and blew it. He didn't hear anything at all, and Catherine didn't respond, so he blew it again, even harder this time.

Catherine's head turned toward him with a terrifying jerk. Her black eyes glared at him with such ferocity that he flinched away. He could see the shadow around her quite distinctly now, and it was less like a shadow than a mask – a snarling animal mask, with its lips curled back in hatred.

Jim said, "*Catherine!*"

A startling look of recognition crossed her face. She said, "What? What's happening?" and even as she spoke the blackness in her eyes began to shrink. The shadow faded and suddenly flowed away, like ink washed away down a sink. She looked around her and saw the trees rearing up on every side of them, and Sharon and Susan with their heads down between their knees.

"*What's happening?*" she shrieked. "*I don't understand what's going on! What's happening?*"

"Get your head down!" Randy shouted at her.

But Jim said, "Catherine – you're Catherine! Catherine White Bird, that's who you are!"

Catherine stared at him for one long moment, and then she raised both hands and touched her forehead, as if she couldn't believe that this head, this hair, this face were really hers.

"You're Catherine White Bird," said Jim, and even

if they all died now, at least Catherine would die with the full knowledge of who she was, and what had happened to her.

She turned to the instrument panel, and rigidly held out her hand. "*Live!*" she demanded. "*Live!*"

Jim saw the lights snap back on again, and the indicator needles suddenly bob back up into position. But the trees were looming so close that they blocked the sunlight out of the cabin, and the Golden Eagle seemed to be dropping even faster, as if it had given up the effort to stay airborne.

"*Randy!*" Jim yelled at him. "*Randy – try the engines again!*"

Randy flicked the starter switches. Nothing.

"Keep trying, for Christ's sake!" Jim insisted.

Randy flicked them again, and then again. And then the starboard engine coughed, and the port engine coughed in sympathy, and suddenly they felt the deep, ripsaw vibration of both engines at full throttle. Randy pulled back on the controls so hard that it looked as if he were physically lifting the Golden Eagle back up into the air. Sharon screamed as branches lashed against the wings. Mark let out a long, eerie-sounding moan of sheer terror.

Jim thought, "*Please, God*", and held Catherine's hand, and now it was smooth and small, the way it should have been, and she interlaced her fingers with his, and whispered, "Gitehe Manitou, save us."

The Golden Eagle burst through the top of the treeline, its propellors spraying leaves and branches in all directions. It continued to climb over the lower slopes of the Cibola Forest, higher and higher, rising to such an altitude that they could see the sun shining across twenty miles of forest and desert, with the Zuni Mountains rising behind them now in a faint purplish heat-haze.

"Well, I don't know what in hell happened back there," said Randy. "But today I can truly tell you that I believe in God. Or Allah," he added, turning to Sharon. "Or Gitche Manitou, whatever."

Mark said, "Whew."

"Is that all?" Randy ribbed him. "Just 'whew'?"

"Yeah, 'whew.' I thought I'd crapped myself but I haven't."

"I guess that's one small mercy," said Randy, and tilted the Golden Eagle toward Gallup.

John Three Names was waiting for them on the hot, sun-glaring airfield. He was a small, dapper Navajo in a brown coat, beige slacks, and a brown wide-brimmed hat with feathers in it. He had one of those crinkled, soft-skinned Native American faces that always reminded Jim of a parcel wrapped in secondhand brown paper. But his eyes were bright and hard, and he spoke in quick, clipped sentences, and there was nothing soft or secondhand about his ideas.

"Hi, I'm John Three Names," he said, grasping Jim's hand. "I gather you had some trouble getting here. They had two firetrucks and an ambulance standing by."

"Well, let's say we've had something of a scare," Jim told him. He turned around and looked at Catherine, who was helping Sharon with her bags. "I'd like to think that it's over, but somehow I don't think that it is."

"I have a car outside," said John Three Names. "Or maybe you'd like to rest up here for a while."

"I think we can go on," said Jim. "How's everybody feeling?"

"Let's go on," said Catherine. "The sooner we get there, the better."

Jim said, "You're sure?" but she reached out and touched his hand, very lightly, and he knew that she wanted nothing more than to get this journey over with. She hadn't thanked him for what he had done in the airplane, but then she didn't need to. Only she and Jim had shared that moment when she had realised who she really was, and that shared understanding was better than thanks. Jim felt very close to her, just then, and as she followed John Three Names, with her long hair shining in the afternoon sun, he could almost have loved her.

"Don't let Dr Ehrlichman see you looking at your students like that," said Susan.

"Like what? I've been worried about her, that's all."

"As you said yourself, she doesn't look like the back of a totem-pole."

"Susan—"

She linked arms with him. "We're alive, that's all that matters. I really thought that we were going to die back there. I suddenly realised how unprepared I was."

She stopped, and lifted her head, and kissed him. Mark and Sharon were walking close behind them and Mark wolf-whistled.

Jim said, "Do you mind? Even faculty members are allowed to make discreet demonstrations of mutual affection."

John Three Names had a blue Ford Galaxy parked outside the airfield, with seats enough for all of them. "I borrowed this from the Navajo Community College. You must drop in and see it, Mr Rook. I think you'll be impressed."

"How come they call you John Three Names?" asked Mark, as they drove away.

"Because I have three names, of course."

"Really? What are they?"

"'John', 'Three' and 'Names.'"

Mark frowned at him for a long time. "You're putting me on, aren't you?"

John Three Names looked at him and laughed. He said, "Nobody laughs louder than a Navajo, when he's tricked a white man." Jim smiled and sat back and tried to enjoy the drive to Window Rock. Once or twice he took out the whistle that Henry Black Eagle had given him and turned it around in his fingers. It had saved him, he understood that. It had saved all six of them. But he still didn't really know why, or how. Catherine didn't seem to have the shadow around her any more, but what were the chances that it might come back? And what might it try to do to them next time? He lifted the whistle to his lips and he was about to blow it when he saw Catherine looking at him with her fingertip raised to her lips.

He said, "What?"

"Better not to disturb him again," she warned.

"Him? Who's him?"

Catherine lifted her hands so that they were covering her face, but opened her fingers so that her eyes could look out. Jim couldn't understand what she meant, but it had a very sinister effect, like a mask, or somebody who was spying on the world from somewhere else.

He lowered the whistle and dropped it back into his shirt. Obviously there were times when it was going to help them, and other times when it was going to bring them trouble.

Susan reached across and held Jim's hand. It could have been a gesture of revived affection, or it simply could have been a way of confirming that they were all still alive. There was one thing that Jim knew for sure – he wasn't going to *fly* back to Albuquerque, not with Catherine, anyway.

John Three Names said, "Any of you ever visited the Navajo Nation before? I think you're going to find it quite an eye-opener. I've lived here for the past twenty-five years and I've seen some changes here, I can tell you.

We still have far too many people on welfare, but we've kept up to date with the modern world in most ways. To me, the most important thing is that we've kept our native language and our national identity. It's just a pity that so much magic has gone out of the land."

They arrived in Window Rock at mid-afternoon, under a flawless blue sky. It was a small Arizona town much like any other, with stores and gas stations and office-buildings. John Three Names had booked them into the Navajo Nation Inn, $73 the night. A calm, handsome woman in a blue dress showed them to their rooms – plain, but sunny, and decorated with *yei* rugs with stylized figures on them. A boy of about five followed them a few paces behind, frowning with shyness and curiosity. John Three Names stopped, and went back to the boy. He held up both hands, which were empty, but then he rubbed them together, and produced a quarter out of thin air. He gave it to the boy and said, "Don't spend it all on candy."

Sharon and Catherine were sharing a bright, big room with a view of the pool. Jim touched Sharon's shoulder as she carried her bag through the door, and said, "Don't forget, will you? Keep your eye on her . . . and if you see anything that worries you—"

"I'll look after her, Mr Rook," Sharon reassured him. "She comes from an ethnic minority that's even more minorer than mine."

Jim and Susan had adjacent rooms with a connecting door. Susan rattled the handle to make sure it was locked. "You know, just in case you start sleepwalking."

"What if I'm awake?"

"If you're awake, you die." She didn't realize how prophetic that was.

John Three Names followed Jim into his room. Jim slid open the patio door and stepped out onto a small terracotta-tiled balcony with a table and chairs. In the distance, the vermilion mountains were washed out with heat. A lizard baked in the dust beyond the balcony, but didn't stir.

"Like the room?" asked John Three Names.

"It's fine, thanks."

"Tell me what really happened on the airplane."

Jim looked at him. "What do you mean?"

"It wasn't just instrument failure, was it?"

"Oh, no? What makes you think that?"

"When we were driving here, I could see you in my rear-view mirror. I saw you take out the whistle. I saw Catherine White Bird caution you not to blow it. Then I saw her cover her face."

"So what did that tell you?"

"It told me that you had probably blown the whistle before, for some reason, and that you were puzzled about the effect it had produced. So maybe you wanted to try it again, to see what would happen this time. But Catherine White Bird said no, you would disturb him – and when you asked who *him* was, she covered her face.

"You know why she did that? She didn't want to speak his name, in case it was carried to him on the wind, and he knew that she was coming closer. But that whistle has only one purpose, to call the spirit called Coyote. And to do *this* –" and here he covered his face in the same way that Catherine had done "– is to warn people that Coyote isn't far away, and that he's listening out for you."

Jim said, "I think you'd better explain this from the bottom up."

John Three Names came and stood next to him. "In days gone by, before the white men came, when you could see spirits by broad daylight, Coyote was the greatest mischief-maker of all the Navajo demons. A killer, a trickster, a raper of women, and a thief. When it came to the grand assembly of all the supernatural beings, the gods would sit facing the south and the demons and other malevolent spirits would sit facing the north. But Coyote was so deceitful that none of the other spirits would allow him to sit close, and he stood by the door, ready to run away before the others ganged up on him.

"Coyote did everything perversely. He profaned against the sacred rites. He tipped his arrows with grey feathers, which is a recognized sign of bad luck. The month of October, which is the month of mishaps and mistakes, was dedicated to him. When the night sky was created, he was given a handful of stars to put in their places, but he was too irresponsible to do it properly, and so he flung them up all in one mass, and created the Milky Way.

"Whenever games were played, Coyote would set one side against the other, and then run off with the prize."

Jim said, "This is all myth, surely. I mean, it's a story – the same kind of story that the Greeks and the Romans used to tell. Zeus hurling his thunderbolts, Neptune with his trident – and Apollo riding his fiery chariot through the sky."

"Not quite," said John Three Names. "There are no records of anybody ever having *seen* Zeus, in the flesh. But Coyote was spotted by Navajo hunters as late as 1861. They turned back from the hunting-ground, of course, because if you ever saw Coyote it meant unhappiness and death. It's all recorded on blankets, if you want to see them."

"I'll take your word for it," said Jim. "I was always a slow reader when it came to blankets."

"The days of the gods and the demons began to die in 1864, after the Navajos had persisted in raiding their neighboring tribes, the Hopi and the Zuni. Colonel Kit Carson went on what you might call a search-and-destroy mission to rout out the last of the Navajo. Carson laid

112

waste their crops and killed their livestock. Then he made eight thousand of them walk three hundred miles from Fort Defiance to Fort Sumner on the Pecos River. Many died. The rest he kept prisoner for four years until the Navajo finally agreed to sign a treaty.

"It was during this time that the Navajos' faith in their spirits was so badly shaken, and their spirits – well, what can spirits do when nobody believes in them any longer? They don't die, they're immortal, but they melt away. The earth gods sank into the ground, and if you go out into the desert you can still see the hills where they did it. The wind gods blew away across the mountains, and caused tornadoes. The river gods ran away to the ocean, although once in a while they come back to flood the Mississipi to remind us of the powers they used to have.

"But mostly the gods were not believed in, so they went their way. There was only one exception – Coyote. When the white men came, and the days of myth and legend were all over, he was wily enough to find a way to live in the open, so that humans would believe in him, and spirits, too. He mated with a human woman, who gave birth to a child that was human and Coyote, both. And this boy gave birth to another child, and so on, from one generation to the next. What this means is that Coyote is still with us today, Mr Rook, and he's very much alive."

"This isn't easy to believe," said Jim.

"Why shouldn't it be? You've seen Coyote's mischief with your own eyes. Henry Black Eagle told me what happened at your college; and he also told me that your apartment had been torn apart, and your cat killed."

"So explain it to me. Why is he doing it, and how?"

"The why is simple. The man that Catherine was supposed to marry went to a wonder-worker and asked him to summon up Coyote's powers, so that Coyote would

113

bring Catherine back to him – and if she fell in love with any other man, to kill him."

"Like a hex, you mean?"

"You could call it that. Except that this hex has taken the shape of a beast, which watches Catherine day and night."

"I think I've already seen it a couple of times," said Jim. "It's like kind of a shadow that seems to follow Catherine around."

John Three Names said, "You're the only man who ever has – and that's why Henry Black Eagle and his family asked you to come here. If you can persuade this man to release Catherine from her promise, the beast will have to leave her – and only you can be sure that it really does."

"Do you *know* this man that Catherine's supposed to have married?" Jim asked him.

"I've seen him once or twice, but I've spoken to him only once. He lives in a trailer up at Meadow Between Rocks. Most of the time he keeps himself to himself, and everybody respects his privacy and leaves him alone. He's supposed to have quite a ferocious temper on him, although I've never seen any of that."

"Does he have a name?"

"Several. But most people call him Dog Brother."

Jim sat down on the end of the bed. "The question is, John, what am I going to offer this – Dog Brother to give up Catherine? She's a beautiful girl. If I had the choice, *I* wouldn't give her up."

"Henry Black Eagle has some property up by Shiprock, as well as stocks and bonds. You're authorized to offer these to Dog Brother in exchange for releasing Catherine from her promise, plus a quarter of a million dollars in cash."

"What if he's not interested?"

"Then we will have to try another way. We will have to find the wonder-worker who conjured up Coyote's curse and see if we can make a bargain with him."

"And supposing *he* doesn't want to play ball, either?"

"I think we should cross that canyon when we come to it."

"What about this Coyote character? If he's half-human, then he must be findable."

John Three Names shook his head. "You wouldn't want to try that, Jim."

"I don't know. Maybe he's more human than you think. Come on, John, how can this be real? A demon who lives for ever by mating with human women?"

John Three Names laid a hand on his shoulder. "How about a drink? I'll bet you could use one, after that journey."

The bar was deserted except for three iron-haired Navajos in ponytails and business suits talking about industrial leases in Tuba City. Jim ordered a beer and John Three Names asked for a Bloody Mary ("I didn't have time for lunch, and this is as good as.") In the background, Nat King Cole sang *Ramblin' Rose*.

John Three Names guided Jim over to a table by the window. "I like to see what's coming and what's going, especially at times like these." He parted the venetian blinds with two fingers and peered out into the glaring street.

"In the original Navajo legend," he said, "Coyote lusted after a very beautiful girl. She had two brothers who tried to protect her. The girl was strong-willed as well as beautiful, and Coyote struggled for months to seduce her, to take over her soul. She hated him at first, and put him through all kinds of tests – literally making him die for her. But each time he died, he buried a flint next

115

to his body so that he could dig himself up again. In the end, he was so persistent that she couldn't resist him any longer, and she allowed him past the hem of her skirt.

"Under Coyote's influence, she became a creature which we call the Changing Bear Maiden, joining Coyote in all of his evil-doing. The stories say that she took a particular pleasure out of snapping men's necks with her jaws, and ripping their chests open with her claws."

"She had only one vulnerability – she couldn't change into a bear when anybody was watching her, so her family protected her by making sure that they kept a guard on her day and night."

"Sounds familiar," said Jim.

"It's a legend. How much of it you care to believe – well, that's entirely up to you."

"What's your part in all this?" Jim asked him.

"I'm an interested party, that's all – apart from being a friend of Henry Black Eagle. I work as a freelance for the Navajo newspaper *Diné Baa-Hané*. A demon hunter by night and a mild-mannered reporter by day."

At that moment, Susan came into the bar, followed by Catherine and Sharon and Mark. "I thought I'd find you two in here," said Susan. "I could murder a Bloody Mary."

Jim moved around so that Susan could sit next to him. Catherine sat opposite, and gave him an odd, worried look, as if she had something on her mind but didn't quite know how to start talking about it.

"What happens next?" asked Susan.

"We'll go up to the Meadow Between Rocks at first light tomorrow," said John Three Names. "We're lucky. They're holding a first laugh rite there for one of my nephews. That's something you don't get to see very often."

"A first laugh rite?"

"When a child first laughs, around its fortieth day, he joins the human race, and he will make a covenant with the laughter gods which will be sealed with salt. There will be prayers and a big celebration. Meanwhile I suggest you all get some rest. You haven't had an easy journey, and there will be much more difficult times ahead of us."

"I'm going out to catch some rays," said Mark.

"Don't burn," Susan told him.

Catherine stayed where she was. John Three Names asked her if she wanted a Coke, but she shook her head. "Something's happening to me," she said. "Something's happening to me and I don't know what it is."

"Go on," said Jim.

"It's just that I keep having these nightmares, only they're not nightmares. They happen during the day."

"What kind of nightmares?"

"They're just like a flash in my head. Flash, and they're gone. But since we've come here to Window Rock I've had three or four of them already."

"Are they all the same?"

"I keep imagining that I'm running very fast. Not running away from anything. I'm not frightened. In fact it's the opposite – I'm chasing something, or somebody. I want to jump on them and attack them. I want to hear them screaming. I'm strong. I can't believe how strong I am. I could tear somebody's arm off just like that.

Tears suddenly welled up in her eyes. "You just talked about a child laughing and joining the human race. I don't know, I have such a terrible feeling. I feel like I'm leaving it."

Chapter Six

During the night, Jim was woken up by the sound of his own heart beating. He placed his hand over his chest, but then he realised that it wasn't his heart beating at all – it was drumming. He sat up in bed and he could hear it quite distinctly – a slow, persistent *throb-THROB-THROB-throb, throb-THROB-THROB-throb*. He listened for a while, frowning into the darkness. Jesus, it sounded like *Drums Along The Mohawk*. He swung his legs out of bed and walked to the patio window, pulling up his newly-bought pajama pants. He slid the window back and stepped out barefoot onto the tiled floor, which was still warm from yesterday's sunshine.

In the near distance he could see a fire glowing, its sparks whirling into the darkness. Up above him, the whole sky was crowded with stars. He hadn't seen stars like this since he was a boy, and his father had taken him fishing off the coast of Santa Barbara. He felt a strange emotional surge – a mixture of nostalgia for days gone by, and regret that he never saw the stars any longer, not like this.

He climbed over the railing that surrounded his patio and dropped heavily down onto the dusty, prickly ground. He heard something scurry in the darkness, and a lizard flickered over his foot. He was beginning to regret that he hadn't put on his sneakers. There were rattlesnakes here, too, and scorpions.

But the drumming went on, resonant and repetitive. *Throb-THROB-THROB-throb*, echoing and flat. Jim looked around. He was amazed that it hadn't woken anybody else – but then again, maybe it had, and they had recognised it for what it was, and ignored it. He hesitated for almost a whole minute, wondering whether he ought to go back to bed and forget about it. But then he saw a dark figure rise from the ground, just in front of the fire, and begin to sway from side to side. It looked as if the figure was wearing an odd, bulky headdress, with horns or ears, and dangling necklaces.

What was more, on the far side of the fire, Jim was sure that he could make out a black, bulky shape. It didn't seem to be illuminated by the flames: it was more like a shadow, except that it couldn't be a shadow, because there was nothing to cast it. He saw two red sparks that might have been sparks, or might have been blood-red eyes. A cool wind blew against his bare back and brought goosebumps all the way up to his hairline. There was something there, he was sure of it. *Something cold. Something old. Something bristling.*

He made his way cautiously toward the fire, trying to step over rocks and dried-up weed and prickly vegetation. He could see now that it was the figure with the headdress that was beating the drum. It was a naked man, his body shining with sweat. He was grasping a tall decorated drum between his thighs and banging it with the edge of his hands. The fire had burned low now: it was nothing much more than a heap of glowing ashes, but it gave off so much heat that the air above it was rippling and distorted. Jim stopped, and shaded his eyes with both hands, but it was impossible for him to tell if the shadow was really there, or whether it was nothing more than a mirage produced by the heat. All the time the drum kept beating *throb-THROB-THROB-throb*, and now Jim could hear the man chanting, too, although he couldn't understand any of the words.

He thought: this isn't getting me anyplace at all. This is probably some kind of Navajo ceremony. Paying homage to the night sky. Thanking the moon for coming up and going down again. Who knew? He felt embarrassed because he was intruding; and he felt slightly paranoid because he kept looking at every slow-dancing shadow around the fire and imagining that it was more than just a shadow. It was the Changing Bear Maiden, with her claws and her teeth, ready to snap men's necks.

He turned back toward the Inn, but as he did so, he saw Sharon rush out onto his patio. "Mr Rook!" she called out, and she was obviously distressed. "Mr Rook? Where are you?"

The man standing by the fire turned around, his pelts and necklaces swinging. Abruptly, the drumming stopped. Jim called out, "Here, Sharon! I'm just over here!"

"It's Catherine, Mr Rook! She's gone missing!"

Jim glanced toward the fire. The man in the head-dress was still staring in his direction, his drum stilled. The heat from the fire was deflected by the wind, and for one split-second Jim was sure that he saw a huge, sloping-shouldered figure, as black as the sky between the stars – just like a bear only three times larger. But then the wind blew up a cloud of smoke and ashes, and the figure vanished.

Jim walked back to the patio, his feet bruised and scratched. Sharon was wearing a voluminous pink T-shirt with a picture of the Care Bears on it. Her hair was thicketed with pink plastic rollers. "I woke up to go to the bathroom, Mr Rook, and Catherine was gone! She was only wearing a nightshirt and she didn't take no clothes with her. I was looking for her along the corridor when I heard that drumming and I was frightened."

"It's OK," said Jim. Behind him, the drummer was still silent, and the fire was beginning to die down. "I don't know what's going on, but the best thing you can do is get yourself back to bed. Catherine's been pretty disturbed since she came back here. Maybe she's gone for a walk to think things over."

Sharon nodded toward the fire, and the silhouetted man with the drum. "What is that, Mr Rook? What's going on here? Is that guy wearing any *clothes*?"

"Erm, no. It doesn't look as if he is. But, you know, this isn't Santa Monica. I guess they do things a little differently here."

"And where were *you* going?" Sharon frowned. "You're not even wearing any shoes."

"I was . . . well, I guess I was going to investigate."

Sharon gave him a narrow-eyed look. "There's something weird about this trip, Mr Rook? I mean, this isn't like your usual college cultural trip. So far I've been scared out of my brain in an airplane and now it's all drums and fires and people shouting in the middle of the night, and nobody's even *mentioned* anything cultural."

"Oh, it's cultural, all right," Jim told her. "I'm just worried that it may be a little *too* cultural."

"What do you mean?"

"Well," said Jim, "the truth is, we're not really here on a field trip. We're here mostly for Catherine's sake. When she was fifteen she was promised in marriage to a Navajo guy called Dog Brother, but now she doesn't want to marry him. I came to Window Rock to see if there's any way to break their engagement. I needed you guys along to keep her company."

Sharon stared at him, distinctly unimpressed. "This Dog Breath, he still wants to marry her?"

"*Brother*, not Breath. But yes, so far as I know, he still wants to marry her."

"But why did she have to come back at all? Why not write him a 'Dear Dog Breath' letter, and forget about it? And why did you have to come? Couldn't her father have brought her?"

"I had to come because of Martin, and what happened in the locker room. I had to come because my home was wrecked and my cat was killed."

"Hunh? I don't get it."

"Sharon, this Dog Brother is a very jealous guy, by all accounts, and he's worked some kind of spell on Catherine. If any guy gets too close to her, Dog Brother makes sure that he suffers. Anything that means anything to him gets destroyed. In Martin's case – well, he was destroyed, too."

"I thought Catherine's brothers did all that. They're in jail for it, aren't they?"

"There's some circumstantial evidence that suggests they might have killed Martin, for sure. But for all of the vandalism and killing my cat they have pretty unshakeable alibis. They claim that everything was done by some kind of a *force* – a force which Dog Brother conjured up when Catherine ran off to LA. It's all to do with Native American magic. I don't even understand it myself. But it looks like the only way to face up to this force is to come here and talk to this Dog Brother face to face."

"When you say 'force,' do you mean like that voodoo guy you had to hunt down?"

"I guess something like that. It's invisible. Nobody else can see it except me."

"Why didn't you tell us before we came out here? Don't you trust us?"

"Of course I trust you. That's the whole reason I wanted you to come. It's just that I didn't know what I was dealing with. The logical explanation is that Catherine's brothers *were* responsible. But I've been seeing things and feeling feelings that make me think that maybe they're telling the truth. Or part of the truth, anyhow."

"What feelings? What things?"

"Nothing specific . . . shadows where shadows shouldn't be. A kind of tension in the air. Maybe I'm just being paranoid."

"Well, next time you see something like that, maybe you'd like to let the rest of us know."

"Sure, I promise," said Jim, trying to be reassuring. "Now, we can talk about this later. Why don't you go back to your room and wait to see if Catherine comes back. I'll go take a look around the grounds and see if I can find her. I doubt she's gone far."

"Just remember – *trust*," said Sharon. Jim gave her a high five and she went back to her bedroom.

Jim started to walk cautiously back toward the fire. He hadn't gone far, however, when he heard Susan's voice calling, off to the right. "Catherine! Sharon! Where are you?"

"Oh, God, that's all I need," said Jim. "Susan! Sharon's fine! She's gone back to her room! I'm just looking for Catherine!"

He couldn't see Susan at first, but then she appeared out of the smoke, halfway between the Inn and the fire. She was wrapped in a light white towelling robe, and she was carrying a flashlight. "Jim?" she said. "Is that you? I've been looking for Catherine and Sharon! Their beds are empty!"

"For Christ's sake, Susan—" Jim began, but he was interrupted by the sharp bang of a hand on a drum. The fire had almost completely died down now, so it was difficult to see the man's figure, except for his dangling headdress and the curve of his glistening chest. But then he banged his drum again, quicker and harder, until he was beating out a fast, insanely complicated rhythm and his hands were a blur. Susan, confused, stopped where she was for a moment. "Jim?" she called out. "Do you have Sharon with you? Where's Catherine?"

She was still more than a hundred feet away. And it was then that Jim saw the black shadow detach itself from the other side of the fire and come rushing toward her, quite silently, with no other trace of its passing than a light whirl of dust and a few small clattering rocks. Susan was standing quite still now, obliviously waving. Yet the darkness was approaching her with all the speed of a charging bull. Weirdly, though, it was totally silent.

"Susan!" Jim shouted. "Susan – watch out!"

He sprinted toward her as fast as he could. He hadn't run like this since he was at high school, when he had almost won the 200m against the school's best athlete, Eddie LaFrance. He could see Eddie's grinning, self-satisfied face even now. Jim had burst his heart trying to win that race and he hadn't been able to believe it when he came second. He had done the unforgivable, and started to cry.

That was why he was running so furiously now. He couldn't fail a second time.

"Susan!" he gasped. "Susan, watch out! On your right, Susan! It's there, on your right-hand side!"

Susan stopped, perplexed. She looked to her right but it was obvious that she couldn't see anything at all. "*Just believe me!*" Jim screamed at her. "*Just get down!*"

The beast was big – much bigger than Jim had imagined. Its shoulders were hunched, its claws were lifted in terrifying curves, already tinged red by the fire. But its speed frightened Jim the most. He was running so fast toward Susan that he was almost flying. His feet skipped from rock to rock and he leaped over bushes like a hurdler.

Yet the huge black shadowy thing was bearing down on Susan and he knew that it was going to be touch-and-go to stop it.

The worst thing was that only *he* could see it. Susan stayed where she was, turning around and around, looking for something which was totally invisible.

Jim reached Susan and flung himself at her in a football-tackle. Astonished, frightened, she stepped back, and he hit the ground with a bruising impact and rolled over into a thicket of thorns. He twisted his head around in time to see the beast almost on top of her, its fur bristling, its eyes smouldering like coke-cinders. Jim could *smell* it: the cold, old bear smell – rank with blood and urine and decaying pelts. He could smell it and he could see it, yet Susan was standing right beneath it, her hands perched on her hips, saying, "Jim – for God's sake – do you mind telling me what's—"

Jim screamed, *"Get down!"* at her, but she was still looking at him in annoyance when a huge claw swept right under her chin and knocked her head right off her body, skying it right up into the night, right up against the stars, with blood spraying behind it like a comet's tail.

For a moment, her body remained where it was, still standing, headless, with her carotid artery pumping out geysers of blood. Her towelling robe turned from white to crimson right in front of Jim's eyes. Then the beast dug its claws into her again, and literally tore her apart – ribcage, pelvis, arms and legs. The crackling of bones was so loud that Jim pressed his hands over his ears, and closed his eyes. He opened them again to see what was left of her collapsing onto the dirt, like a broken bird's nest, rags and sticks and branches.

He looked up at the beast. For a moment, he thought that it was going to strike him down, too. It stood over him for a moment, blotting out the night sky. Jim lowered his head and closed his eyes and he was sick to his stomach. But then he heard the drums start up again – *throb-THROB-THROB-throb* – *throb-THROB-THROB-throb*. He looked up, and saw the beast turn its head. Then its outline appeared to waver, and soften, and one by one he saw the stars begin to shine through its bristling fur. The drum persisted – *throb* – *THROB* – *THROB* – *throb* – and the beast began to move away, or perhaps to *melt* away, disappearing into the darkness in the direction of the fire.

Jim was sure that he saw it cross in front of the fire, because the fire momentarily dimmed, but then it vanished altogether, and all he could see was the man and his drum and the hot, dying embers, and all he could hear was Sharon calling him.

"Mr Rook? Mr Rook? I heard somebody shouting. What's happening, Mr Rook?"

Jim climbed to his feet. He was bruised and shocked and hyperventilating. Thank God it's dark, he thought, and she can't see Susan's body. Thank God I can't, either.

"It's OK, Sharon," he told her. "I was just trying to find Catherine, that's all. She hasn't come back yet, has she?"

"Not yet, Mr Rook. Maybe I should help you look."

"No, no. Go back to your room. Please. You'll be doing me a favour."

Sharon waited on the patio a little while longer, straining her eyes out into the night, but then she reluctantly went back inside. It was just after three o'clock. Jim walked back to the place where Susan's body had fallen. Then he walked over to the fire, and the man with the drum.

The fire may have been low, but it gave off so much

126

heat that Jim couldn't stand very close. The man had stopped playing now, and was crouched next to it, completely covered from head to foot in a grey-and-white Navajo blanket.

"Who are you?" Jim demanded. "What's been going on here? Do you know what's happened? A woman's been killed." His voice was trembling like a loose bandsaw.

The man reached into a leather pouch and tossed a handful of powder onto the fire. It briefly sparkled, and gave off the smell of dried herbs, along with another smell, less definable, more like memories. Jim saw himself playing in a wood beside a lake, and then he didn't.

"I'm going to have to call the police," he said.

The man threw another handful of powder onto the fire. Then he tightened up his leather pouch, and stood up, winding the blanket around him so that he looked like a pilgrim, or a monk. It was John Three Names. His face was impassive. His eyes gave nothing away.

"You've killed my friend," Jim insisted. He was very close to tears. "She's – you took her head off – and then you just – *snapped* her."

"I didn't do that," said John Three Names. He walked past Jim to a smooth flat rock, where he had left his clothes. Unabashed, he took off the blanket and proceeded to dress himself in a checkered shirt and jeans, with a bolo necktie.

Jim said, "That thing was here. That beast. What did you do, conjure it up?"

"I didn't see anything, Jim. The only person who can see that creature is you."

"So how do you think that Susan was torn to pieces? It took her head off, John, right in front of me!"

John said, "I'm sorry. I saw her go down, and I'm deeply sorry. But that's all I can say. This is a struggle, and when you have struggles, people get hurt. Particularly when you start struggling with powers that you don't really understand."

"I'm still calling the police. I came here as a favour. Now my girlfriend is dead. Jesus, what's the matter with you? What the hell do you have to be so calm about?" He was almost screaming.

John Three Names said, "I'm not calm, Jim. I'm not calm at all. I'm as shaken as you are. But that beast is going to go on killing people until Dog Brother can be talked into letting Catherine go, and calling it off. And only you can do that."

"I'm calling the police."

"Oh, yes? And what are you going to say to them?"

"I'm going to tell them the truth, what else?"

"The truth? An invisible beast came along and took your girlfriend's head off? I saw you run up to her. I saw her fall. But as far as I'm concerned, there was no invisible beast. So what conclusion do you think the police are going to draw from that?"

"It ripped her to pieces. I couldn't have done that!"

John Three Names shrugged. "They're still going to hold you under suspicion, aren't they? They're Navajo, Jim, the cops around here, and they're always very intolerant with whites. After all, they have plenty to be intolerant about."

Jim looked around in desperation. "You didn't see *anything*? You didn't see the shadow? It was here, by the fire, while you were drumming."

John Three Names touched one eyelid with his fingertip. "I don't have the eyes to see such things, Jim. Most of the time, I'm glad that I don't."

"So what were you doing here, lighting this fire and beating that goddamned drum?"

"I was making a prayer to my ancestors. I was asking them to help us when we go to see Dog Brother tomorrow, so that we should be successful, and that Dog Brother should let Catherine go."

"So why do you think that the beast showed up?"

"Perhaps to show me that tomorrow's confrontation will not be easy, and that we still have much to fear."

"There won't be any confrontation tomorrow. After tonight, I quit."

John Three Names looked taken aback. "How can you quit, when you are the only person who can make sure that the beast who killed your girlfriend is sent back to the world in which it belongs? How can you quit, when so many others might die?"

Jim looked back in the direction of Susan's body. "How do you expect me to go on with this, after what's happened tonight?"

John Three Names took hold of his arm. "Jim, you have to go on. You don't have any choice. Destiny only goes forward. It can never go back. The door behind you is closed. The door ahead of you may be difficult to open, but it is the only way out."

"So what can I do with Susan's body?" asked Jim. "It'll be dawn soon."

John Three Names nodded toward the fire. "It's very hot now, Jim. We can cremate her."

Jim took a deep breath. Hiding a body was illegal, and deeply incriminating, if it were ever found. But shocked as he was, he knew that there wasn't a court in the country that would believe that Susan had been killed by an invisible spirit-beast – not until he could prove that it existed, if he ever could. He said, "All right, then. But I'm going to need your blanket, to wrap her up in."

"This is a Ganado," said John Three Names, clutching it tight.

"I don't care if it's the Turin Shroud. I need it."

John Three Names reluctantly handed over his rug.

129

Jim trailed it over to Susan's remains, and laid it on the dirt beside her. He reached out once to touch her, and found that he couldn't. But then he quickly tugged at her bloodsoaked bathrobe and rolled her onto the rug. The noise of bones and sloppy viscera almost made him sick – but what was worse was that, headless, she *sighed* as he rolled her over – a faint, regretful sigh.

"Just a little air left in her lungs," said John Three Names, pragmatically.

Jim wrapped up the blanket and John Three Names helped him to carry it over to the fire. It swung heavily, like somebody in a hammock. They raked back the embers with sticks and lowered the blanket right into the hottest part. Jim's eyes watered, not only from heat. The blanket scorched and flared and there was a choking smell of burned wool.

"We have to find her head," said John Three Names, grimly.

Jim said, "I don't know. I don't think I can." He was so overwhelmed by grief and shock that he could hardly stay standing.

John Three Names gripped his wrists. "You have to. What do you think you're going to do – leave her head here for the dogs to find?"

They spent the next twenty minutes bent double, peering into the darkness for any sign of Susan's head. The sky began to lighten and the stars began to fade away. The noise of cicadas was almost overwhelming. At last, his back aching, Jim looked up. Along the back perimeter of the Inn there was a corrugated-iron fence, with a top that had been cut into serrated spikes. Three-quarters of the way along it, he saw a pale, cross face. For a split-second he thought that a woman was watching him, over the top of the fence, and he half-lifted his hand to wave at her. Then he realized that he was looking at Susan's head.

It had fallen with appalling neatness and landed on top of the fence, and it was still frowning at him in the same way that she had frowned at him before she died.

He said, "John," in a hollow voice, and approached the fence with knees like water. As he came closer, he realized that her head was nearly seven feet off the ground. Her eyes were open, and if he hadn't known that the rest of her body was burning in the pit behind him, he could have easily believed that she was still alive.

He couldn't touch the head himself, and he had to turn away as John Three Names used a dry stick to dislodge it. All the same, he heard it thud to the ground. John Three Names picked it up by its blood-matted hair and carried it over to the fire. Jim couldn't look. He stayed where he was, gasping for breath, with tears running down his cheeks.

After a while, however, John Three Names called him, and he managed to compose himself enough to rejoin him beside the embers. John Three Names said, "We'll have to let this burn itself out . . . then I'll come and cover it with dirt. I asked the Inn management if I could light a ceremonial fire here tonight . . . there's no reason for them to get suspicious about it."

"But what happens when Susan doesn't appear for breakfast?"

"You'll just have to persuade your students that she was taken sick in the night, and decided to go back home. I'll take her clothes and her suitcase and keep them hidden."

"But if anybody finds out what we've done, they're going to think that *we* killed her."

"Exactly," said John Three Names. "Just as the police in Los Angeles think that Paul and Grey Cloud killed Martin Amato."

"So what the hell are we going to do?"

"We're going to have to do what we always intended to do . . . what you came here to do. We're going to have to talk to Dog Brother and see if he'll be prepared to let Catherine go."

"That still won't prove our innocence."

"It'll prevent any more killings. And maybe we can discover a way of *proving* what Dog Brother did."

Jim looked down at the fire. It was still very hot, but it was much more ashy now, and the early morning breeze blew some of the ashes across the ground, so that they clung in the thorn-bushes. He said a quiet prayer for Susan's soul, and hoped that wherever she was, she could find it in her heart to forgive him.

It was then that he heard Sharon calling him again, "She's back, Mr Rook! Catherine just came back!"

While John Three Names continued to rake over the ashes, Jim returned to to his room and quickly dressed in jeans and a blue checkered shirt. His fingers were trembling so much that he could hardly fasten his buttons. Then he went across to the girls' room and knocked on the door. Sharon opened up immediately. Jim walked in and found Catherine sitting on the end of her bed in a green nightshirt, thirstily drinking from a can of Coke. He looked down at her feet and they were dusty with ashes.

"Do you want to tell me where you've been?" he demanded. "We've all been worried about you." He paused, and then he said, "Ms Randall's been so worried it's brought on her asthma, and she may have to fly back home."

Catherine looked up at him and there was the strangest expression on her face. Dark, suspicious, almost creepy. "Asthma?" she said.

"That's right. She suffers very badly when she's stressed."

132

"You mean she has difficulty breathing?"

"Yes."

Catherine lowered her head again and Jim had a suspicion that she hiding a smile.

"You still haven't told me where you've been," he insisted.

"I couldn't sleep, that's all. I went for a walk."

"That wasn't particularly wise, was it, under the circumstances?"

"Sometimes wisdom is a matter of opinion," said Catherine. "You told us that yourself."

Jim hated it when his students quoted his own words back at him, particularly when he didn't agree with what he said. He opened his mouth but then he closed it again without saying anything. He had intended to ask Catherine if she had heard the drumming outside, and if she had seen the fire. But he decided it would be better to hold his tongue, just for the moment. If Catherine were involved in Susan's death in any way, then she knew about it already. If she weren't, then it was better that she didn't know anything about it.

Mark appeared, his hair all scruffed up, wearing a T-shirt and droopy shorts. "What's going on?" he wanted know. "I keep hearing people shouting and doors banging and stuff. Any chance of getting some sleep?"

Jim took his arm. "I'm sorry, Mark. Catherine went for a walk and I guess we all got a little over-excited."

"OK, then," said Mark, "but keep the noise down, hunh? I was having this terrific dream that I was the drummer for REM."

Jim met John Three Names in the corridor and took him back to his room. Susan's door was locked, and the interconnecting door was still locked, too, but Susan had left her sliding patio door slightly ajar. They climbed

133

over the railings that separated the two patios, and let themselves in.

Jim immediately went to the closet and took down Susan's dresses. They smelled of her perfume and he had to bite his lip to stop himself from bursting into tears. He took down her case, opened it up, and quickly packed. John Three Names came out of the bathroom with her toothbrush and her toiletries.

"Is that everything?" said Jim. "Look under the bed, in case she's left anything there."

John Three Names ducked down and came back up with a pair of flowery cotton mules and a dog-eared copy of *The San Andreas Fault.*

"Geography teacher," said Jim, flicking through the book. "She's a geography teacher."

John Three Names picked up the case. "OK," he said, "I'll take this back to my house. Why don't you go back to bed for a couple of hours? Even if you don't sleep it'll give you a chance to settle your nerves. I'll meet you back here at eight thirty, say."

Jim said, "It's unbelievable. You didn't see that thing at all? Not even a shadow of it?"

John Three Names shook his head. "I only saw your girlfriend die . . . and I know that you couldn't have done it, not like that."

"It was . . . *huge*," said Jim. "It was *black*, and *tall*, like a bear. And *fast*. Susan didn't stand a chance."

"You mustn't blame yourself. There was nothing you could have done to stop it."

"I shouldn't have asked Susan to come to Arizona in the first place."

"Jim . . . life is always dangerous. She might have stayed in Los Angeles and died in a traffic accident. Only Gitche Manitou knows the ways that we're going to walk."

Jim couldn't think of anything else to say. He looked around Susan's empty room, and then he opened the door. He checked that there was nobody in the corridor, and then he beckoned John Three Names to follow him out.

"Eight thirty," he said, and went back into his own room. He went to the bathroom, switched on the light, and stared at himself in the mirror. There were two ashy smudges on his cheeks, but apart from that he looked completely normal, as if nothing exceptional had happened at all. Behind him, through the patio windows, he could still see the smoke rising from the fire, and it was almost impossible to believe that it was Susan's funeral pyre, and that he would never, ever see her again. Just at the moment he was beyond tears.

He tried to watch some television, but all he could find was *The Prisoner of Zenda* in black-and-white, and a Mexican program about the Day of the Dead. He switched the television off and closed his eyes. Almost immediately, he opened them again. Under his eyelids, he had seen the dark, bristling beast rushing toward him, its claws upraised.

He thought: it's Thursday already, the day I'm supposed to die. He lay back, staring at the ceiling, with a sweaty sensation of dread. He couldn't begin to imagine what it must be like, to have your head ripped off, or your body slashed open. You must feel something, surely, if only for an instant. Weren't there stories of people's eyes moving, after their heads had been cut off – staring in horror at their own severed neck?

He climbed off the bed and went to the mini-bar. He poured two miniatures of bourbon into one glass and drank both of them, straight down. He coughed, and wiped his eyes. He was shaking so much that he dropped the glass onto the floor.

At a quarter past eight he went to the girls' room and knocked. After a while, Sharon answered it. "Just thought I'd give you a wake-up call," he said. "John Three Names is picking us up in forty-five minutes."

"How's Ms Randall?" asked Sharon. "Did she get over her asthma?"

"Her asthma? No – no she didn't. It got worse. Terrible. She could hardly breathe. I sent her back to Albuquerque. She's going to have some treatment there, and then she's going to fly back to LA."

"That's too bad," said Catherine, sitting up in bed and swinging her hair behind her.

Jim said, "Yes. But anyhow, I'll see you after breakfast."

He closed the door. He didn't know what to make of Catherine at the moment. She seemed to be changing. When she had first arrived at West Grove, she had always been open and friendly. She had been first in class to put up her hand and ask questions, and she had never been afraid of expressing her feelings. She had loved the poetry of Delmore Schwartz, and recited in class: '*The heavy bear who goes with me, A manifold honey to smear his face, Clumsy and lumbering here and there, The central ton of every place.*' At the time, he hadn't thought anything much of it, but after what had happened tonight, it seemed to have a new and threatening significance.

Here, on her own territory, Catherine had become remote and prickly, and had withdrawn deeply into herself. This morning he hadn't seen any sign of the shadow over her, but her tension was almost visible, like the heat waves that had risen from John Three Names' fire.

Mark came up to him, wearing a baggy faded pair of plaid Bermuda shorts and a Delco/Bose T-shirt, which his father had probably been given for free. "Hey, Mr Rook.

I want to thank you for this. This is the best time I ever had in my life."

"I hope so, Mark."

"You seem like you're down, Mr Rook, if you don't mind my saying so."

"Well, it's Susan – Ms Randall. She had an asthma attack and she had to go on back home."

Mark said, "You like her, don't you, Mr Rook? I've seen you looking at her. You really like her."

It was the hardest thing in the world for Jim to smile, but he put his arm around Mark's shoulders and said, "Yes, I really like her."

They walked together to the Inn's cafeteria. There was a pungent smell of fresh coffee and muffins, and a severe-looking Navajo woman in a long print dress was serving out platefuls of bacon and eggs and pancakes. Jim and Mark sat down by the window. Outside, Jim could see a hazy spiral of smoke still drifting upward, and he thought to himself, that's the last of Susan's spirit, rising into the sky.

Mark was fiddling with the sugar and the Sweet'n'Lo. "You know something, Mr Rook, before I met you, I never knew half of the feelings that I had inside me. You know what I mean? I always thought that poetry sucked. But the way you teach it, it's like you can understand what it means. It's like your own feelings, put down on paper. And there's something else you showed me, too. There's a whole wide world outside of Santa Monica. I mean not just Arizona, but all of those places that people write about, like France, and Russia, and who knows where.

"Like, if you live on this planet, you have to know where you live, because once you know where you live, you know who you are."

He paused, and then he said, "You're friends with Ms

Randall. Do you think she could maybe take a little time to teach me some geography? You know, just to *orient* myself."

The severe-looking Navajo woman had arrived at Jim's elbow. "Coffee?" she demanded. "Juice?"

Jim looked at Mark and said, "I'll talk to Ms Randall about it when we get back to LA, OK? I'm sure she wouldn't mind." The words felt like ashes in his mouth, Susan's ashes.

He sat and sipped a cup of black coffee while Mark enthusiastically dug into a plateful of eggs and bacon and hash browns. He didn't look out of the window again. He didn't want to see the smoke. He didn't want to think that he would never see Susan again, as long as he lived.

The morning was glaring and dusty as they drove across the high plateau toward Fort Defiance. John Three Names did most of the talking, telling them all about the history and the culture of the Navajo people.

"The Navajo weren't a 'tribe' as such, back in the old days. The basic unit of economic support was the biological family – a man, his wife and their unmarried children. Each family lived in its own fork-stick house, or *hogan*.

"You'd see a few *hogans* loosely grouped together, because some of their daily tasks needed more than the members of one family could manage. Quite a few of the men used to have more than one wife, or else they'd marry sisters."

"I can't see any Navajo wanting to marry *my* sisters," put in Mark. "They never stop talking about lipstick and clothes and boys and who's cool and who's a dweeb."

John Three Names said, "A Navajo husband would

have great authority over his wives. If they displeased him, he would thrash them."

"Is that a violation of women's rights, or what?" said Sharon. "If my boyfriend ever tried that, I'd break his arms."

"You're not in Los Angeles any longer," John Three Names reminded her. "This is a people who go back thousands of years, before white men or black men were even dreamed of. This is a land that used to be a land of great magic. Most of that magic has gone now, but not all."

With that, he gave Jim a meaningful glance.

Sharon was chatty and inquisitive all the way. Mark came up with one or two subliminal jokes. But Catherine remained silent, staring out at the reddish-colored mountains.

"Are you all right?" Jim asked her.

She gave him a quick, humourless smile. "I think so. I just want today to be over."

Not too damn soon, thought Jim. This could be my very last day on earth.

They reached a trailer park with a wooden sign over the entrance that read *Meadow Between Rocks Homes.* John Three Names turned into it, and drove slowly past the trailers that lined the main strip on either side. Most trailers had their own small gardens, with herbs and vegetables and flowers. Small children ran around everywhere, chased by yapping brindled dogs. As they passed, a woman lifted her washing to the line that was tied to the side of her trailer, and her eyes caught Jim's with such steady familiarity that he felt as if she had been expecting him.

About two-thirds of the way along the main strip, John Three Names drew the Galaxy to a stop outside one of the larger trailers. There were seven or eight cars and trucks parked outside it already, and a small crowd of people gathered around it. Young families in freshly-washed jeans and plaid shirts – older men and women in traditional costumes. A barbecue had been set up behind the trailer, as well as two long trestle tables.

As they climbed out of the Galaxy, John Three Names was approached by a tall, smiling man carrying a small baby in his arms. "Jim," said John Three Names, "I want you to meet my cousin Dan. And this little fellow here is the reason for all of today's celebrations."

"I'm real glad you could make it," said Dan, ushering them up the steps and into the trailer. Although it was quite large, it was already crowded with neighbors and friends and relatives. Dan's wife Minnie passed them cans of beer and they all stood jostling each other in the kitchen section.

"Tell me about the first laugh ceremony," said Jim, tickling the baby under the chin. The baby chuckled and wildly pedalled his arms and legs.

Dan smiled. "When he made man, the Great Spirit gave man two gifts, life and laughter. Animals have life, but no animal laughs. Laughter is what makes man human. Laughter is what makes man closer to the Great Spirit. Every day that a man fails to laugh, he takes one day's journey further away from his spiritual birth-place.

"Today we celebrate my son's arrival in the human race, and his joining together with the spirits."

John Three Names said, "Unfortunately, Dan, we won't be able to stay for very long."

"After you've driven so far? You can't be serious!"

"Actually, we came here on other business," said John Three Names, pressing himself back against the kitchen cabinet as a very generously-proportioned woman in a fringed buckskin dress pushed her way past him. "We came to see Dog Brother."

"Dog Brother? What business do you have with Dog Brother?"

"Family business."

"Not to do with—?" said Dan, nodding his head toward Catherine.

John Three Names nodded. "He refuses to let her go. He says that a bargain was struck, and a bargain must be honoured."

"I warned Henry at the time," said Dan. "I warned him but he wouldn't listen. He was crazy with worry for his wife. He said, 'Don't worry, when the time comes for Catherine to go to him, I'll take her away, and Dog Brother will never find her.' I told him that Dog Brother would always find her, wherever she went.

"Henry didn't seem to understand that Dog Brother himself could have given his wife the cancer."

"Excuse me," said Jim. "You may be able to give people the 'flu but you can't give them *cancer*."

Dan looked at him as if he had just said something spectacularly stupid. "This is Dog Brother we're talking about here."

"So? He's only a man."

"*You're* going to see him, too? A white man?"

"Sure. That's why I'm here. Henry asked me to try to buy him off. A hefty payment in stocks and bonds in place of Catherine."

Dan shook his head and kept on shaking it. "Are you crazy? Do you think he'll really give up Catherine in return for money? You don't know what kind of individual you're dealing with here."

John Three Names laid a hand on Dan's shoulder. "Come on, Dan. Let's not get alarmist here. Most of what

141

people say about Dog Brother is superstition, hearsay. He's just an ordinary guy."

"So why do people go to him when they want somebody cured of cancer?"

"Dan – everything's going to be fine. Everything's going to work out. We'll go see Dog Brother, and then maybe we'll be back in time for the prayers."

"You'll need them, believe me," Dan told him.

Chapter Seven

Toward the end of the main strip, the trailers began to look shabbier and more weatherbeaten. Some had half-collapsed verandahs built onto them. Others had scabby tarpaper roofs. In place of the meticulously-tended vegetable beds there was nothing but scrub-grass and dust and all of that indescribable detritus that seems to collect around trailer-parks as if they were some kind of Sargasso Sea of useless junk. Heavy, rusty objects that had no apparent purpose whatsoever. Car seats, right in the middle of nowhere at all. Heaps of worn-out tyres.

The neat lines of trailers began to straggle, and then there were long gaps in between them. Outside one of them, its windows bedecked with filthy net curtains, a handpainted sign said, *Keep Away. Owner Has Gun & Itchy Trigger Finger.* A dog was tearing at a dead buzzard.

At the very end of the strip, parked askew to all the rest of the homes, was a large black-painted trailer with blacked-out windows. The heat shuddered from its roof, distorting the distant vermilion mountains behind it. There were empty cans and automobile parts strewn all around it, as well as a stack of what looked like old newspapers gummed together with some black substance like tar. Whatever it was, a host of flies were crawling all over it.

Not far away, an old blue Buick Electra was shaded

under a single tree, while high above, two buzzards lazily circled in the flawless sky.

John Three Names stopped the Galaxy at a respectful distance. Immediately, two black Dobermanns got up from the grass in which they had been lying and pricked up their ears. Jim was relieved to see that they were both chained to one of the trailer's rear wheels.

"This is where Dog Brother lives," said John Three Names. "From now on, we should take this very, very easy."

"What do we do if he's not home?" asked Mark.

"Oh, he'll be home. He's *always* home."

Jim said, "OK, then. Let's screw our courage to the sticking-place."

"Let's screw what?" frowned Mark.

"Shakespeare, Mark. *Macbeth.* You should have read it."

"I did. I remember 'out damned spot.' The first time I read it I thought he meant, like, zit."

Sharon clucked her disapproval. "I'll tell you something, Foley. I used to think that I was stupid till I met you. Then I graduated to genius overnight."

John Three Names said, "I'd better go first, then you and Catherine can follow. But don't worry: Dog Brother isn't especially prejudiced against whites. He hates everybody equally."

"What shall we do?" asked Sharon.

"Just stay in the car for a while, if you don't mind. You can leave the motor running to keep the air con on."

"Hmph," said Sharon. She was very strong-willed and she didn't like being left out of the action, whatever it was.

John Three Names led the way across the dust toward the trailer. The Dobermanns twitched and quivered and strained at their chains. They looked as if they were ready

144

to rush over and take a leg apiece, but they didn't bark. John Three Names climbed the steps to the trailer's door. There was a knocker on it, with a face like a snarling wolf. John Three Names gave three cautious knocks, and then waited.

Jim shaded his eyes. "It's odd how Dog Brother's trailer is set at an angle from all the others," he remarked.

Catherine said, "His door faces east, where the demons come from."

"I thought that Native Americans avoided doing that."

"Dog Brother is different, Mr Rook. Dog Brother positively welcomes them."

After a while, John Three Names knocked again. There was a long paused, and then the trailer door swung open, on its own. Inside, Jim could see nothing but pitch-blackness. No sign of Dog Brother. No sign of anything at all. He suddenly began to feel alarmed, and he could sense his pulse-rate quickening. Just remember what the Indians used to say, he told himself. "Today will be a good day to die."

John Three Names peered inside the trailer, then turned back and beckoned Jim and Catherine to come closer. "It's OK, I guess."

Catherine suddenly snatched hold of Jim's hand. She was startlingly cold, and she was trembling. He looked at her and her face was as white as paper.

"Listen," he said, "you don't have to go through with this if you don't want to. Nobody's going to force you, least of all me. All we're going to do is see if we can't persuade this Dog Brother guy to forget your father's promise."

"I don't know – I don't know if I can do this," Catherine gasped. "I don't know if I can face him. I want to see him. I really want to see him. Don't you understand me, I'm *burning* to see him – but I don't know – I'm afraid of him

145

– I'm so afraid of him, Mr Rook – and I'm so afraid of myself."

Jim put his arm around her. "Do you want to turn around and go back to LA? I don't mind. I don't know what will happen if you do. I guess this whole problem is going to stay unresolved, and your brothers are going to stay in prison. But you have to think about *you*. Otherwise, the way I see it, this whole mess is going to go on being a mess, and more people are going to get hurt."

Catherine stared at him. "Ms Randall – did *she* get hurt?"

"What makes you say that? She had asthma, that's all."

"No she didn't. She got hurt, didn't she? She got hurt!"

"Catherine—"

"You can't say she didn't because I saw it! I'm sure that I saw it! I saw her fall to the ground!"

John Three Names called, "Are you coming or not? He's waiting for you."

"So what do you think?" Jim asked Catherine. "Are you coming inside or not?"

Catherine's eyes were filled with tears. "I saw her fall and it was all my fault. I saw her fall and I was glad that she fell, I don't know why."

Her confusion was almost total. Her eyes were unfocused, and her movements were abrupt and jerky. What was more, Jim was sure that he could see the shadow beginning to form around her – dim, blotchy traces of darkness that clung in the air like bloodclots.

"Jim!" called John Three Names.

"Catherine, you can say no if you want to," Jim repeated. "Just say the word, and we're out of here."

"I can't," she said, and her voice was suddenly deep and harsh. "A promise is a promise. An oath is an oath."

146

With that, she began to walk stiffly toward the trailer. Jim called, "Catherine!" but she mounted the steps and disappeared into the darkness. John Three Names beckoned Jim yet again, and said, "Come on, Jim. This is the only way."

Jim looked back at the Galaxy, where Sharon and Mark were waiting for him. Then he took a deep breath and walked up to the trailer. "It's all right, Jim," said John Three Names, holding out his hand. "He's agreed to talk to you, even if you are white."

Jim peered into the darkness. An odd smell was wafting out of the trailer. It reminded Jim of stale sweat and dogs, but there was another fragrance mixed up in it, too – a fragrance like burning leaves, and woods, and long fall days, and *leather* for some reason, the smell of a leather watchstrap that you've worn too long.

"Go ahead," said John Three Names, and Jim took a step into the darkness. It was a heavy black sheet, hung over the doorway so that the light couldn't penetrate. Inside, the trailer was painted as black as it was on the outside, with black-upholstered furniture, and it was lit only by tiny lamps with bulbs no bigger than beads.

Catherine was already seated on one of the couches, her hands held across her chest in her familiar 'parachute-jump' position, her hair shining in the lamplight. She was facing a tall, thin man who was sitting cross-legged in a large antique chair with faded, gilded arms, and a seat that must once have been the finest midnight-black velvet, but which was now reduced to a faded collection of grey strings.

The man was naked to the waist, and his body was very lean and muscular, with no excess fat at all. Both of his nipples were pierced and hung with various beads and bird's-wings. He had long black hair that draped over his shoulders. His eyes were concealed behind small spectacles with yellow lenses. His face was hard and angled and vulpine, as if his great-great-grandfather might have been a wolf, but he was handsome, too, in a very primitive way. He wore a tight pair of black leather britches, half-unlaced at the front.

"Jim . . . this is Dog Brother," said John Three Names. "Dog Brother . . . this is Jim Rook."

"You are the one who sees?" asked Dog Brother. He spoke slowly and harshly, as if he weren't used to making much conversation.

"I guess you could call me that," said Jim. "And you . . . you're the one who puts hexes on people?"

"Jim—" John cautioned him.

"No, no. That's the whole reason I'm here," said Jim. "I've come here to prevent any further killings by this spirit-beast of yours."

Dog Brother lifted his right hand. On the palm of it was tattooed a picture of the dark, bear-like creature that had attacked Susan back at Window Rock. "You are a wise man, for a white. Not many Navajos still believe in spirit-beasts these days, let alone whites."

"I believe in it because I've seen it."

"You've actually seen it with your own eyes? Do you want to tell me what it looks like?"

"Like many bears, with claws. And with eyes like coals from a furnace."

"You *have* seen it, haven't you?" said Dog Brother, with a smile that revealed crowded, pointed teeth. "I never thought that anybody ever would. Well . . . you can go back to your lodges now and tell them that it was all a bad dream. Tell them it's over, and that the Changing Bear Maiden will never trouble them again. Unless, of course, it chooses to. But then you can never tell with the Changing Bear Maiden. She's always so spontaneous."

He laughed, a crackling laugh like dry twigs breaking.

148

In the dim light, Jim could see Catherine sitting hunched on the sofa, her hands lying in her lap, upturned. Next to her sat John Three Names, conspiciously tense. He kept drumming his fingers on his knees and shuffling his feet. If a ticker-tape had come out of his brain, it would have read, 'Come on, come on. Let's get going. For Christ's sake, Jim, let's cut the niceties and get the hell out of here.'

Jim leaned forward so that he was looking directly into Dog Brother's glasses. "Let's cut straight to the chase, shall we? Henry Black Eagle has authorized me to make you an offer of stocks, bonds and ready cash. All you have to do is name your price."

Dog Brother stared back at him for a long, long time without saying anything. Then, as if had just woken from a coma, said, "Price? What are you talking about, price?"

Jim reached into his pocket and took out his organizer. In it, he had clearly written a list of all of Henry's stocks, bonds and insurance investments. He had also jotted down that in the last resort, Henry would give him a percentage share in his next contract with Fox TV, and a percentage share in all of his royalties, 'in perpetuity and for ever,' as they like to say in Hollywood contracts.

"Henry can raise $950,0000. Just say the word, and it's all yours. No more living in a trailer, hunh? You'll be able to build your own house for this, with pool."

"Is this some kind of . . . *dowry*?" asked Dog Brother.

"No, no. I don't think you get it. Henry is offering you this $950,000 so that you won't chase after Catherine any longer."

"I won't chase after her. I promise. Why should I need to? She'll be here, sitting by my side."

Jim took off his reading-glasses and tucked them into his shirt-pocket. "Dog Brother, we're talking at cross-purposes here. Henry Black Eagle is offering you this money to set Catherine free – to tear up your marriage agreement. The money isn't a dowry, sir. It's a form of compensation. A goodwill gesture, if you like."

Dog Brother turned to John and snapped, "You told me this white man was bringing Catherine White Bird back to me."

"Well, he is, and he has."

"Excuse me," said Jim. "You're not thinking of taking both of them, are you? The girl *and* the money? Because I'm afraid that this is a 'tick one box only' situation. Either you get to keep Catherine, who has made it perfectly clear to me over the past few days that she wouldn't live back on the reservation if you gave her all the peanuts in Georgia. Or, you can take the money. But not both."

"No," said Dog Brother.

"No, what? No, you're quite aware that you can't have both? Or, no, you don't want the money but you do want the girl? Or, no, you want the money but you do—"

"Enough!" said Dog Brother. "You've done well to bring me back this woman. Now you can go."

He climbed out of his chair and took hold of Catherine by the wrist. "You see this scar?" he said. "That was where our blood was mingled when she was fifteen years old. She belonged to me from that day onward. You can't change that with money."

"Mr Dog Brother," said Jim. "I know that you feel that Catherine belongs to you, but the fact is that in the eyes of the law your betrothal doesn't mean squat."

"Take it easy, Jim—" John Three Names cautioned him.

"What do you mean, 'take it easy'?" Jim demanded. "Are you part of this, too?"

"We couldn't fight it, Jim. You've seen it for yourself. After your college boy died, and Paul and Grey Cloud were accused of killing him – Henry knew that he didn't have any choice."

"You mean that he didn't send me here to bargain at all? All he wanted me to do was to take Catherine back to this feather-nippled yahoo?"

"Jim! They couldn't risk any more killing!"

"Then why didn't they come back here and turn this creep over to the cops?"

"Because who would believe them? Even the Navajo cops wouldn't believe them."

Dog Brother was still holding onto Catherine's arm, still grinning widely. His teeth looked as if he could take a bite out of a three-inch mahogany tabletop. "John Three Names is right. Nobody would believe that you had seen the Changing Bear Maiden. You would be locked up by the same people you had asked for help, and they would throw away the key."

Jim said, "You refuse the money?"

"I would be happy with the money, if Henry Black Eagle wishes to give it to me."

"But you're not letting Catherine go free?"

"Absolutely not. She's going to be my wife. She's going to bear my children. She's going to feed me and bathe me and worship me. She's going to lick the sweat from between my toes."

Catherine was staring at him. There was a turmoil of darkness around her. John Three Names obviously couldn't see it, but Jim could, and the way in which Dog Brother was taunting her made Jim wonder if *he* could, too – or maybe *sense* it, at the very least.

"I don't want to marry you!" Catherine retorted. "I won't ever marry you!"

"Of course you'll marry me. You'll grow to love me so much that you'll cry every time I'm out of your sight."

"I won't! I hate you!" The darkness began to leap and dance with a life of its own, and to coagulate around her shoulders in hunched, shadowy knots.

151

Jim said, "Come on, Dog Brother, let her go."

"You!" said Dog Brother, contemptuously. "You've been warned, haven't you? This is your day to die!"

"I've heard enough of that for one week," Jim told him. He was angry now – angry and tired and frustrated. "All you have to do is let her go and then we can negotiate this situation like reasonable men."

"You think you were sent here to *negotiate*?" Dog Brother sneered at him. "You were sent here for two reasons only – to bring Catherine White Bird back to me, and to see that the Changing Bear Maiden returns to the great outside, where she came from, because you're the only one who can. That was the one single condition that Henry Black Eagle asked for, before he returned his beautiful daughter, and who was I to refuse him? A promise is a promise."

Jim said, "John, is this true?"

John Three Names nodded. "I'm sorry, Jim. I didn't like deceiving you, believe me, but there was no other way. Dog Brother and Catherine are supposed to be exchange their marriage-promises – and when they do, you're supposed to witness the spirit-beast disappearing back to the spirit-world."

"Oh, I see. Then you've been telling me lies right from the start."

Dog Brother smiled. "They weren't exactly lies, Mr Rook. They were just a way of getting you out here, and to make sure that Catherine got here, too. You've seen the beast. You've seen what it can do. Even *I* can't control it sometimes."

"Oh, I've seen it, thanks, and I've seen what it can do. It killed a promising young student. It wrecked my apartment and killed my cat. It turned the West Grove locker room into a disaster area. And yesterday it killed – a woman I was very fond of."

152

"So you'd like to see it go for good?" said John Three Names.

"Are you kidding me?"

"Then let's see Dog Brother and Catherine married, and that'll be the end of it."

"And what about Paul and Grey Cloud?"

"You can go back to LA and testify to what you saw."

"Oh, sure, and a jury's going to believe me?"

"You can take a polygraph test."

"Inadmissible as evidence. You know that."

"But what if somebody else were killed in exactly the same way, hundreds of miles distant, while Paul and Grey Cloud were still in custody?"

Jim stared at him. "You're talking about *Susan*?"

"Too badly burned, I'm afraid. You see, Susan was a necessary sacrifice to Coyote. You don't walk on the master's territory without paying him homage."

"You mean that Susan was a *burnt offering*?"

John Three Names shrugged. "That was why I built the fire. I expected her to come out looking for Catherine, but I didn't expect *you*. All the same, you were quite a help. Pity about the blanket."

"You mean you summoned up that beast? You did it on purpose? Just so that Susan could be murdered and burned?"

Dog Brother said, "Coyote always appreciates the smell of human flesh, burned in his honor. It makes him more amenable to the human race. In the old days, they burned virgins, and buffalo, and they burned them alive."

"Just a minute," said Jim. "If you're not talking about Susan being killed in exactly the same way, who *are* you talking about?"

Dog Brother said, "You brought some friends with you, didn't you, just like Henry Black Eagle asked you to?"

153

"Hey – wait a minute," said Jim. "Nobody touches one hair of those students' heads. You talk about promises? I made three promises when I agreed to come here. I promised Henry Black Eagle that I would try to negotiate Catherine's release from her marriage vows. I promised my students that I would take care of them. And I promised myself that I wasn't going to die. Not today."

"Pretty hard promises to keep," said Dog Brother, slowly approaching him, until Jim could see every blackhead in every pore of his nose. "I'm taking Catherine, don't you have any doubt about that; and I'm going to give Henry Black Eagle all the evidence he needs to free his sons from prison; and if you raise any objection whatsoever, then so help me I'll hunt you down for the rest of your life, and destroy everything that means anything to you, and kill anybody you love. That's what it means to die, my friend. That's what it *really* means to die. That's what the white men did to us, not so very long ago. Destroyed our houses and burned our crops and killed our cattle. Our women and children starved and what did you care? You spat on our graves.

"Today, you die," Dog Brother repeated. "Tomorrow, you die. Every day for the rest of your life, you die."

Jim stared back at him and thought, Christ, what am I going to do? He looked across at John Three Names, who held his gaze for only a moment before he uncomfortably looked away. Then he looked at Catherine, whose expression was a tangle of confusion and fright.

"All right, then," he said. "I guess if it's Catherine you want, you can have her. What can I do?"

Dog Brother slowly grinned. "That's good. I like a realist. Now, which of your students can we have, or shall we take them both?"

Jim was appalled at Dog Brother's cold-bloodedness.

How can I possibly sacrifice one of my class? And even if I could, which one would it be? Sharon, who had a future ahead of her as a social worker or even a local politician for black causes; or Mark, who would probably end up just like his father, beating automobile panels, but whose humour and poetic insight would break the mould of his father's ignorance, and make sure that *his* son had a chance?

"Maybe I should ask them to toss a coin," he said. "They don't need to know what it's for."

Dog Brother seemed to like that. "I knew that you were an intelligent man, when I first saw you. Henry Black Eagle chose wisely."

"Catherine?" said Jim. He tried to catch her full attention – tried to appeal to Catherine White Bird, instead of the shadowy shape that was forming all around her. "Catherine, I'm sorry. You see what kind of position I'm in."

Catherine said, "I – I don't know what you mean. What are you trying to say to me?"

"I'm trying to tell you that you have to marry Dog Brother. I don't have any choice."

He stepped up close to her and took hold of her hand. Already he could feel the prickle of harsh, invisible hair, like static electricity.

He leaned forward as if to kiss her cheek. "I'm going to grab your hand real tight," he murmured. "When I do that, *run*, you understand?"

He stood up straight. There was nothing in her face to tell him if she had understood him or not – just the same bewilderment, the same fear.

"Okay, then," he said to Dog Brother. "I guess I'll go out and ask my students to decide which of them is going to live and which of them is going to go the Happy Hunting Ground."

John Three Names said, "I guess I'll be going, too. I've seen enough blood for one week, believe me."

He turned, and Dog Brother stepped back to let him pass, and at that moment Jim pushed Dog Brother flat in the chest, so that he lost his balance and fell back against the armchair. John Three Names turned back again, but Jim shouldered him roughly out of the way. He gripped Catherine's hand and shouted, "*Now!*"

He tried to pull at her hand, but as he did so Dog Brother let out a high, unearthly shriek. Catherine's hand seemed to explode inside his. One second her fingers were slim and smooth – the next he was holding a gigantic, bristly claw. He cried out, "*Ahh!*" and whipped his hand away. There was no longer a slight, long-haired girl behind him, but a bulky bearlike shadow that reached almost to the trailer's ceiling. It had tiny eyes that glared red like the perforations in a furnace-door, and claws that literally clattered as it lifted them up.

Jim dropped to the floor, shielding his face with his arm. As he did so, one claw whisked past him, so close that it tore the skin along his knuckles. It struck the side of the trailer with a thunderous crash, breaking a Formica cabinet in half and puncturing the aluminum wall, so that five jagged stars of daylight suddenly burst through.

"*Catherine!*" Jim yelled at it. But the beast lurched forward yet again, so that the whole trailer shook. It swung at Jim again and again, but Jim rolled away across the floor and slid beneath one of the couches. He heard Dog Brother howling and whooping, and singing some kind of high-pitched, repetitive chant. "*Aheeiioo – ahane – aheeiioo – saabate –*"

The beast lashed out in all directions, its claws tearing through upholstery, metal and laminate. The noise was ear-splitting, and it didn't stop. It felt to Jim as if a bomb had detonated in slow-motion. The foam seating

156

over his head was torn apart; the flooring was ripped up; glasses smashed; furniture was wrenched limb-from-limb. The air was filled with a blizzard of broken china and shreds of upholstery, and with every blow the Changing Bear Maiden ripped her way through the sides of the trailer, so that sunlight came criss-crossing in from every direction.

The trailer's framework began to give way. The walls were all battered and dented, and even ripped open, in places. The entire structure tilted, and suddenly its wheels collapsed, which threw Dog Brother back onto the floor, hitting his head against the television stand. John Three Names had been struggling to reach the door, and had to cling onto the drapes to prevent himself from tumbling backward. Jim – under the couch – was forced into an awkward corner, his legs doubled-up. He managed to push his back against the side of the trailer and force himself free, just as the Changing Bear Maiden's claw detonated through the cushions on top of him and slammed through the wall with all the force of a fork-lift truck.

Jim knew that he had to make a run for it. He might not survive, but anything was better than waiting here to have his head torn off, the way that Susan had. He took a deep breath, counted to three, and then he jack-knifed out from under the couch, rolled across the floor, and grabbed hold of the first support that he could find – which turned out to be John Three Names' ankle. John Three Names, panicking, screamed, "Let go of me! Let go of me!" He tried to kick Jim's hand away, but Jim wouldn't let go. He dragged himself forward until he and John Three Names were lying side by side.

"Do you know what you've done?" Jim yelled at him. "You've killed two innocent people, just because you were too frightened to stand up to some sly, treacherous,

157

out-of-date demon! Did you really think that I was going to allow you to kill any more?"

John Three Names struggled to get himself free. "What do you white men know? This whole country is Navajo country and always will be! We're waiting for the time, that's all! We're taking care of our spirits, we're bringing them all back out of hiding, one by one, we're reviving the old beliefs, and we're waiting for the time! Let me tell you something, Mr Rook – it won't be long now before every white community between here and Los Angeles is populated by nothing but corpses. Blowfly heaven, that's what it'll be."

The floor shook beneath them. Jim glanced up. The Changing Bear Maiden was looming over them, cold and dark. Its stiff fur bristled and its eyes burned red and it uttered a sound in its throat like men being strangled. It lashed out at Jim, ripping his shirt and tearing his shoulder open. He felt blood springing wet down his back. John Three Names struggled with him and kicked him and tried to lift him up from the floor, so that the beast's next blow would hit him in the head. Jim tipped himself backward and rolled John Three Names over on top of him. John Three Names gripped his wrists and tried to wrestle him over again. Jim felt his sweat dripping on his face and the smell of stale coffee on his breath.

"We were supposed to forget, were we?" he roared. "We were supposed to forget about what you did to us? All those women and children who died here at Fort Defiance?" His anger was so intense that he seemed to have forgotten all about the spirit-beast that was shaking the trailer all around them.

Over his shoulder Jim saw a paw lifted – a shaggy black paw with claws that caught the criss-cross sunlight. Even though John Three Names was shouting at him and struggling with him, he tried to push him sideways, out of the way. But there was a *whakkk!* and a sharp gristly noise like somebody twisting the leg off a raw chicken, and Jim was suddenly spattered with warm blood. John Three Names fell off him, clutching the side of his head. "My ear! It's taken my ear off!"

The trailer seemed to blow up. The beast tore down its ceiling and ripped away its walls. Torn fragments of aluminum hurtled everywhere, along with a billowing cloud of foam and feathers and shredded sheets. Dog Brother, unconscious, was showered in rice and flour and dried fettucine.

John Three Names tried to climb to his feet, his face streaked with blood. He reached for a wall that was no longer there, and teetered. At that moment the Changing Bear Maiden gripped him in both of its claws, and lifted him high over its head. John Three Names screamed. His legs bicycled. The beast's claws had penetrated his ribcage on both sides, deep into his lungs and his liver.

"No!" he screeched out. "No! I served you! I saved you!"

But then the beast pulled its claws wide apart, and with a loud crackling noise it tore open his body from his neck to his crotch, and then violently shook him, so that he was emptied out all over the floor of the trailer, heart and lungs and stomach and intestines, in a sloppy, splattering heap. The beast then dropped his gutted, flaccid body, all arms and legs like a marionette, and turned toward Jim.

Jim was already running. As soon as the beast had caught hold of John Three Names, he had scrambled toward the door, dropped to the ground, and headed for the Galaxy where Sharon and Mark were waiting.

It was hot, and he was badly shocked. He could hear his shoes chuffing in the dust and it sounded as if somebody were two steps behind him. Sharon was out of the vehicle already, staring in shock at the wildly-exploding trailer.

159

Mark was sitting in the back seat, punching wildly at John Three Names' mobile phone.

"Sharon! Get back in!" Jim shouted at her, as he ran toward her.

"What? What about Catherine?"

"*Get back in!*"

He looked back over his shoulder and the spirit-beast was already running toward him, in the heavy, sinister lope of a grizzly bear. It was enormous, almost three times the size of a real bear, and its claws made a clashing noise on the ground as it ran, like somebody sharpening carving-knives.

"Sharon, for Christ's sake! Get back in!"

He reached the Galaxy and pushed Sharon back into her seat. He climbed behind the wheel, slammed the door and gunned the engine.

"But Catherine!" Sharon shrieked at him. "What about Catherine?"

Jim violently reversed the Galaxy and swung it around so that it was facing back toward the trailer-park. "Catherine isn't Catherine," he told her. "Not any more, anyway."

"But she's there!" said Sharon, taking hold of his arm and shaking it. "Look, Mr Rook, she's there!"

Jim kept his foot down and the Galaxy slithered in the dust. Jim looked up in the rear-view mirror and he could see Catherine running after them, her hair swinging as she ran. But when he twisted around in his seat, all he could see was the huge dark shadow of the Changing Bear Maiden, relentlessly trying to catch up.

"Mr Rook, stop!" begged Sharon. "You're leaving Catherine behind!"

Jim jammed on the brakes. "Sharon, it isn't Catherine. It's something else. It may look like Catherine to you, but to me it looks like something else altogether."

"I called the cops," said Mark, hopefully, holding up

160

the mobile telephone. "They said they'd try to get here in a half-hour, if they could."

Catherine was still running toward them. In his mirror, Jim could see that her expression was fixed, her eyes were glazed. She was running like somebody who was determined to catch up with them, no matter what.

"Hold tight," he said, and stepped on the gas. The Galaxy's tyres slewed sideways on the dirt, and then they were speeding away. At that moment, however, they felt a catastrophic bang at the back of the vehicle, and the rear window shattered inward. Then they heard a hideous scraping, followed by a jarring, wrenching sound, and Jim felt the Galaxy's steering wheel twitch in his hands as if it had a mind of its own.

"What's happening?" said Sharon, in terror.

Jim looked back and saw the Changing Bear Maiden running after them, faster and faster. It lunged at the back of the Galaxy and tore off the rear door panel, which bounced away over the dusty ground. Then it smashed the brake lights and pulled off more of the trim. Fragments of red plastic were scattered all over the ground.

"It's *Catherine*," said Mark. "What the hell is she doing? She's tearing the whole damn car to pieces!"

"It's just like I said, Mark," Jim told him. "It isn't Catherine, not at the moment. It's kind of a beast. The same beast that killed Martin Amato. The same beast that wrecked the locker rooms."

"What are you telling us?" said Sharon. "You're trying to say that *Catherine* killed Martin? You're trying to say that *Catherine* did all of that damage?"

Jim turned around and saw the beast running up closer. It collided with their rear bumper with a heavy thump and he had to swerve wildly from side to side. They were speeding down the main strip between the trailers now, and there were children and dogs scampering everywhere.

161

Yet he didn't dare to slow down. The back of the Galaxy was already battered and torn and scored with scratch-marks, and he knew that if he stopped now, the beast would hurtle through the back window into the passenger compartment and tear them into pieces before they had time to open the doors.

"*Mr Rook!*" screamed Sharon.

Ahead of them, an old Navajo woman was crossing the main strip with a Zimmer frame. She was accompanied by a little girl of no more than six or seven, who was smiling to her and chatting to her and offering her wildflowers.

Jim saw them like a photograph – utterly clear, utterly detailed. He was already hitting 70 mph and he had no chance of stopping before he hit them. He just had time to shout "Hold tight!" before he swerved off the main strip and crashed through somebody's picket fence, mowed down their garden planted with beans and squash and pumpkins, collided with a water-butt, tore up another length of fence like a giant zip-fastener, skidded around the back of another trailer straight through a line of freshly-hung washing, and then bounced back onto the main strip.

He drove out of the trailer-park, hung a howling right turn, and sped back toward Window Rock with his foot flat against the floor.

He checked his rear-view mirror. Catherine wasn't running after them any longer. She standing outside the trailer-park watching them speed away. He turned his head around and she was still Catherine. The beast had vanished. He had an almost irresistible urge to U-turn and go back to her. Christ, he was her teacher, he felt responsible for her. He couldn't imagine what she was going through, what fears she was feeling. But he did know that until she was released from Dog

Brother's influence, she was capable of killing all of them.

"You're just going to *leave* her here?" asked Mark.

"I don't have any choice. This man she's supposed to be marrying has put a spell on her, for want of a better word. Back then, when she was running after us, you saw Catherine but I saw a huge black beast."

Mark turned around and looked back along the road, just in time to see Catherine turning back toward the trailer-park. "A beast. It's hard to believe it."

"Look at the damage she did to the van. If she wasn't possessed by this *thing*, whatever it is, she couldn't even have dented it."

"Come on, Mark," said Sharon. "You know that Mr Rook can see things like spirits and ghosts and all."

"Yeah, but a *beast*, man – in broad daylight! Wish I'd seen it!"

Jim said, "Listen," and told them the legend of the Changing Bear Maiden, the way that John Three Names had told it to him. What he didn't say was that John Three Names was dead; or that Susan had been killed, too, and burned as an offering to Coyote.

They reached Window Rock and drew up outside the Navajo Nation Inn. "What are we going to do now?" asked Sharon.

"We're going to pack our bags and get the hell out of here, that's what."

"What's Catherine's old man going to say when you come back without her?" asked Mark.

"I'm very much looking forward to finding out."

"Wait up a minute. You mean – he didn't *expect* her to come back?"

"I don't think he expected any of us to come back. Only me, so that I could confirm that the beast was gone

163

for good. And I doubted if I would have lasted long, after that."

"I don't get it. We were all supposed to die, *all* of us?"

Jim nodded. "Henry Black Eagle took his family to California to duck out of his promise to give Catherine to Dog Brother. But he underestimated how powerful the magic was, and how far it could reach. After Martin was killed, and Paul and Grey Cloud were arrested for murder, he realized that he had to honour his promise. He wanted us killed by the Changing Bear Maiden so that he would have evidence that his sons couldn't possibly have murdered Martin. Which, of course, they didn't. They went down on the beach that night to try to find Catherine before she hurt anybody."

Sharon pushed the revolving glass door into the reception area. "It seems terrible, leaving Catherine behind like that. I mean whatever she's turned into now, she was always such a totally sweet person."

"Sharon, there's nothing else we can do right now. If we go near her, she'll rip our heads off. And I'm beginning to think that Dog Brother doesn't have the slightest intention of sending the Changing Bear Maiden back into limbo, or wherever. I think he likes her fine the way she is."

Jim rented a Pontiac station-wagon and they drove all the way from Window Rock to Gallup, where they stopped for cheeseburgers; and then 138 mph nonstop to Albuquerque. They arrived in time for an American Airlines flight direct to Los Angeles and they took off into the sun. Sharon and Mark slept for most of the flight. Jim was exhausted but he was still suffering badly from shock and he didn't want to close his eyes for fear of what he might see.

He took out the silver whistle that Henry Black Eagle had given him. He wasn't tempted to blow it, but he wondered exactly what it was for. Catherine had warned him that it would alert Dog Brother and give away their location, but Jim didn't really see the point of a whistle that did nothing more than that. It had snapped Catherine out of her Changing Bear Maiden trance when their airplane had been nosediving into the Cibola Forest, but Jim couldn't understand how. He had quite a list of questions for Henry Black Eagle when they returned to Los Angeles.

He drove both Mark and Sharon home, and by now it was dark. "Listen," he said, "I think it would be better if you didn't tell your parents what happened at Fort Defiance. They're bound to want a police investigation, and if there's one situation that the police won't be able to handle, it's this. I'm thinking of Catherine, more than anbody else. If the police find her and she goes berserk the way she did at the trailer-park . . . well, you can use your imagination."

"We'll see you tomorrow in class, Mr Rook," said Sharon, and she unexpectedly gave him a kiss on the cheek. "Thanks for getting us out of trouble."

"I shouldn't have gotten you *into* trouble to start with."

"Hey, what's life without a few scares?" said Mark. "I had the best time ever. Better than sitting on your duff watching TV, anyhow."

"You didn't think that when we was headed for those trees," Sharon retorted.

"I didn't crap myself, did I?"

"If you had, I would have been the first one out of there, with or without a parachute."

"Listen," said Jim, "you don't have to show up for

college tomorrow if you don't want to. Maybe you could use the rest."

"Try and stop us, Mr Rook. Just try and stop us."

Chapter Eight

He drove to George Babouris' house and found George sitting on the porch strumming his bouzouki. "Jim – you're back already! How about a glass of retsina? You should listen to this song I've composed. It's called *How We Danced In Aspropirgos*."

"Catchy title," said Jim. "Is it OK if I stay here tonight? The super is supposed to be clearing up my apartment, but I'm not sure that I can face going back there, not till tomorrow."

"Of course you can stay. Are you hungry? I made stuffed peppers yesterday, all they need is a couple of minutes in the microwave."

"That's all right, George. I think I just need a drink."

George led the way inside. To be fair, he seemed to have tidied the place up since Jim had last stayed there. The goldfish were still swimming through a dense turquoise murk, and there was a pair of discarded socks on the back of the couch, but George had thrown out most of his waste paper and empty beer cans and there was even a bowl of oranges on the table.

"Don't tell me you're in love," said Jim.

"Well, not exactly," George confessed. "But I've met this woman and we've been getting along pretty well. I think you know her, as a matter of fact. Well, you *would* know her. She lives in the same apartment block as you do."

167

"Go on," said Jim, suspiciously, setting down his bag.

"You left my number with your super, right, in case he had any questions? So he called and said that he couldn't replace the kitchen cabinets with exactly the same doors, but would these other doors be OK? So I went around there and they were fine, the doors I mean. They were just like your old ones only better quality. Except that I met your neighbour from downstairs. The woman."

"You mean Miss *Neagle*?"

"That's it. Valerie! And I can tell you something, Jim, two people never got on better than Valerie and me. The spontaneity! It was great! And she's crazy for Greek café music!"

"Well, George. I hardly know what to say. I'm very happy for you – both of you."

"I'm going round to see her later this evening. Say – why don't you join me? You could see how your apartment's coming along."

"I don't know. I don't want to get in the way."

George opened the fridge and took out two cans of Pabst. "You won't. So how was Indian country? Did you manage to get everything sorted out?"

"To tell you the truth, George, it was a disaster."

"Hey – how come? I thought you were looking forward to it. Acting as a marriage guidance counsellor to Native Americans. Smoking peace-pipes. Dancing round the totem-pole."

"Henry Black Eagle was lying to me all along. He didn't want me to take Catherine back to the reservation to break off her engagement. He simply wanted me to chaperone her, to make sure that she returned there safe, and married this guy.

"He made a deal with a devil, George, and then he found he couldn't go back on it."

"When you say '*devil*'—?"

"I mean exactly that. Devil, or demon, or evil spirit, or whatever you want to call it. The man that Catherine is supposed to be marrying has some way of invoking the worst of all the Navajo spirits, called Coyote. His name's Dog Brother. He can turn people into beasts."

"He can turn people into *beasts*?" George repeated, raising one black bushy eyebrow.

"I know it doesn't sound very believable, but there are dozens of mythological stories from all kinds of cultures about demons turning men and women into animals. In Ireland, there's a jealous fairy who turned men into dogs. In Africa, there's a demon who makes women into monkeys. I don't know whether any of these myths have any basis in fact, but here in America there's a spirit who can turn a young girl like Catherine into a huge black creature like a bear. It was Catherine who wrecked the locker rooms. It was Catherine who trashed my apartment. It was Catherine who murdered Martin Amato. Worse than that, she's killed two other people, too."

"I'm finding this difficult," said George. "Who?"

"John Three Names, the Navajo guide who took us out to meet Catherine's prospective husband. She tore him apart." He hesitated, and he found that he could hardly speak. "The other was Susan."

"Susan? Susan Randall? You're kidding me!"

Jim's eyes were suddenly blurred with tears. This was the first time that he had allowed himself to show his emotions since Susan had been killed. "The beast just went for her, George. It took off her head. It ripped her apart. I was shouting at her to warn her but I couldn't do anything."

"So what – so where did this happen?"

"Window Rock . . . in back of our hotel. We burned her body on a fire."

169

George pressed his beer-can against his forehead. "Jesus Christ, Jim. Catherine turned into a beast and killed Susan and then you burned Susan on a fire?"

Jim took off his glasses and said, "I swear to God, George. It's true. All of it. It's true. You only have to ask Sharon and Mark."

"And what about this John Three Names?"

"It happened in Dog Brother's trailer. I was trying to get her out of there. She just – well, one second she was a pretty girl and the next second she was a raging black creature who could tear holes in steel."

"Jesus Christ, Jim. What are you going to do?"

"There's only one thing I *can* do. I have a responsibility to Catherine, for what I did, taking her back to the reservation. All right, I was deceived, I didn't know what I was getting her into. But she's an innocent party in all of this, George, and I helped to take her back to a life she doesn't want and a man she doesn't love."

"But she *killed* Susan."

"Not her, George. The Changing Bear Maiden – the beast – that's what killed Susan."

"What are you going to tell Dr Ehrlichman? What are you going to tell Susan's family? You think they're going to believe you? Like, I know you, and I trust you, but even I'm not sure if I believe you."

"What I tell people is going to have to wait. Right now there's only one way to see justice for Susan and to save Catherine from a whole lifetime of living on the reservation with this Dog Brother character – and that's to exorcize her, or whatever the hell you're supposed to do when somebody's possessed with a ten-foot invisible creature with claws like goddamned scimitars."

George said, "You're upset, you know. I wouldn't go so far as to say deranged. But you should think about this in the morning."

"I can't stop thinking about it now."

"Well, let's go around to see Valerie and see if the sight of your newly-decorated apartment can take your mind off it."

Jim took hold of George's hand, and gripped it tight, and George was vaguely embarrassed. "You know something, George. I never saw anything like this before. I've seen ghosts, and spirits, and I've seen a man leave his body and walk through the city for hours on end, with cars passing right through his body like he wasn't even there. But this – no, this is different. This isn't just a spiritual parlour-trick. This is a force that comes right out of the air we breathe and the ground we tread on. This is serious power, George. This is real Native American magic."

George clapped him on the back. "I'll say one thing for you, Jim. You never do things by halves. When you go bananas, you go *seriously* bananas. Did you try Prozac yet?"

"Don't you think I have enough ups in my life?"

"Right now, probably yes."

"Just let me ask you something. Even if you don't believe a single word I've said, will you accept that I'm sincere?"

"Sure, yes, I believe you're sincere."

"Then support me, help me. Even if you think I've lost the plot."

Quite unexpectedly, George put his arms around him and hugged him. His belly was enormous. His beard scratched, and he smelled of kebabs and Sure deodorant. "Don't you worry, Jim. Whatever gibberish you talk, George is right behind you."

They drove to Electric Avenue in George's huge old Silverado pick-up. For Jim, it was very strange going back there, after the feline formerly known as Tibbles had been killed, and his apartment had been wrecked. He felt as if this wasn't his home any more, and in a sense it wouldn't be, ever again. Once you've been burgled, once you've been vandalized, your home loses its sense of safety, and adding more locks makes it feel even less secure.

"Go take a look at your apartment, then come on down," George told him. "They're doing a great job for you. You'll like it."

Jim climbed the steps to the second-story landing and walked along to his front door. He saw a blind twitch just opposite, and he knew that it was Myrlin spying on him, to make sure that he wasn't spying on *him*. He hesitated for a moment and then he inserted the key into the lock. There was a strong smell of fresh paint and carpentry. He switched on the lights and saw that George was right: the walls had been newly decorated in a color that Jim could only describe as "faded camel". All of the gouges in the plaster had been smoothed over and the kitchen cabinet doors replaced.

Underneath a large dusty sheet of heavy-duty plastic all of his possessions were heaped: his books, his pictures, his CDs, even one of his cardigans. He felt as if he were walking into the apartment of somebody who had recently died.

He turned to leave when he saw his grandfather standing by the window. He looked very much older tonight, his shoulders hunched, his hands deep in his pockets. Jim approached him and said, "Grandpa? What did you come back for? Are you all right?"

"All right? No, I don't think I am," said his grandfather.

"Then what's wrong? Tell me. My friend said that relatives don't come back unless it's something serious."

172

"How does your friend know that?"

"Because she's dead, just like you. Her name's Alice Vaizey and – well, you probably won't believe this, but she talks to me through the woman who took over her apartment when she died."

"Why shouldn't I believe it? It's the kind of thing that happens all the time. The dead, clinging onto the living."

"So what's wrong?" asked Jim. He was so tempted to touch his grandfather – just to take hold of his hand, and feel those dry old fingers and those veins like wriggling roots. Just to feel that soft, well-shaved cheek. He could even smell his grandfather's hairdressing lotion, and his tobacco.

"That thing I warned you about – it came, didn't it?" said his grandfather. "That old, cold bristling thing."

Jim nodded. "It came all right. Look around you. They've just finished cleaning up the mess."

"This isn't the only mess, is it, Jim?"

"No, grandpa, it isn't. There was a woman that I was in love with. Susan Randall. The thing killed her, too."

His grandfather sucked at his false teeth. "I've seen Susan: that's why I came."

"You've *seen* her? Like, where?"

"Jim, there isn't any *where* when you're dead. One minute bells are ringing and you're looking out over these wet, tiled rooftops. Next minute you're riding the Eighth Avenue Local. Then, before you know it, you're walking by the shore at Hilton Head, tossing sticks for your dog."

"How was she?" Jim wanted to know. "Come on, grandpa. I tried to save her. I hope she knows that."

"She didn't know anything much. She was very shocked, as folks usually are when their bodies have been beheaded. It takes them quite a while to get over the way they died. But

173

she said one thing to me, and she meant it, Jim. She said, 'Tell Jim to go as far away from West Grove College as he can. Tell him to go to Europe. Tell him to go to Japan. Tell him to go anyplace that beast can't reach him, because it will.'

Jim said, "Do you think you might see her again? Do you think you might pass on a message?"

His grandfather gave him a quick, impatient look. "I'm not a go-between, Jim. I'm not some kind of spiritual mail-carrier."

"All the same, do you think you could tell her that I love her, and that I won't stop loving her? Do you think you could tell her that I'm going to make sure that she gets justice?"

"Justice doesn't mean too much to the dead, Jim. Justice is only for the living."

"All the same, can you tell her?"

His grandfather shrugged. "I guess I could try. No guarantees, though."

At that moment there was a knock at the door and Miss Neagle came in, dressed in a black ruffled negligee and strappy high-heeled slippers. "Jim?" she said. "George and I were wondering if you'd like to come down and join us for a drink. He said you had a *very* interesting time in Arizona."

She suddenly stopped and blinked and stared at Jim's grandfather. "Oh—" she said. "I'm sorry. I didn't realise you had company."

Startled, Jim said, "You can *see* him?"

"Of course. He keeps flickering in and out of focus like an old TV, but I can see him, for sure."

"Who are you to call me an old TV?" Jim's grandfather demanded.

"Mrs Alice Vaizey, I think, grandpa," said Jim. He turned to Miss Neagle and said, "Right?"

Miss Neagle smiled. "That's right. I couldn't see him, not on my own, but Mrs Vaizey can. That's why he's so flickery."

"What's going on here?" asked Jim's grandfather, suspiciously. "Is this the friend you were telling me about? The one who's dead?"

"That's right, grandpa. Miss Neagle here took over her apartment, and her spirit, too."

Jim's grandfather slowly approached Miss Neagle and stood right in front of her. He lifted his left hand and held it an inch or so away from her forehead. It was obvious that he wanted to touch her, but he couldn't. "I can see her," he said. "I can actually see her. It's like there are two women standing here, one inside the other."

Without any warning, tears formed in Miss Neagle's eyes and ran down her cheeks. "Do you know something?" she said, "That's the first time that anybody's seen me, since I died. I was beginning to think that I was invisible to everyone, even to other spirits."

"Well, now, you shouldn't have to worry about that," Jim's grandfather comforted her. "*I* can see you . . . I can see you as clear as daylight."

"So what do I look like?" asked Miss Neagle, in the same coquettish way that Mrs Vaizey would have said it.

"You're slim, very slim, like a dancer. Not like this lady at all. And you're a very handsome woman indeed."

"Well, you're very complimentary," said Miss Neagle. "And even if we never meet again—"

Jim's grandfather smiled at her, and blew her a kiss. Jim said, "I don't believe this, grandpa. You come here to give me a warning and you end up flirting with the spirit of the woman who used to live downstairs."

"Jim, that's not flirting. When people die they need comfort – more comfort than they ever needed when they

175

were alive. It's bad enough for a woman to grow old and lose her looks, so that nobody notices her any more. What do you think it's like when you die, and you can't get any kind of response from anybody? You're nothing; you're invisible. You think that's good for your morale? You don't know how lucky I am that I have a grandson who can actually see me."

He suddenly looked more serious. "Listen, Jim, this thing wants your blood and you're going to have to do one of two things. Either you're going to have to pack your bags and go someplace where it can't follow you; or else you're going to have to find a way of beating it."

Miss Neagle said, "Today was the day you were supposed to die, Jim; and you're not dead yet, are you? So if I were you I'd have courage."

"I'm as good as dead," Jim told her. "So long as that thing is still in this world, it's going to be coming after me."

"Then go," said his grandfather. "It's the only answer. Go."

Jim suddenly realized why his grandfather had said that he was a failure. He *was* a failure. Whenever any kind of challenge appeared on the horizon, his answer had always been to turn on his heel and walk very quickly in the opposite direction. Jim wasn't like that. Jim was his mother's son, and his mother had always stood up for herself. She had refused to help his father when he had started up his marine insurance business, and taught herself to play the piano instead. "If you don't get rich on your own, then you don't deserve to be rich. But you do, and you will, and if I don't learn to play the piano, what will all your rich friends listen to, when we we entertain them at dinner?"

Jim said, "No, grandpa. I'm going to stay. The Native Americans are always talking about tribal honor. Catherine's my student. She belongs to Special Class II. That's enough of a tribe for me to feel honourable about."

His grandfather looked at him for a long time, and then nodded. "That's bravely spoken, Jim. It looks like all I can do is to wish you all the luck in this world; and a hundred times more in the next."

"Goodbye, grandpa," said Jim. "I won't forget this, I promise you."

His grandfather went to the open door and stepped out into the darkness. Jim followed him and watched him walking along the balcony. His image seemed gradually to fade, so that by the time he reached the steps the streetlights were shining right through him. He stopped, turned, and looked back at Jim, and gave him a wave. He hadn't even taken one step downward before he vanished, and there was nothing in the night but streetlights and automobile horns and somebody laughing.

"Jim," said Miss Neagle. "Come down for a beer."

"I don't think so, Valerie. I'm tired enough already."

"But George can't dance any of those Greek dances by himself."

"All right," Jim acquiesced. He guessed that anything would be better than lying on George's couch listening to the icebox rattling all night – unable to sleep, and thinking about Susan's head flying off.

Miss Neagle entwined her arm around his. "I was never sure about Greeks, you know. But then I met George, and I thought to myself, 'What was good enough for Jackie must be good enough for me.' You don't happen to know the Greek for 'I love your beard,' do you?' '

*   *   *

Before he went back to college the next morning he called Susan's brother Bruce, who was a screenwriter who lived in Sherman Oaks.

"Susan's staying in Arizona for a few more days."

"Oh, yes?"

"Well, I thought I'd better tell you, just in case you were worried."

"Why should I be worried? She's a grown-up now, the last time I looked."

"OK, then. But I thought I'd better tell you, that's all."

There was a pause. Then, "There's nothing *wrong*, is there?"

"Wrong, what do you mean?"

"Well, Susan and me, we hardly ever speak to each other. We have a very different view of life, if you understand me. She thinks I'm a trashy materialist and I think she should try sailing round the world with one of her antique maps and see where *that* gets her."

"Oh. Well, OK."

He drove to college feeling strange, mainly because everything looked so normal and familiar. The morning smog hadn't yet cleared and the day had a soft, blurry appearance, like an Impressionist painting. He parked in the faculty parking-lot and waited for his car to backfire, which it didn't. He climbed out, and he had almost reached the main entrance when it let off a tremendous detonation that echoed all around the buildings.

Everybody in the staff room was eager to find out all about his trip to the reservations, but he found it very hard to talk about it. He kept repeating, "Sure, it was great. Fascinating. Susan loved it so much she decided to stay out there for a few more days."

Richard Bercovici, the social studies lecturer, came up smelling strongly of pipe-tobacco. "What was your view of Navajo alcoholism? From what I've read, drunkenness is the blight of the reservations."

Jim said, "I think, Richard – if you saw what I saw, you'd need a drink, too."

At last, however, it was time for his first class, and

he walked with some relief along the corridor to Special Class II. Almost the whole class were already there, except for Jane Firman, who always had difficult periods, and Jim was sensitive enough not to ask where she was. Sue-Robin was finishing off painting her nails in pearlized pink and Sherma was noisily rustling a large brown grocery bag.

"Sherma? Any chance of hearing ourselves think?"

"I'm sorry, Mr Rook. I'm supposed to be baking applesauce cookies with Mrs Evers afterward and I think I forgot my raisins."

Mark was sitting behind David Littwin, looking uncharacteristically pale and subdued – much to the frustration of his best friend Ricky, who kept trying to tell him stupid jokes. "'Doctor, I keep thinking I'm a spaniel.' 'Well, just get up on the couch.' 'I can't. I'm not allowed.'" Sharon was wearing a tight black dress with jet necklaces and black ribbons in her hair. When Jim came in, they both looked at him with the intensity of people who had shared a traumatic experience, and needed very badly to talk about it.

Jim said, "You'll be pleased to hear that our short field trip to Arizona was extremely arduous and that you didn't miss much except some spectacularly breathtaking scenery and some spectacularly disgusting food. We did however learn quite a lot about Navajo mythology and I'm very keen to discover what you were able to find out from your resources here.

"Unfortunately, Catherine White Bird decided to stay on for a while to – well, to visit some people she knew. So we're missing her input, which is a pity. And we're also missing Ms Randall, who wanted to stay for a while, too, so that she could—"

He hesitated, and saw Mark and Sharon looking at him and frowning. He hated lying – especially to his class –

179

but he knew that there was no alternative, not until the Changing Bear Maiden had been exorcized for good.

"– so that she could look for some historical maps, you know what she is about maps."

Beattie McCordic put up her hand and said, "How did you find, like, the way that Navajo women are as opposed to the men? Do you think they're as equal as we are – you knew, here in California – or not so equal?"

"Nobody's as equal as you are, Beattie!" said Seymour Williams.

"Good literary reference," said Jim. "What's it from, Seymour?"

"What?" asked Seymour, in bewilderment.

"George Orwell's *Animal Farm*. 'All animals are equal but some animals are more equal than others.'"

"Oh, right," said Seymour, with a grin, and the whole class hooted in derision.

"Anyway, to answer your question, Beattie, from what I've seen the Navajo woman has a very different standing within her family to that of women in other parts of the country. Navajo men still seem to think that they're the undisputed head of the household. That's a traditional, historical view. But the reality is that there's so much unemployment that it's the women who hold the family unit together – the women who have the strength – the women who make the really fundamental day-to-day decisions."

Mark said, "That may be, but you have to admit that it's pretty tough trying to be a great warrior and hunter and everything when there's nobody to fight and nothing to hunt. I mean, what are you going to do, maraud the 7-Eleven?"

"But let's go back a bit and talk about their history and their mythology," said Jim. "Some of them say that it's the collapse of their magic that led to their present plight.

180

Did anybody manage to find out anything about Navajo legends?"

Sue-Robin said, "I found about a giant demon called Big Monster. He was half as tall as the tallest fir tree, and had an ugly face with blue and black stripes. He wore a suit of armour made from flint stones knitted together with all the guts and the sinews of the people that he killed."

"That's disgusting," said Amanda.

"It's all right," Jim told her. "It's only a story." Thinking, as he said it, of the way that John Three Names' body had been pulled apart, and all his insides emptied onto the floor.

Sue-Robin said, "Big Monster was finally caught by two brave gods called the Twins. They tried to sneak up behind him while he was drinking a large lake, but he saw them reflected in the last drops of water. He shot two enormous arrows at them, but they caught hold of a rainbow and used it as a shield. Big Monster ran after them, but just as he was about to catch up with them, a bolt of lightning struck him dead. The Twins cut off his head and threw it to the east. It took root in the ground, and it's still there today, called Cabezon Peak."

"I found out about Big Monster, too," said Titus, putting up his hand. "There's a web site all about Native American mythology. It said that Big Monster wouldn't have been killed by the lightning, but another demon had cut off all his hair, which left his head unprotected. The other demon was called . . . I wrote it down here someplace . . . Coyote."

Jim felt the back of his neck prickle, as if an insect were crawling down it. "Coyote, huh? Did anybody else find out about Coyote?"

"Hey, I did," said John Ng. "To me, he was one of the most interesting of all the Native American spirits, because there are spirits just like him in Japan and

Vietnam. He was very cunning and tricky, you know? And he really liked human women. He was always chasing after them and trying to get up their skirts. I found this Navajo song that goes: *'One day walking through a mountain pass, Coyote met a young woman. What have you in your pack, she said. Fish eggs. Can I have some? If you close your eyes and hold up your dress. She did as she was told. Higher, said Coyote and stepped out of his britches. Stand still so I can reach the place. I can't there is something crawling between my legs. Don't worry it's a bee, I'll get it. The woman dropped her dress. You weren't fast enough. It stung me.'"*

"Typical male," put in Beattie. "Even when you're demons you can't keep your things to yourselves."

Ricky Herman said, "Play another tune, Beattie." But Jim interrupted and said, "Go on, John. What else did you find out about Coyote?"

"Well, he was different from all the other spirits because he had power over death. This happened because he loved this one woman so much that he agreed to die for her. The only thing was, he buried his lungs, his heart, his blood and his breath deep in the ground, so that he could dig them up again. He died four times for this woman and each time he came back to life again. So in the end the spirits of the underworld said that he would never have to return."

"Presumably, then, he's still alive today?"

"If you believe in spirits, I guess he is. But it says in *Navajo Legends* that he only managed to survive when the white men came by mating with a human woman. Every generation that goes by, he picks the most beautiful Navajo woman that he can find, and gives her a son; and that son is him, too, so that when he dies he's still alive, if you get what I mean.

"In the old days he was so frightening to look at that he

used to wear a coyote skin on his back to disguise himself, which is why he was nicknamed Coyote. His real Navajo name is First One To Use Words For Force. These days, he looks like any ordinary man, except that he has to wear yellow glasses so that people can't see that he has yellow eyes like a dog."

Jim had a sudden flash of Dog Brother, sitting in his trailer. The feathers, the leather pants, the yellow spectacles. John Three Names had lied to him, because he must have known that he wouldn't have taken Catherine to see him if he had suspected the truth.

Dog Brother wasn't a man at all. Or rather, he was only half human. He hadn't needed to find a wonder-worker to put a hex on Catherine. He hadn't needed to call on Coyote. Dog Brother was Coyote.

Jim suddenly realised that John had stopped talking and was looking at him expectantly.

"Go on, John. I'm listening. You've done really well."

John said, "Coyote is supposed to choose his wives on their fifteenth birthday. He cuts his hand and he cuts her hand, and they exchange blood."

"Doesn't he know about HIV?" asked Seymour.

"It's a *legend*, for crying out loud," said Ray. "Legends don't get sick."

"Superman gets sick when he's exposed to Kryptonite," Ricky objected.

"Yeah, but Superman is a comic character, not a legend. Besides, he wouldn't get HIV because he isn't gay."

"He *looks* gay."

"So do you but I don't make a class discussion out of it."

"That's enough," said Jim. "John – you finish telling us what you've found out."

"Once Coyote's blood is flowing inside the woman's

veins, he can control her with magic, wherever she goes, even if she tries to run away from him."

"What did I tell you?" said Beattie. "Typical domineering male behavior."

Jim walked slowly and thoughtfully to the back of the class. "You've done very well. That's all very interesting research. I wonder, though – even though Coyote was apparently exempt from death – did anyone find out if it was possible to get rid of him? Banish him, maybe, to a place where he couldn't escape? Or rob him of some of his magical strength, the way that he cut Big Monster's hair and robbed him of his?"

"*Navajo Legends* says that in the old days, wonder-workers used to call Coyote with a whistle, and they would make bargains with him to defeat any opposing tribes. It says here, 'In 1837 a Navajo wonder-worker whistled up Coyote and agreed to give him five virgins in exchange for invincible strength against the Hopi. The next day the Navajo attacked the village of Oraibi, which had a claim to being the oldest continuously populated community in America, and they wiped out almost everybody living there.'"

He ran his finger down the page, and then he said, "It looks like the only way to deal with Coyote would be to have him killed by one of his fellow-spirits . . . and men dig up his heart before he could, and hide it where he could never find it."

Beattie said, "Mr Rook? I found out about a woman who turned herself into one of those big furry animals that live in the forest." Beattie suffered from anomia, which meant that she had difficulty in remembering what things were called.

"You're talking about the Bear Maiden," said John. "She was the one that Coyote was really in love with."

Jim said, "I don't think we need to discuss Navajo

184

legends any more for today. After this week I'm all Navajoed out. But next week I'd like you all to write a modern-day story based on an old Native American myth. Bring it up to date, so to speak."

"Oh, I see," said Beattie. "Just when we get to women demons we have to stop."

The students gathered up their books and papers and noisily left the class. Jim went back to his desk and looked through his schedule for the rest of the mouth. He was still bent over it when Mark and Sharon came up to him. Both of them looked serious.

"Hi, you two. I think I know what you're going to say."

Sharon said, "What's the story, Mr Rook? Did Ms Randall really have an asthma attack, like you told us back in Arizona, or is she still on the reservation, looking for old maps? Or is it neither?"

"I owe you both an apology," said Jim. "You know how I usually feel about telling the truth. But back there in Window Rock I didn't want to upset you more than I had to."

"What happened?" asked Mark. "Ms Randall's OK, isn't she?"

"I'm going to have to ask you guys to keep this to yourselves, for the same reason I kept it from you. This business with Catherine isn't finished yet, and unless I have freedom of movement I'm not going to be able to help her.

He paused, and then he said, "Ms Randall was involved in an accident. I'm afraid she was killed."

"She's *dead*?" said Sharon, shocked.

"What kind of an accident?" asked Mark.

Jim gave them a small, helpless shrug. "It was something to do with Catherine, but right now I can't really explain it. As soon as I can, though, you'll get the whole story. I promise."

185

"But you told everybody that she was still back in Arizona – even Dr Ehrlichman."

"I know, and when the time comes, I'm going to have to apologize to them, too."

"Jeez," said Mark. "I just can't believe that she's dead. I can still see her face."

Jim laid a hand on his shoulder. "Believe me, Mark, so can I."

Jim was packing up at the end of the day when Dr Ehrlichman came into his classroom. "I'm glad you had an interesting trip, Jim. I have to admit that I wasn't sure about your ethnic adventures to start with. I didn't really see their relevance to remedial English studies. But I've heard some approving noises from the board of education, and I gather that your test results have been improving."

"Communication is communication," said Jim. "I just believe that if everybody in my class can understand each other's background, and what makes them think the way they do, then they're going to be much better at explaining their own background, and their own ideas."

"Well, that's good. That's very good. It seems like *The Los Angeles Times* may even be interested in running a piece about it."

"I think my students could do without that sort of publicity," said Jim. "Between these four walls they don't mind admitting their shortcomings, but they don't want the whole world to be told that they're slow."

"A story like that would do the college good, you know . . . especially after last week's tragedy."

"Well, we'll see. I'll think about it over the weekend."

"We're going to see you tomorrow afternoon, I hope?"

"What for?"

"The game against Azusa tomorrow. Ben Thunkus thinks we have a better-than-even chance of winning."

"You're still going to play? After what happened to Martin?"

Dr Ehrlichman dry-washed his hands with a particularly unpleasant squeak. "I talked to his parents. They're all for it. I talked to the team. They all want to play this game as a tribute to everything that Martin did for them."

"OK . . . if that's the way they feel."

"It is, Jim. It is. And it's the way *I* feel, too. This college has had a very shaky semester, very shaky. I'd like to see us back on track again. Remember the West Grove motto – 'Achievement Through Enjoyment.'"

"I think the student version is 'Getting It All By Having A Ball,'" said Jim.

Dr Ehrlichman said, "I didn't know that, and I wish I didn't know it now."

"I'll see you at the game," Jim told him.

Chapter Nine

Early that evening he drove over to see Henry Black Eagle. A pretty young Hispanic woman was standing on his doorstep, busily polishing his brass doorplate.

"Mr Black Eagle at home?" asked Jim.

"No, *senor*. But you can find him at the Cafe del Rey."

"You seen him today?"

"Sure. He wasn't working today. He said they were shooting around him."

"What kind of mood was he in? Can you tell me that?"

"*Que?*"

"Well, was he happy, cheerful, humming songs? Or was he sad and depressed?"

"He was very itchy."

"He was *itchy*? You mean like scratching himself all the time?"

"No, no, itchy like he was waiting for something. Every time the telephone rings he goes voom! to answer it."

"Voom," Jim repeated, thoughtfully. "OK, that's helpful. Thank you."

He climbed back into his car and drove toward the ocean. It was an hour before sunset and the streets were striped with marmalade light. He turned into Admiralty Way and drove toward the marina with the warm sea air blowing in his hair. If he hadn't been so worried it would have been a perfect evening.

He found Henry Black Eagle sitting at the cafe's dining bar, where singles can look out over the yachts jostling at anchor in the marina and eat in peace. He was halfway through a steak and a fennel salad, with a large glass of red wine. Jim approached him from behind and slipped onto the empty stool next to him.

"How's the steak, Mr Black Eagle? Bloody enough for your taste? Or do you prefer something more like a burnt offering?"

Henry Black Eagle jerked back, his eyes wide with shock.

"Oh, excuse me," said Jim, "did I surprise you?"

"What are you doing here?" asked Henry Black Eagle. Then he looked around the busy cafe as if he were searching for somebody. "Where's Catherine?"

"You want to know what I'm doing here?" Jim told him. "I'm here to settle a score, that's what I'm doing here. As for Catherine – well, mission accomplished, for the most part. I managed to get her to Fort Defiance trailer park and hand her over to her prospective husband, which was exactly what you wanted me to do, wasn't it? The only trouble was, it all got a little messy."

"Messy? What are you talking about?"

"Hasn't your friend John Three Names called you and told you? Well, I'm not totally surprised. Right now, John Three Names looks like that steak probably looks like, inside of your stomach."

"John Three Names is dead?"

"That's right. And so is Susan Randall, who came with me to help look after your daughter."

"How about your students?"

"Oh, thanks for your consideration. They're fit and

189

well, no thanks to you, or to the Changing Bear Maiden, or to First One To Use Words For Force."

"Listen," said Henry Black Eagle, pushing his plate away. "I didn't have any choice. If I hadn't sent Catherine back to Coyote, she would have gone on killing. What was I supposed to do?"

"Sending Catherine back to Coyote was one thing. But you sacrificed the life of a completely innocent woman and you were quite prepared to sacrifice the lives of two completely innocent young people, just to get your sons out of jail."

"That wasn't the only reason, Mr Rook. Coyote knew how much you cared for that woman, and he knew what those students meant to you. He wanted to show you that if you ever set yourself against him, or tried to take Catherine away from him, you would be as good as dead."

"Then he wasn't going to kill *me*?"

"It depends on your definition of death, Mr Rook. He would have killed everybody that you love and destroyed everything that you cherish. That's his way."

"But what for? What the hell have I ever done to him?"

"You're a white man, Mr Rook. That alone would be quite enough. But more than that, he knows that you have the gift of sight. He would have sensed it from the moment you first came near Catherine. His blood runs in her veins, remember."

"And?"

Henry Black Eagle lowered his eyes for a moment and then looked up again and gave Jim a narrow, piercing look. "And he's just a little bit afraid of you, that's what."

"What can I possibly do to him, when he's got the kind of magic that can turn your daughter into a beast like the Changing Bear Maiden?"

190

"He remembers what the white men did to all of the other spirits, Mr Rook. He's alone now, the last spirit who can actually walk on the earth. Maybe 'afraid' is an exaggeration, but he's certainly wary of you. He thinks you must be in contact with the white man's spirits, and he doesn't want to risk offending a demon who might be stronger than him."

Jim looked at Henry Black Eagle for a while and didn't know whether to feel disgusted or sympathetic. In the end, he said, "What are you going to do now?"

"What *can* I do? You've found me out, and I can't even begin to tell you how ashamed I am, how guilty I feel. I will have the death of your woman on my mind for the rest of my life; and the deaths of my sons, too, if the courts find them guilty. If I had known when my wife was dying that this was what would happen if I made a bargain with Coyote, then I would have preferred to have done nothing, and let her die."

"I may have found you out, but there's nothing I can do about it," said Jim. "You haven't broken any laws, have you, except the laws of common humanity."

"My head is bowed," said Henry Black Eagle.

"Well, maybe you can unbow it by helping me to get your daughter back. I think we owe her that much, don't we?"

"It's impossible. Coyote will only transform her into the Changing Bear Maiden again and again, and each time it happens to her, the beast grows larger and the transformation lasts longer. In the end, she will be a beast for ever, and she will have to roam the reservations every night looking for men to kill. Can you imagine what a nightmare that would be? And every fresh killing would be on my conscience, too.

"If we leave her alone, Mr Rook, Coyote will take the curse off her and treat her well. She will be treated with

191

great respect by everybody on the reservation. She will lead a much better life than most Navajo women."

"Mr Black Eagle, that's not the life she wants to lead. We owe it to her to get her away from him."

"It's impossible," Henry Black Eagle repeated. "And who knows what revenge Coyote would take?"

"God almighty," said Jim, "no wonder the Indians lost the West."

"Mr Rook – if I knew how to get my daughter back – if I thought that there was a way to make some kind of amends for what I've done—"

"There is. You can arrange for you and me to fly back out to the reservation tomorrow and we can beard this Coyote character in his den."

"To do *what*? You don't have any idea how powerful he is."

"The legend says that you can keep him under control by having him killed by another spirit and then taking his heart and hiding it from him. You must know some wonder-workers who could conjure up another spirit, surely."

"Grey Cloud does. But even if you could find a wonder-worker who was prepared to do it, you wouldn't find another spirit that would kill Coyote for nothing. Spirits always demand a payment."

"Then maybe a human could kill him. Maybe *we* could kill him."

"I'm sorry, Mr Rook, we wouldn't stand a chance in hell. Nobody challenges Coyote unless they're dead drunk or tired of living."

"I can find a way, I'm sure of it."

Henry Black Eagle lifted his hand to call for the check. After he had paid, he said, "Okay, Mr Rook, I'll arrange two flights tomorrow afternoon. If I can't stop you from going, then the least I can do is go with you. Maybe if the Changing Bear Maiden kills both of us, the police will let Paul and Grey Cloud go free."

Jim scribbled George Babouris' number on a paper coaster. "You can call me here before twelve. After that, you can catch me at college. There's a football game tomorrow afternoon."

Henry Black Eagle stood up and held out his hand. "I don't know what to say to you, Mr Rook. I don't expect you to forgive me. All I ask is that you try to understand."

"Well, there is one thing," said Jim. He lifted the silver whistle out from under his shirt. "What exactly does this thing do?"

"It attracts Coyote's attention. All the old wonder-workers used one, when they wanted to summon him up from the underworld. It's set at the same pitch as a bat's squeak, and in the days before he became half-human, Coyote used to have a taste for bats."

"Let me tell you – we were flying from Albuquerque to Gallup when the airplane lost all of its power. No engines, no electrics at all. Catherine was staring at the controls and I could see the beast's shadow around her. It was a miracle that we didn't nosedive into the forest. But I blew the whistle and it seemed like she woke up, and we got all of our power back. If we'd have hit those trees we would have been dead for sure."

They left the cafe and walked out onto the sidewalk. The sun was melting into the ocean, and a chilly wind was beginning to blow. Waste paper tumbled between the gliding wheels of the day's last rollerbladers, and the sun caught the spokes of a passing bicycle. Henry Black Eagle looked thoughtful.

"What you've said . . . that's very strange. Coyote would have done everything he could to make sure that Catherine reached him safely. He wouldn't have wanted her to crash the plane like that. He didn't want any of you dead until you had reached Window Rock, and he didn't want *you* dead at all.

They walked a little further and then Henry Black Eagle said, "You know, it seems to me that someplace inside of her, Catherine knew what was going to happen to you. After all, she had Coyote's own blood in her veins. She knew what was going to happen to you and she knew that it would be far more terrible than dying quickly in a plane crash. So she used Coyote's own powers to shut down the plane's electrics. He can do that, you know. In the old days, when the white men first set up their telegraph lines, he could silence them just by staring at them, the same way that some men can silence a dog with just a look."

"So when I blew the whistle—"

"That's right. You alerted Coyote, and when he realised what was happening, he stopped her."

"But that means that Catherine has some kind of will of her own, even when she's turning into the Changing Bear Maiden."

"Perhaps. But even if she has, I doubt if Coyote will let her exercise it ever again. Remember what I said. The more times she changes, the more of a beast she becomes."

Jim reached his car. "Call me tomorrow," he said, and Henry Black Eagle nodded. Jim glanced at him in his rear-view mirror as he drove away. He decided that he didn't feel any sympathy for him, not after what he had done, but he did think that he looked like the loneliest man on God's earth.

Jim slept badly that night. He kept dreaming about the thin man with the yellow glasses, and his dream was filled with a stomach-dissolving sense of dread. He thought that he woke up, and looked across the room, and saw a figure in a charred, smoking blanket sitting on the armchair opposite. He thought, God, it's Susan, she isn't dead after all, and he climbed off the couch and approached her. But the blanket-figure didn't move, and he was too frightened to open it to see what was inside it. He reached out his hand but then he woke up and realised that this was a dream, too. He was soaking with sweat and he was shaking.

Over breakfast, George looked at him through the haze of frying bacon and said, "You're looking rough, Jim. After everything's that happened, you ought to take a break, you know that."

"I'm probably going back to Arizona tonight."

"Really? What the hell for?"

"Well, let's just say that I've got some unfinished business."

George sat down opposite and began to fork up mouthfuls of bacon and runny fried eggs. "Don't do anything stupid, Jim. I know you. You've got kamikaze written all over you."

"Oh, and you don't think that a 4,000-calorie breakfast is suicidal?"

"Jim – I have to keep my strength up. That Valerie, I'll tell you. She's a very demanding woman."

"You haven't—?"

"She kept me dancing till ten after two. Polka, foxtrot, waltz, shimmy, shake, Charleston, twist, frug, locomotion, turkey trot, you name it."

"You enjoyed it, didn't you?"

"Sure I enjoyed it. And let me tell you something else. I think I'm in love."

Jim left him to his bacon and eggs and drove to the college. After last night's dreams he wanted to take another look through the book that John Ng had been reading – *Navajo Legends*. He needed to know as much

195

as he could about Coyote's possible weaknesses – his vanities, his petty jealousies, the way he played tricks. He was convinced that the only way to beat a deceiver was to out-deceive him.

The college campus was almost deserted this morning, apart from three or four students who were hanging up the bunting for this afternoon's game. West Grove had a long-standing grudge against Azusa Commmunity College, mostly because Azusa had never beaten them by less than 38 to 7. Jim looked up as he crossed toward the college building. The sky was strange, with heavily-building clouds. He had a feeling that something threatening was in the air.

He walked along the wax-polished corridor toward Special Class II. Mr Wallechinsky, the security guard, was just coming out of Sue Randall's room, and locking the door behind him.

"Ah – Mr Rook! Any idea when Ms Randall's coming back? She borrowed a projector from the science department and I know they're pretty keen to have it returned."

"I think she's going to be a few more days yet, Mr Wallechinsky. Why don't you just give it back to them?"

"Sure thing."

Jim unlocked his classroom and opened the door. Immediately, he stopped dead. The room had been totally wrecked. All of the desks had been toppled over, and some of them had been completely dismembered. Personal computers lay everywhere, their screens smashed, their keyboards ripped apart, their printers crushed. The portraits of Shakespeare and Mark Twain and Walt Whitman had been pulled from the walls and torn apart. The fluorescent lights dangled down from the ceiling. Jim's own desk had been tipped on one side and its contents strewn all over the floor.

Worst of all, though, were the marks on the walls. There were criss-cross gouges everywhere, like the gouges of giant claws. Whole furrows of plaster had been dragged out, in deep parallel stripes, and one clawmark went right through the frame of the blackboard, and across its surface – not just scratching it but cutting it almost through to the wall behind.

Jim took two or three steps into the room, and sniffed, the way that Mrs Vaizey would have sniffed. He could pick it up now. Animal – or maybe two different animals. The heavy funky smell of bear, and the sharper, rancid odour of wild dog. He picked up a first edition, his own, of John Peale Bishop's *Green Fruit*. His father had given it to him when he had graduated. Now its spine was broken and half of its pages fell out onto the floor.

She's here, he thought to himself. It had never occurred to him that she might follow him back to Los Angeles, but she obviously had. She's here, and she's making sure that I suffer.

He heaved his desk back onto its feet. For some reason, it had never occurred to him that the Changing Bear Maiden might come after him. No wonder his grandfather had been warned him to go away – as quick as he could and as far as he could. Coyote was obviously not willing to forgive and forget, even though he had now had his bride-to-be, and he had no reason to suspect that Jim would try to set her free. Although maybe he did. Maybe he had sniffed out in Jim that burning sense of consideration that had made him want to teach a remedial class in the first place. Maybe he knew that Jim would never let Catherine go.

Jim started picking up chairs and desks, one by one. The floor was strewn with ripped-up poems and essays

197

and broken glass. God knows it was hard enough for most of these students to write one coherent sentence. Now most of their semester's laborious work had been thrown all over the floor. Jim picked up Mark Foley's essay on Rip van Winkle: 'Rip van Winkle let his childrin run wile they never wore no shos and his suns pants was alus fallin down.' When he thought of the essays that Mark was capable of writing now, only a few months later, it really hurt him that somebody could have treated his first efforts with such disrespect. He picked up another sheet and it was Mark's latest piece of work on Walt Whitman: "Walt Whitman was gay. He kissd dyin soldiers durin the Cival War which was part human but it exited him too. Still he loved his mother and was never rude about women. He rote about 'a merry housefull of young ladies' and 'I never saw so many fine-looking grey hair'd women . . . such as no time or land but ours could show.' "

Mark's spelling was still erratic, but his ability to read and to *comment* on what he had read had increased enormously. Henry Black Eagle had been right: Coyote knew how to attack his enemies where it hurt. He knew what they valued the most, and he had no compunction about destroying it.

He was still picking up papers and books and pieces of broken glass when Mr Wallechinsky came in. "What the hell happened here?" he demanded.

"Our vandal came back," said Jim.

"Look at the state of this place. I don't believe it. I only looked in here about an hour ago."

"And you didn't hear anything, and you didn't see anybody?"

"Only that big fat student of yours – what's his name, Gloach?"

"Russell Gloach, that's right. And I'd prefer it if you

198

didn't call him big and fat. Think of some other way to describe him. Like, think of his hair."

"OK, I saw that big fat crewcut student of yours. He was in here maybe fifteen minutes ago."

"Anybody else?"

"I don't know. Let me see . . . there were two or three of them wandering in and out. That Indian girl, she was one of them."

"Catherine White Bird? Catherine White Bird was here?"

"I saw her with my own eyes, walking down the corridor. She was brushing her hair."

"Do you have any idea where she went afterward?"

"How should I know? Wherever it was, though, she wasn't in any kind of a hurry."

She's back, thought Jim. And now she's come to get me.

"OK, Mr Wallechinsky," he said. "Take it easy. Let's lock this room up for now."

"You don't want me to clean it up?"

"No, I want you to leave it just the way it is. After the game this afternoon I'm going to call the cops, and I don't want any of this evidence swept up or tampered with."

"In that case, maybe you should stop tidying it up yourself, Mr Rook. I bet by now you've left so many fingerprints they're going to be able to prove that *you* did it."

Jim dropped Mark's essay on Whitman onto the floor. "You're right," he said. "But there's something I *am* going to tidy up."

He went back outside and walked around the buildings, but there was no sign of Catherine anywhere. He went down to the football field. Greg Lake was there, sitting on the bleachers talking to Sherri Hakamoto.

"Hi, Mr Rook. Looking forward to the game this afternoon?"

Jim shaded his eyes with his hand and peered all the way around the field.

"You seen Catherine today?"

Greg's face went through a complicated series of contortions before finally deciding to look mildly puzzled. "Catherine? No. I thought she was still in Arizona."

"Well, so did I, Greg, but apparently not. By the way, I'm going to have to ask you to stay out of the home room today. There's been some more vandalism."

"Hey, none of my stuff's been damaged, has it? I left all my project in there."

"I don't know. You'll have the chance to look later. But meanwhile, keep an eye out for Catherine, will you?"

"Okay, Mr Rook."

Jim borrowed Mr Wallechinsky's spare set of keys and spent the next twenty minutes combing the college grounds. Because it was Saturday, many of the buildings were locked, but he checked the art studio, the design block and the gym complex. He even searched the girls' locker-rooms (making sure he shouted "halloo!" loudly before he went in). He opened Catherine White Bird's locker but there was nothing inside it to suggest that she was back. Books, magazines, T-shirts, cosmetics – as well as cut-out pictures of fashion models and moody-looking young rock stars. Kurt Cobain grinned from beside her mirror, and Jim thought, if you think that what happened to *you* was bad . . . wait till you see what the Changing Bear Maiden can do.

In the end, he had to give it up. He gave Mr Wallechinsky's keys back and went to the faculty lounge and picked up the phone. He waited and waited and at last Henry Black Eagle answered.

"Mr Black Eagle? Jim Rook. No, it doesn't matter that you haven't booked the tickets yet. No, I'm glad that you didn't. We don't need to go to Arizona. Catherine's here."

"What do you mean?" asked Henry Black Eagle, in a chilled voice.

"Catherine's here. My classroom's wrecked, the same way the locker room and my apartment were. Our security man told me that he saw her in the corridor."

"But don't you see – now that's he got her – Coyote wouldn't let Catherine out of his sight."

"I don't understand."

"It's simple, Mr Rook. If Catherine's here, then Coyote must be here, too."

"I hope you're kidding me."

"No, Mr Rook. I've told you how possessive he is."

"So what do you think he wants?"

"I think, Mr Rook, that you must have left him feeling very angry. Coyote likes to think of himself as the trickster, not the tricked. He might be wary of you, as I said, but it looks as if he's come to show you who's boss."

"I don't understand it. Why should he bother? I'm only one white man."

"He's seen how much you care for your students, Mr Rook. Maybe he knows that you're not going to rest until you get Catherine away from him."

Jim thought: that can't be the whole story. Even if I came after Catherine, Coyote could set the Changing Bear Maiden on me, or use all kinds of magic to kill me before I could get anywhere near him. He doesn't have anything to fear from me, not really. So why has he come all this way to hunt me down?

201

And then it occurred to him. Maybe he *does* have something to fear – something that he knows about but I don't. Maybe I *can* kill him, after all.

It must be something to do with the fact that I can see spirits. Not only white man's spirits, but Native American spirits, too.

"Are you still there?" Henry Black Eagle asked him, impatiently.

"Yes, yes, I'm still here. Listen, I'll tell you what I want you to do for me. Go see Paul and Grey Cloud and ask them which Native American spirit is Coyote's deadliest enemy. Ask them which spirit could be most easily persuaded to kill him."

"There are many. I don't know them all."

"Well, go ask your sons. Then come up to the college, and make it as quick as you can."

"But Mr Rook—"

"No buts, Mr Black Eagle. You owe me. And more than that, you owe your daughter, too. This could be the only way of saving her."

The Azusa team and their supporters arrived in a procession of coaches and people carriers just after twelve. Dr Ehrlichman had arranged a cookout under the trees on the north side of the college, and the air was already pungent with the smell of mesquite. Jim circled the school grounds, his coat slung over his shoulder, looking from right to left for any sign of Catherine or Coyote. If they were still around, they were keeping themselves well out of the way, but Jim was sure that he could sense their presence. He kept seeing furtive movements behind the trees, and flickering shadows where no shadows ought to be cast. He felt a prickling sensation in his skin, too, and thought of *Macbeth*: '*By the pricking of my thumbs, Something wicked this way comes.*'

He walked between the wooden picnic tables where the West Grove team were eating their lunch. Mitch Magro, the new captain, was trying to work the Fumblers up into a serious fighting mood. "We owe this to Martin, OK? He didn't die so that we could lose to Azusa. He trained us, didn't he? He really inspired us. So we're going to go out there this afternoon and we're going to beat the living crap out of those guys.

"If we catch it, we run with it. If it hurts, we think how bad Martin got hurt. If we feel like giving up, we don't. I'm going to tell you this: I would rather die than lose this game, and I want you all to feel the same way."

Russell Gloach was sitting a little way apart from the others, cutting up a bunless hamburger into very small pieces.

"How's the struggle going, Russell?" Jim asked him.

"Oh, great. I love these diet burgers. It's just that I could eat about four hundred of them."

"Come on, Russell. You're doing good."

"I'm weak, Mr Rook, I promise you. I'm so goddamned weak I can hardly stand up, let alone play football. I haven't had a Twinkie since two weeks Tuesday. I can't remember what peanut butter tastes like."

"Listen, Russell," said Jim. "Something pretty weird is happening here today. Catherine's back."

"What's weird about that?"

"Well, she's not exactly herself. She's having some kind of a breakdown. The point is, if you see her, I want you to make sure that you grab hold of her and send somebody off to find me."

"Grab hold of her? Supposing she doesn't want to be grabbed hold of? Especially by me. Why don't you get Brad Kaiser instead?"

"Grab hold of her all the same. And for God's sake don't let her go."

Russell said, "You're right. This *is* weird. Do you want to tell me what's going down here, or what?"

"I'm not at all sure," Jim told him. "But I'm worried that it's something real bad."

"It's not like that voodoo business, is it? I mean that scared me. I had nightmares about that for weeks."

"I don't know. But if I can depend on you to grab Catherine if you see her, and to tell me if anything really bizarre happens—"

"Sure thing, Mr Rook. I'll do it. You don't have to worry about me."

It was then that Jim looked up and saw a figure silhouetted between the trees. The air was hazy with barbecue-smoke, and a lot of students and parents were coming and going, right across his field of sight. He looked again, and frowned, because the woman had disappeared, but all the same he said, "Excuse me," to Russell, left the table, and began walking right toward the trees. He stopped, and looked around. He caught the faintest smile of white musk on the wind, as well as that tingle of psychic electricity. He thought he could hear a hand-slapped drumbeat, too: one beat, then a pause, then another beat.

He went back to the table. Russell had already finished his hamburger and was writing down how many calories he had consumed on his diet chart.

"They tell us to be totally honest – just like this was confession or something."

"What happens if you secretly eat a whole pack of Reece's Pieces? What happens then?"

Russell flushed. It was obvious to Jim that he *had* eaten a whole pack of Reece's Pieces, or something similar, and kept it all to himself.

"You jog five times round the football field and hope you've burned it all off, that's all. These diets, these days they're very forgiving."

"OK . . . but just remember this. Forgiving is not a mood I want to see from you this afternoon. I want you to go out there and kill those guys. You're a battering-ram, Russell. I want you to batter. I want people in twenty years to say, 'Do you remember that Saturday? That was the Saturday that Russell Gloach single-handedly road-rollered Azusa into the turf. He was great. He was like a one-man elephant stampede.'"

"You watch me," grinned Russell.

But Jim said, "Something else may happen, too. Something totally unexpected. And if that happens, I want you to be ready for that, too."

"Something unexpected? Like what?"

"Like – I don't know. As bad as that voodoo thing, maybe worse."

Russell suddenly looked serious. "You mean this, don't you, Mr Rook?"

"Yes, Russell, I do. Today isn't going to be a normal day, believe me. Look at those clouds, over in the east. The wind has changed around. Whatever happens this afternoon, remember your class, remember your friends, and do whatever you think is right."

"I'm not sure I get it, Mr Rook."

"You'll get it when the time comes, believe me."

"OK, Mr Rook." He stared down sadly at his empty plate. "Do you know what I used to have for breakfast, only six weeks ago? Two peanut butter and jelly sandwiches, with crispy bacon and french-fried potatoes."

"That's what killed Elvis," said Jim.

"Oh, sure, I know that. I wouldn't go so far as that. I made sure I had a tomato and a lettuce-leaf with it."

By three o'clock, when the game was due to kick off,

205

the sky had become completely overcast. In the distance, over the Santa Monica mountains, lightning was flashing behind the clouds like a curtained-off photo-booth. The West Grove college band was playing *Pasadena* as if they were anxious to get it over with, and their pom-pom girls were leaping and strutting. There was a strong smell of electricity in the air.

Jim sat on the bleachers at the south end of the field and kept on checking his watch. Henry Black Eagle hadn't turned up yet, but he tried to tell himself not to be so anxious. There was no sign of Coyote or Catherine, and for all he knew they had decided that it was enough to vandalize Jim's classroom, without causing any further damage. But he didn't want to bet on it.

Just as West Grove kicked off, George Babouris arrived, with Valerie Neagle. George was wearing a purple windbreaker that was two sizes too tight for him and Valerie Neagle was dressed in a leopard-print dress with a *décolletage* that was two inches too low for her age. As the crowd stood up and applauded, Jim manoeuvered his way next to Valerie and said, "Hi. You're looking very striking."

"Why, thank you," said Valerie, and printed a big red kiss on his right cheek. "I always knew you had taste."

"Listen," said Jim, "this isn't really the time and the place, but I wondered if I could talk to Mrs Vaizey?"

Valerie blinked her mascara-speckled eyelashes at him. "You want to talk to Mrs Vaizey? What about?"

"Something's going to happen here today . . . something bad. I need Mrs Vaizey to talk to the spirit world for me."

Valerie's next words were drowned in a roar of applause as Azusa scored their first goal. George covered his face with his hands and Ray Vito, who was sitting three rows behind them, let out a long string of Italian expletives, many of them involving mothers and hunchbacks and paraplegics.

"What did you say?" asked Jim.

"I said that Mrs Vaizey has left me. She decided that it was time for her to fade away."

"*Now*? She decided to fade away *now*?"

Valerie shrugged. "I couldn't stop her, Jim. She said she'd clung on long enough, and it was all becoming too tiring for her."

"But *now*? Just when I really need her?"

"I'm sorry, Jim. She was talking to your grandfather, and they both faded away together."

Jim said, "I don't believe this. They both warned me that I was in danger. They both predicted that I was going to be killed. And now they've gone, and left me to face up to this situation on my own."

"Mrs Vaizey left a message for you."

"Oh, yes? What was it? 'Rest in peace'?"

"No. She said that you really didn't need her any longer. You had powers enough of your own. She said that you ought to have faith in yourself, and what you can do."

"That's terrific. The trouble is, I don't *know* what I can do. I was very much hoping that Mrs Vaizey could tell me."

"Well, search me," said Valerie. "That's all she said. Then she just . . . melted away, you know? I had the sweetest sensation – the sweetest, most blissful sensation – and she was gone."

"We've scored!" George bellowed, so close to Jim's ear that it almost burst his eardrum. "Magro's scored! Did you see that run! That boy's a genius!"

Jim took hold of Valerie's hand and kissed her.

"Thanks, Valerie. If you ever feel Mrs Vaizey again, you can tell her how much I miss her."

He sat down again. The afternoon was even darker now, and the clouds began to trail across the sky like sheets soaked in Indian ink. George said, "Hope it doesn't rain. I've left my sandals out in the yard."

"Your sandals?"

"They're Greek. I bought them in Agnos Ioannis. They're great so long as you never get them wet. Otherwise they curl up like dried fish."

While George was talking, Jim looked across the football field, past the ducking, tackling, helmeted players – past the crowd of supporters from Azusa, waving Azusa Community College pennants and banners. Standing at the very top of the bleachers on the opposite end of the field were two dark figures, almost silhouetted against the threatening sky. Catherine White Bird, her long hair flying loose, in a big-shouldered black leather coat; and Dog Brother, in a long grey poncho, his eyes concealed by yellow-tinted glasses. Coyote, the First One To Use Words For Force, here at West Grove Community College.

Jim said, "You'll have to excuse me, George," and pushed his way along the row of cheering West Grove students until he reached the aisle. He kept his eyes on Dog Brother and Catherine as he circled the football field. He wasn't sure whether they had seen him or not, but the likely betting was that they had.

"Hi, Mr Rook!" said Sue-Robin Caufield, as she jiggled her pom-poms by the touchline. "Isn't this a great game? Isn't that Azusa full-back just swoony? I think I'm going to the wrong college. For boys, anyway," she quickly corrected herself. "Not for education."

Jim gave her a smile and a nod, although he hardly heard her. One of Azusa's guards had ducked through

208

the West Grove defence for a touchdown, and suddenly everybody was on their feet. For a moment he lost sight of Dog Brother and Catherine, and he had to keep jumping up to see if he could catch sight of them. But then a last ray of sunshine reflected like a heliograph from from Dog Brother's yellow glasses, and he located them again. He didn't quite know what he was going to do when he reached them, but they were dangerous, both of them, and he didn't want them here at West Grove, threatening his students.

He had almost reached the other end of the field when he felt a tremendous slap on the back. He turned around and instinctively lifted his arm to protect himself, but it was only Ben Hunkus, the football coach. "What a game, Jim! I got a feeling in my water we're going to win this one! Pass it, Beidermeyer, for Christ's sake, you're not married to the damn thing!"

"Ben, I want you to keep your eyes open," said Jim. "The person who killed Martin is here."

"You know who it is? I thought it was them Indian boys."

"No, it wasn't. But I can't explain who really did it, not just yet."

"Just give me the name, Jim, and I'll have my boys pile on top of him, until you can call the cops."

"Not as easy as that, Ben. All you can for now is to watch out for anything unusual."

"OK, Jim. Whatever you say."

Jim had reached the bleachers where Dog Brother and Catherine were sitting. As he climbed the aisle, however, West Grove were awarded another four downs, with only 15 yards to go to the Azusa goal line. The crowd stood up in unison, and started cheering and whistling and chanting, and in the confusion he lost sight of Dog Brother and Catherine for a second time.

209

He picked the row in which he guessed they were standing, and elbowed his way along it. "Pardon me, excuse me. Sorry. Pardon me. Sorry."

When he reached the place where he had last seen them, however, they were gone. He desperately looked all around him. He caught the arm of a large man with a golfing hat on backward, so that his hair sprouted out of the front. "Pardon me, sir. Did you see two people standing here a moment ago? A girl in a black coat and a man with a pair of yellow sunglasses."

The man turned around and looked behind him as if he expected them to be hiding behind his enormous rump. Then he looked back at Jim and dumbly shook his head.

Jim pushed his way further along the row. Azusa had regained control of the ball and the excitement had subsided. As everybody sat down again, Jim was able to see all around the field. He couldn't understand how Dog Brother and Catherine could have escaped without his seeing them.

Well, he thought, there's one sure-fire way to find out where they are.

He lifted the whistle from around his neck and blew it. The large man in the golfing hat stared at him in dull curiosity. He waited, his eyes scanning the field and the college grounds beyond. Nothing – no sign of Dog Brother or Catherine anywhere. He blew the whistle again, and then again.

It was then that Dog Brother raised both his arms and Jim caught sight of them, although he couldn't believe where they were. They were standing on the opposite side of the field, only a few rows away from the place where Jim had been talking to George Babouris. It was impossible. Nobody could have made their way all around the field in only a few seconds, not even an Olympic runner. Yet there they were, and now they knew for sure that he was here, and that he was watching them.

At that moment, Jim began to understand the immense occult power of what he was up against, and for the first time in a long time he felt profoundly afraid.

Chapter Ten

He climbed down from the bleachers and walked toward the college buildings. The sky was completely dark now, and a strong wind was buffeting the bushes. He wasn't at all sure what he was going to do. He couldn't call the police, because he couldn't prove that Dog Brother and Catherine had done anything wrong. And now that Mrs Vaizey had faded away, he couldn't even call on his only adviser from the spirit world.

He had almost reached the main entrance when Henry Black Eagle appeared from the direction of the parking-lot, dressed in his black fringed buckskin jacket and wearing a headband. He was carrying a small rolled-up parcel of buffalo-hide, tied tightly with waxed cords and decorated with faded old feathers.

"I managed to talk to Paul and Grey Cloud," he said. "They're both very worried that Coyote has come here. He's very vengeful, you know, and they think that he intends to kill many people to show you that he is greater than all of your white man's spirits."

"Did they give you any ideas how to stop him?"

"They say the same as all of the legends. Coyote must be killed by one of his own kind, and his heart must be taken away from him. The only spirit who hates Coyote more than he fears him is the Rain Spirit. The story says that Coyote tricked his daughter into having sex with him, and that after she had done so, she died of shame, because she was supposed to be keeping herself pure for a noble hunter called Deer Slayer."

"So how do we go about enlisting the help of this Rain Spirit?"

Henry Black Eagle lifted the buffalo-hide bundle. "In here, there are sacred bones which Grey Cloud brought back from the Wide Ruins reservation. They were used to call the Rain Spirit in times of drought. This time we shall have to ask him to do us another kind of favour."

"Won't he want something in return?"

Henry Black Eagle said, "Yes. He will want a gift. What do you think you could offer him?"

"It depends what kind of gift he likes. I mean, what do you give to a Rain Spirit who's probably got everything?"

"You could give him your gift of supernatural vision."

"He'd really take it?"

"Why not? It's a gift like any other. One man gave his singing voice to the Buffalo Spirit, in exchange for bringing his family plenty to eat."

Jim frowned. When he first discovered that he could see spirits, he would have given his vision away to anybody who could have taken it, and been glad to be rid of it. But now it seemed so natural and normal that it would be like having one eye taken out. All the same, a man could still see with one eye, and what was important was saving Catherine and ridding the world of Coyote.

"All right," he said. "He can have my vision, if he wants it. I don't really have anything else."

"You're lucky you have that," Henry Black Eagle told him. "Sometimes a spirit will ask for a hand or a foot, or even a man's virility."

"The vision, OK? He can have the vision."

"Then we must hurry," said Henry Black Eagle. "Have you seen Coyote and Catherine here already?"

213

"The last time I saw them was in the crowd. I tried to go after them, but when I got to where they were standing, they were way over on the opposite side of the field."

"What would you have done, even if you *had* caught up with them?"

Jim shrugged. "I don't know. I hadn't really thought it through."

"With Coyote, you *must*. He is too cunning to be faced head-on. Now, let's get under those cedars, and see what we can do to call up the Rain Spirit."

There was more cheering from the football field as Russell Gloach caught a perfect 20-yard pass from Micky McGuiver.

"Run with it, Russell!" the captain was screaming. "Get those goddamned legs moving!"

Jim didn't try to see what was happening. He could imagine Russell lumbering along at his usual elephantine pace, and knew that he would be lucky to cover more than a yard before the Azusa quarter-backs brought him down. He followed Henry Black Eagle to the three tall cedars which stood on a rise at the north-west corner of the college. Underneath their overhanging branches it was quiet and dark and sheltered from the wind.

Henry Black Eagle sat cross-legged on the ground and untied the buffalo-hide parcel. Jim stood beside him and watched. "I'm not a wonder-worker myself," said Henry Black Eagle, "so I will have to rely on *your* spiritual gifts to contact the Rain Spirit. All I can do is to perform the ritual."

He rolled the hide out flat. Inside were five yellowed bones, which looked to Jim like old human arm-bones. The ends of each of them were tied with hanks of hair and faded red ribbons. Henry Black Eagle picked up two of them and tapped them together, in a quick, hesitant rhythm.

"Sit in front of me," he instructed Jim. "Empty your mind of any thoughts about Coyote and Catherine. Empty your mind of any thoughts about yourself – any fears, any questions, any doubts. Your mind should become as dark and as empty as the universe beyond the stars, where there are no more stars, only blackness, and that is where the Great Old Ones live, far beyond the reach of men."

Jim eased himself cross-legged onto the dry turf. He hadn't sat like this since he had last eaten at Koto, the Japanese restaurant, and then he had spent the rest of the evening walking like Groucho Marx. Henry Black Eagle tapped the bones again, and then again, and each time the rhythm because faster and more frenzied. He began to hum, and then to sing, both in Navajo and in English.

"The Rain Spirit walks in the west . . . He lives on top of the highest mountains, wrapped in clouds for a cloak . . . He carries water in his cloak and spreads it on the dry ground . . . He is generous and just, the protector of all life . . . We ask him now to appear so that we may honour him, and to ask of him a special favor . . ."

This went on and on, in a monotonous warbling sing-song. Jim didn't need to make much of an effort to empty his mind – Henry Black Eagle's singing was so hypnotic that it emptied it for him. He kept his eyes open, but he could feel all conscious thought sliding out of his head. Soon there was nothing but blackness and emptiness.

"Rise now, O Rain Spirit and lend us your strength . . . Rise up, so that we may see you . . . Throw back your cloak of clouds and stand in front of us, so that we can witness your return . . . Rise up, Rain Spirit! Rise up! Rise up!"

Henry Black Eagle was chanting this so loudly that two passing students stopped to give Jim and him the most peculiar looks. But they had hardly turned away when there was a blinding flash of lightning and a deafening

215

crack, and the cedar tree under which they were sitting was split halfway down its trunk, and instantly burst into flames.

"Henry! For God's sake, let's get out of here!" Jim shouted, trying to untangle his legs.

But Henry Black Eagle stayed where he was, tapping and tapping the bones, murmuring and singing, while sparks drifted down all around him, and the cedar tree crackled and spat.

Several people started running toward them. It was then, however, that Henry Black Eagle lifted the bones right over his head and let out a howl like a triumphant animal.

"Let us see you, O Rain Spirit! Let us see you! Rise up and be our guardian! Rise up and be our protector!"

As he clacked the bones together one last time, the ground shook with the reverberation of a massive peal of thunder, like all the kettle-drums of all the orchestras in the world, all rolling at once. Even before the first helpers could reach them, rain came blasting out of the sky in a vicious, slanting torrent that almost stopped them in their tracks. The rain drowned the fire in the cedar tree and came rattling down through the branches. Jim looked down toward the football field, and he could see some people running for cover and others holding coats or newspapers over their heads. The game, however, was still going on. West Grove and Azusa were battling for their honour, and neither team was going to let a rainstorm put them off. West Grove were looking for their first victory this season, and Azusa were determined not to be beaten by the Fumblers at any cost. Swathes of rain trailed across the football field like soaking-wet net curtains, and in only a few minutes the grass was half-flooded. The players dodged and kicked and scrimmaged in showers of spray, with rain dripping from their helmets and water spraying from their boots.

Jim yelled at Henry Black Eagle, "What the hell's going on? There's plenty of rain, but where's the Rain Spirit?"

"Believe!" Henry Black Eagle shouted back at him. "You have to believe!"

The rain was so heavy now that Jim could barely see the football field. It spouted off the college guttering and filled up the rosebeds beside the main entrance, until muddy water started to pour over the top of the brickwork and run down the path toward the parking-lot. Many parents and supporters had convertibles, and they had all rushed to the parking-lot to put up their tops.

Another devastating crack of lightning jumped across the sky, and then the ground shook again.

"*Believe!*" screamed Henry Black Eagle. "*You have to believe!*"

Jim stood up and walked out from under the cedar tree. He was instantly soaked in freezing rain – his coat hanging from him, his hair plastered flat against his forehead. There *is* a Rain Spirit, he said to himself. There *is* a Rain Spirit and I believe in him. I have the gift. I have the vision. I believe in him and I can see him. I believe in him and—

I can see him!

There, in the pouring rain, right in front of him, Jim could make out the watery outlines of a tall creature – almost like a man, yet not a man at all. It had a proud, remote face, as colourless as rain, and a body swathed in tumbling, smoking cloud.

Jim felt its power – cold and sharp and stinging like the rain itself. He had never believed that such spirits existed – that the elements themselves were controlled by living, thinking beings. But here in front of him was the proof,

217

its watery features wavering and pale and distorted, a face from the times when America was being created out of rock and wind and water.

He dropped to his knees on the grass. He felt exhausted and humble. He felt as if everything he had ever taken for granted had been swept away, like the mud and the leaves that were being swept away by the Rain Spirit's storm.

Henry Black Eagle came up and laid a hand on his shoulder. "You can see him, can't you?" he said.

Jim nodded. "He's there. He's just like the rain."

"You don't know how much I envy you," said Henry Black Eagle. "To see what a spirit can do, that's one thing. Rain, thunder, lightning, that's impressive enough. But to see a spirit's face—"

"What do we do now?" Jim asked him. "How do we get him to kill Coyote?"

"We ask. That's the only way."

Henry Black Eagle knelt down beside him and raised both hands. "O great spirit," he said, "we have been wronged by the First One To Use Words For Force. He is here today, with my daughter, Catherine White Bird, whose hand he wants to take in marriage. He has deceived me in the same way that he deceived you, O spirit. For my sake, and for my daughter's sake, I beg you to kill him for me, and take away his heart."

Jim kept his eyes on the Rain Spirit but he didn't see any response. The spirit continued to drift in the rain, its cloud-cloak billowing and fuming. Sometimes it was almost impossible to see if there was anything there at all.

"Please, great spirit. I abase myself in front of you." And with that, Henry Black Eagle laid himself flat on the ground, his arms outstretched, while the rain continued to pour down on top of him.

A black senior called Mo Sharp came up to Jim, his

college T-shirt soaking. Mo was academically slow, but he was almost a genius at cabinet-making. "You okay, Mr Rook?" he asked, looking down suspiciously at Henry Black Eagle.

"Sure, Mo, everything's cool. You get back down there and cheer us on."

"Never saw it rain like this before, Mr Rook."

"No, well, neither did I. Maybe you should start building us an Ark."

Another crackle of lightning lit up the falling rain like a strobe light. Mo scampered off and Jim turned back to the Rain Spirit. It looked to Jim as if he were fading, as if his cloud-cloak were breaking into fragments.

"You have to help us!" he shouted. "You can't leave us to fight Coyote alone! You have to help us! I've got the gift of vision! You can have that, if you kill Coyote for us!"

Jim heard a blur of words in his mind. It was like somebody with a very deep voice whispering very close to his ear. Henry Black Eagle lifted himself from the ground, and said, "Thank you, great spirit. Thank you."

"What?" Jim wanted to know.

"The Rain Spirit has agreed to do it. He will kill Coyote for us. All he wants in return is your gift of vision and one of my fingers."

"You're kidding me. One of your *fingers*?"

"Mr Rook – it will be a very small price to pay to get my daughter back."

"But you can't let it take one of your fingers!"

Henry Black Eagle lifted up his right hand. "It already has," he said. His middle finger was missing, except for a quarter-inch stump of broken bone. Blood was pouring down the back of his hand and into his sleeve.

Jim touched his forehead. "He hasn't taken my vision yet, has he?"

"Not until he has killed Coyote. He wants you to see him doing it."

Jim heard more blurred words. Henry Black Eagle dragged a handkerchief out of his pocket and wrapped it around his hand. "We should follow him," he said. "He is going to find Coyote and rip his heart out."

The blurry Rain Spirit turned around and began to move down the slope toward the football field. The rain was still driving down just as fiercely as before, and Jim found it difficult to follow it. It kept fading away, and then reappearing, no more substantial than a drift of smoke from a garden fire.

They followed it all the way around the back of the bleachers, until it reached the far side of the field. There – almost alone at the very top – stood Dog Brother, his hair streaked with rain, and Catherine, with her collar turned up. Jim walked up the rows of bleachers and stood in front of them, with rain pouring from his chin like a faucet.

"So – what do you want?" asked Dog Brother. "Haven't you caused me enough trouble?"

"I've come for Catherine," said Jim. "If you let Catherine go, then maybe I'll let you go."

"I came here to kill you," said Dog Brother. Droplets of water quivered on his yellow-lensed spectacles. "I came here to destroy everything you touch and everybody you love. Your class of young people are going to die first. Then I'm going to kill anyone who ever meant anything to you, *ever*. Remember your cousin Laura, whom you loved so much? You remember that poem you wrote her, *My Golden Girl*, and she couldn't even read? You'll know what's happened to Laura in the next few days, when your mother's sister calls you up and tells you that she's dead."

"What are you trying to do to me?" Jim yelled at him.

Dog Brother grinned. "Nothing that you white people didn't do to me. You killed my people, and when you killed my people, you killed me. Well, now it's *your* turn to find out what it's like."

Jim turned to Catherine. Her long hair was dripping in the rain and she looked extremely pale. "Catherine," he appealed. "Are you just going to stand by and see innocent people killed?"

"And not just any innocent people," smiled Dog Brother. "Your fellow-students, Catherine. Your precious Special Class II, where you've been learning to forget the Navajo way and the Navajo beliefs – where you've been learning to forget *me*."

"If you harm any one of my students—" Jim began, but Dog Brother raised his hand. It was a long, narrow hand – more like a claw than a hand, with a thin, hairy wrist. Dog Brother said, "I'm going to slaughter them all, Mr Rook. David and Sharon and Muffy and Mark. There's going to be so much blood, you'll think that you're drowning in it."

"Catherine," said Jim. "Catherine, please. Think what you're doing. Those are your friends he's talking about. He wants to murder all of your friends."

Catherine turned her face away but Jim could have sworn that he saw a flicker of response.

"Catherine," he repeated. "Listen to me, Catherine."

"You can't stop me," said Dog Brother. "Your spirits are all much weaker than mine."

Jim took three steps back down the bleachers. Thunder bellowed directly overhead, which made him feel as if the sky were falling in. "*My* spirits may be weaker than yours, Coyote. But *yours* aren't. I summon you, great spirit, to rise up and see what Coyote has become. And I bid you destroy him – extinguish his breath, tear out his lungs, pull out his heart."

221

A father with a gingery moustache turned round to Jim and said, "Excuse me, mister. There are kids here. You two guys want to say things like that, take your argument someplace else."

"Yes, sorry," said Jim. But then he flung his arms wide and shouted, "*Great spirit, come and kill Coyote! Great spirit, come and tear out his heart!*"

"Jesus," said the father with the gingery moustache. "The principal's going to hear about this."

But at that moment, a sharp gust of rain snapped across the bleachers, and Jim saw the Rain Spirit climbing up the aisle, its watery face grim with the look of revenge. In one hand it carried a huge and complicated spear, with water continuously pouring from its tip, and raindrops falling from its shaft.

"*Your time has come, Coyote*," said the Rain Spirit, somewhere inside of Jim's head. "*And this isn't a good day to die.*"

"Wait," said Dog Brother, raising his hand. "Can't you allow me one last wish before you kill me?" Catherine clung close to his arm, and even though Jim said, "Catherine! *Catherine!*" again and again, she wouldn't look at him.

The Rain Spirit said, "*Why should I grant you any last wishes, after what you did to my daughter?*"

"I simply want to choose the way I die," said Dog Brother. He was still grinning. All around them, the few spectators who had braved the rain were cheering West Grove toward another touchdown. "Go West Grove! Go West Grove!"

"*You may die any way you wish*," said the Rain Spirit. "*Choose, but be quick, My spear is growing impatient for your heart.*"

"You're the spirit of storms – kill me by lightning! Let me hold up your spear and take the full force of your anger! I'm half a spirit, but I'm half a man, and that will kill me as quickly as snuffing out a torch."

The Rain Spirit hesitated for a moment. "Don't listen to him," said Jim. "Just stab him, and take out his heart."

"If an enemy asks to die in a particular way, then it is shameful not to grant him his wish."

"You're going to give him your spear? That's good thinking!"

"I am water, my friend. I am nothing but rain. My own spear cannot harm me."

"Well go on, then. Do it. But do it now. And you – Dog Brother – you make sure that Catherine stands well away from you."

"Do you think I would harm the most beautiful girl I have ever known?"

"Just make sure she stays clear, you got it?"

The Rain Spirit tossed his spear to Dog Brother. Nobody but Jim could see any of these things. They couldn't see the Rain Spirit, in his tumbling cloak of clouds. They couldn't see why Dog Brother suddenly lifted his hand as if he were catching something. But Jim could see him standing on the top row of the bleachers with the Rain Spirit's spear held high in his right hand, pointing up at the hurrying black clouds.

"I'm ready," said Dog Brother. He took off his yellow spectacles and revealed eyes that were yellow, too.

The Rain Spirit lifted one finger to the skies. There was a moment's pause, while the rain continued to lash down all around them. Then a leader-stroke of lightning came forking out of the clouds, heading right down toward them. Jim stepped back, and pushed back the father with the gingery moustache.

"Who are you shoving, buddy?" the father demanded, just as the blinding bolt of lightning hit the tip of the Rain Spirit's spear. How Dog Brother had the split-second

223

timing to do it, Jim would never know. But he threw the spear back at the Rain Spirit, and the Rain Spirit instinctively caught it – right at the instant when the lightning's return stroke hit it, with more than a quarter of a million volts.

Jim saw the Rain Spirit's expression for only a fraction of a second – an agonized mask. Then it exploded into steam, like the ear-splitting blast from a locomotive. Scores of people turned around to see what had happened, but all they saw was the last stray fragments of steam drifting away.

It kept on raining, however, as if the skies were in mourning for the loss of their spirit, the one who had guided them for century after century, even when the white men came.

Dog Brother replaced his spectacles and said to Jim, "No spirit can touch me. No man can kill me. Now I'm going to show you what Coyote can do to you, if you make him angry."

He turned to Catherine and laid a hand on her shoulder. "*No*," said Henry Black Eagle. "Leave her alone."

"She isn't yours any longer, old man," said Dog Brother. "She's mine, and she's going to stay mine. Catherine, let's see what pain you can inflict on Mr Rook's team here. You told me they've never won a game. Well, let's see how badly they can lose this one."

"*Catherine, no!*" Jim shouted at her. But already he could see the shadows forming around her head, her shoulders hunching, her eyes beginning to shrink and smoulder scarlet.

"*No!*" he said, and tried to grab hold of her arms, but they were already thick and hairy and she pushed him aside.

Henry Black Eagle couldn't see Catherine's transformation, but he knew what was happening to her. He

224

climbed up the bleachers to Dog Brother and tried to seize hold of his coat. "You can't do this! She's a child! She can't change when people are watching her! Leave her alone!"

"When I'm here, she can change whenever I want her to. And I want her to." With that, Dog Brother grasped hold of Henry Black Eagle's lapels, and head-butted him, so that he fell backward and tumbled halfway down the aisle. There were screams and shouts and George Babouris called up to Jim, "What the hell's going on, Jim? What's happening?"

"Call an ambulance! Call the cops!" Jim told him. "Stop the game! Get everybody out of here!"

"I just want to know what's happening!"

"Do it, George, that's all I ask! Just do it!"

Dog Brother came down the bleachers, took hold of Jim's shoulder, and slapped him across the face. Jim tried to punch him back, but Dog Brother slapped him again.

Behind him, Catherine had grown taller and darker and now she was *bristling*, just the way that Jim's grandfather had predicted. Her claws were like black crescent moons, and she had rows and rows of hideously hooked teeth.

Dog Brother said, "This is my revenge, white man. This is what happens to people who try to cross me. Catherine White Bird is mine. She was always mine, and she always will be, even when she has given me the child I need, and she becomes nothing more than a beast."

George had gone down to the field waving his arms to stop the game. Ben Hunkus was shouting at him and so was the Azusa coach. The players were standing around in muddy bewilderment. The crowd had shrunk away from Dog Brother and Jim, but they would have shrunk away even further if they could have seen the beast that Catherine was gradually becoming.

"I'm going to murder your children now," said Dog

225

Brother. "I'm going to murder your children just as the white men murdered our children."

He waved his hand, and the Changing Bear Maiden began to descend the steps. All that anybody else could see was Catherine – walking stiffly perhaps, with her shoulders hunched. But Jim could see a huge black shadow-creature with claws and teeth – a creature that could slaughter every young man on the football field and tear their bodies into shreds.

"*Catherine!*" he roared. "*Catherine, listen to me!*"

Dog Brother kept hold of him, but grinned at him even wider. "It's no use, Mr Rook. It's time for the bloodshed."

"Catherine," Jim repeated. "Catherine, this creature isn't you. It's only an illusion. Magic, trickery, that's all it is. You're still inside there, Catherine, someplace. Catherine White Bird, who's free. Catherine White Bird, who wants a life of her own."

"You can't stop her, Mr Rook," smiled Dog Brother. "Why don't you sit down and enjoy the spectacle, mmh? It's going to be better than the Roman games."

"Catherine," Jim pleaded. "You never wanted to go back to the reservations, did you? You never wanted to be Dog Brother's bride? Come on, Catherine, listen to me. You have to break free. You have to be *you*!"

He paused for breath, and then he recited,

'*Thus in the winter stands the lonely tree*
It cannot say what loves have come and gone;
I only know that summer sang in me
A little while, that sings in me no more.'

The shadowy spirit-beast hesitated. It turned its head toward Jim and there was a look of hurt in its eyes, a look of deepest hurt.

"Go!" Dog Brother commanded it. "Go and rip their

lungs out! Go bite off their heads! Come on, heads! I want to see some heads!"

But the Changing Bear Maiden stayed where she was; and then she turned, and came back toward Dog Brother and towered over him, her fur streaked with rain.

"Kill," said Dog Brother, unconvincingly. But the Changing Bear Maiden loomed over him and wouldn't move.

"*Kill!*" Dog Brother screamed at her. "*Kill the bastards before I kill you!*"

Without warning, the Changing Bear Maiden slammed her claws into Dog Brother's shoulder. He let out a high-pitched shriek and tried to wrestle himself away. But the Changing Bear Maiden lifted him completely off the bleachers until his feet were kicking in the air like a hanged man.

"*Let me go!*" he shouted. "*Let me go!*"

But he was half a man, as well as half a spirit, and he didn't have the strength to tear himself free. And even though it needed one of his own kind to kill him, she was the same – half-beast, half-spirit – and that was what he had forgotten.

She let out a roar that made Jim's skin prickle all the way down his back. Then she ripped open his chest with a single catastrophic blow, tearing through skin and muscle and ribs, and she dragged out his living heart. She held it up in one bloodstained claw, and roared again.

Jim heard more screams all around him. To the horrified crowd, it must have looked as if Catherine had pulled out Dog Brother's heart. There was blood spraying everywhere, and Dog Brother staggered and slipped and fell on the bleachers, clutching his chest, coughing and gasping.

He held up his hand toward the Changing Bear Maiden, to give him back his heart, but she took one step backward and downward, and then another, and with every step the shadows around her the bristles began to fade, and the shadows melted more. The claws shrank and the eyes stopped glowing. By the seventh step, she was Catherine again, her face white with shock, still holding Dog Brother's heart, but Catherine again.

Dog Brother heaved himself up and grasped hold of the metal handrail. "Catherine," he said, "give me back my heart."

Catherine stood with his heart held up in the air. Blood and rain were running down her sleeve. She turned to Jim and looked at him in desperation.

"I love you, Catherine," said Dog Brother. "Please, give me back my heart."

Jim mouthed one word. *"Don't."*

Dog Brother came down the steps, one by one. His bloody hands slid down the handrail, inch by inch. "Please, Catherine, I'm begging you."

Catherine took another step back and Dog Brother lunged at her, but he lost his footing and tumbled at her feet. He lay sprawled across the bleachers, one foot shuddering. Then he lay still. Blood ran down the steps onto the grass below. Henry Black Eagle went across and put his arm around Catherine's shoulders and held her tight. "I'm sorry," he said. "You don't know how sorry I am."

"Is he dead?" asked Catherine.

"He's half-human but he's half-spirit, too. He can survive for quite a time without a heart."

"He *looks* dead."

Jim looked around the football field. The spectators were all standing in the rain staring at them, confused and frightened. He could sirens in the distance. On the field itself, the players stood like statues. Dog Brother lay on the steps, broken and silent, with the rain soaking

228

his coat and his blood dripping from the bleachers onto the ground below.

"Come on," Jim told Catherine, holding out his hand. "You'd better give me that."

At that moment, however, Dog Brother lashed out and caught hold of Catherine's ankle. She stumbled, colliding against her father, who stumbled too. Dog Brother struggled up onto his feet and seized hold of her arm, trying to snatch his heart away from her.

"*Catherine!*" shouted Jim, and held both hands up, even higher. He didn't realise that Catherine had thrown him the heart until it came flying toward him, spraying blood like a pinwheel. He caught it and it landed in his hands with a sharp flap, with its protruding arteries still attached. Cupping it closely, he jumped and bounded down the wet bleachers, trying to avoid the dumbfounded spectators, some of whom caught at his coat in a half-hearted attempt to stop him, simply because they didn't understand what was happening.

Dog Brother came leaping after him, and both of them slithered and tripped on the wet woodwork, although Jim managed to keep his balance until he reached the field. He cannoned his way through a crowd of milling spectators, and then he ran up the field as fast as he could, dodging in between the players. The rain lashed his face like a bucketful of cold salt, and his shoes splashed in the puddles.

He thought he was clear. He thought he *must* be clear. But then he glanced back over his shoulder and saw that Dog Brother was only five or six yards behind him, and closing. His chest was hanging open. His lungs were blown up like bloody balloons. Yet he kept on running and his yellow eyes were glaring with hatred. Jim suddenly realised that he didn't have the speed or the stamina to get away.

"Mo!" he shouted, to one of West Grove's tackles, Mo Newton. "Mo, take this and run with it!"

He threw the heart to Mo and Mo caught it before he realized what it was.

"What the hell is *this*, man? This is gross!"

"*Run with it!*" Jim yelled at him.

Mo started to run and Mo was fast, but Dog Brother was faster, even with his body ripped open. He swerved past Jim and just had time to say, "Bastard!" before he was running through the rain after Mo. Like Jim, Mo must have thought that he was clear, and by the time he reached the 20-yard line he started to ease off. But then Dog Brother lashed at his football shirt, and tore the back of it wide open, and Mo realised that he didn't have a chance of getting away. He called, "Ron!" and threw the heart to Ron Hubbard, one of their half-backs, who caught it one-handed and started running back toward the Azusa goal with it.

All around the field, the crowd watched it disbelief as Dog Brother came running after Ron Hubbard, gaining on him yard after yard. He was half-human, and he couldn't survive for very long without a heart, but he was running for his own survival, and that made all the difference. Ron Hubbard threw the heart to Keith Altham, the quarter-back, who passed it on almost immediately to Denzil Green, another tackle. Denzil was quick-footed and liked to play football for laughs, and he danced and skipped in front of Dog Brother, holding up his heart like a football trophy, and then twirling around just out of his reach.

But then Dog Brother caught hold of his helmet and wrenched it around, and all Denzil could do was hurl the heart wildly in any direction. The only player anywhere near was Russell Gloach, who caught it neatly, stared at it in complete disgust, but then went lumbering off up the field, his big legs working and his boots kicking up spray.

"*Run, Russell!*" Jim bellowed at him. "*For God's sake, run!*"

Russell kept up his heavy, measured jog; and all the time Dog Brother was catching up with him, his coat-tails flying, his teeth gritted, his face a mask of complete hatred. He was only three yards behind Russell when Russell looked around and saw him coming.

It was a transformation. Russell arched back his head, filled out his chest, and began to run faster. Dog Brother lashed out at him, but missed him, and Russell ran faster still. The rain gradually began to clear as he sped through the puddles, past the 35-yard line, past the 50-yard line, kicking up fountains of spray. Everybody cheered and whistled and clapped, even though most of them didn't understand what was happening, and didn't realise that Dog Brother's chest was gaping open.

Dog Brother lost his footing by the 50-yard line, and tripped, and fell to his knees. Russell ran all the way to the goal line and performed a little triumphant ballet of his own. The clouds had almost passed over now, and the air was warm and steamy. Jim walked over to Dog Brother and stood beside him. Dog Brother was close to collapse. He took off his yellow spectacles and wiped them, and then he looked up at Jim and there was an expression on his face which wasn't hatred, or anger. It was more like resignation.

"Well, white man, it seems like you've beaten me, after all."

Jim said nothing. Three policemen were approaching, across the grass, and he lifted his hand to warn them to keep their distance.

"Maybe I should have realised that times have changed," said Dog Brother. He spat a string of blood onto the ground.

"Maybe I should have realised that the world doesn't have a place for creatures like me any longer."

"You want me to feel sympathetic? Because of you, an innocent young boy was murdered, and I lost a woman I loved – and whatever I think about John Three Names, he didn't deserve to die, either."

"If I could have my heart back—" said Dog Brother.

"I'm not giving you your heart back. Your days on this earth are over, Coyote."

"But you forget. I have power over death. Lives are taken away – yes. But lives can be given back again, can't they?"

"What are you talking about?"

"I'm talking about a deal, white man. I'm talking about getting my heart back."

"You mean you can bring these people back to life? What are you talking about? The woman I loved, she had her head taken off, and then her body was burned. She was a sacrifice to you."

"What's a sacrifice? A gift, that's all. And gifts can always be returned."

"I don't believe you."

Dog Brother lowered his head, and coughed more blood. "That's your privilege. But wouldn't it be wonderul if it *were* true?"

Jim was silent for a very long time. He looked around the field and saw the spectators all anxiously milling around. He saw the teams watching him in bewilderment. He saw the clouds blowing away and the sun coming out.

"If I give you back your heart," he said, "you have to promise me one thing. You have to promise to leave Catherine White Bird alone, for ever. You have to go back to Fort Defiance, and if you want a bride, you have to find yourself a Navajo girl who really wants to marry you.

232

"If I even smell you anywhere near Catherine White Bird again, then by God I'll come after you and you'll wish that you were never even thought of."

Dog Brother nodded. "Don't worry, Mr Rook. I won't touch her again."

Jim beckoned to Russell and Russell brought the heart over. "You deserve a medal," said Jim, and gave Russell an affectionate cuff. Then he handed the heart to Dog Brother, who looked at it for a moment, and then took it, and stowed it into his chest like a man putting his wallet away. He passed his hand down the front of his body and his bones knitted together with an odd creaking sound, and his skin mended itself over his wound like melting wax.

He stood up. "Perhaps I should have realised that times have changed," he said, almost regretfully. "So many of us died, but that was a long time ago now, the way you humans look at things, at least. Maybe it's time to forget."

He lifted up the whistle that was hanging around Jim's neck. "If you ever feel the need for some spiritual reinforcements, why don't you whistle?"

At that moment, Catherine White Bird came up, closely followed by Henry Black Eagle. "I don't know how to thank you," she said.

"You can start by forgiving your father," Jim told her. "And then you can get the best English grades ever."

He turned around to talk to Dog Brother, but Dog Brother had vanished. He hadn't even left any footprints. The sun shone on the wet football field and there was a sharp smell of ozone. The game had been played in which both sides had lost; and his encounter with Coyote was over.

Catherine took hold of his hand and walked back to the college with him. She was wet and her hair was straggly but she was still very beautiful. "Do you ever date your students?" she asked him, squeezing his hand. He smiled at her and squeezed her hand back. "No," he said. "Never."

Later that evening, in the West Grove mortuary, the body of Martin Amato, the football captain, suddenly twitched and stirred. In another mortuary, in Window Rock, Arizona, the body of John Three Names, the Navajo journalist, uttered a low, vibrant moan.

And behind the Navajo Nation Inn, the wind started to blow like a small tornado, and blue lights started to flicker. Dust and ashes were blown up into the air.

Then, slowly, a woman's hand appeared out of the ground.